Praise for Victoria Cooke

'Funny and poignant with a gloriously realistic cast of
characters. I followed Charlotte's journey avidly, cheering
her on all the way. An unputdownable read'
Rachel Burton, author of *The Many Colours of Us*

'Buy this book now and read it!'
Rachel's Random Reads

'A truly fantastic read, I couldn't put it down'
Jessica Bell

VICTORIA COOKE grew up in the city of Manchester before crossing the Pennines in pursuit of her career in education. She now lives in Huddersfield with her husband and two young daughters. When she's not at home writing by the fire with a cup of coffee in hand, she loves working out in the gym and travelling. Victoria has always had a passion for reading and writing, undertaking several writers' courses before completing her first novel in 2016.

Also by Victoria Cooke

The Secret to Falling in Love
The Holiday Cruise
Who Needs Men Anyway?

It Started with a Note

VICTORIA COOKE

ONE PLACE. MANY STORIES

HQ
An imprint of HarperCollins*Publishers* Ltd
1 London Bridge Street
London SE1 9GF

This paperback edition 2019

First published in Great Britain by
HQ, an imprint of HarperCollins*Publishers* Ltd 2018

ISBN: 978-0-00-832305-9

Typeset by Palimpsest Book Production Ltd, Falkirk, Stirlingshire

For my great-grandfather, Private Thomas Edward Fitton, who served with the 1st Battalion in the Borders Regiment and was killed in action on 1/7/1916 in the Somme Valley aged 24.

And, my grandmother Rose (his daughter) who was six years old when he was taken from her by the Great War. She became a much-loved grandmother who always had time for her grandchildren.

***

In loving memory of my grandad, Kenneth Taylor Cooke, (1926–2018) a Second World War Royal Marine, spared from fighting the Japanese in the Pacific as the war ended during his training. Grandad is remembered for his bravery, patience, kindness, generosity and love.

Rain

Rain, midnight rain, nothing but the wild rain
On this bleak hut, and solitude, and me
Remembering again that I shall die
And neither hear the rain nor give it thanks
For washing me cleaner than I have been
Since I was born into this solitude.
Blessed are the dead that the rain rains upon:
But here I pray that none whom once I loved
Is dying to-night or lying still awake
Solitary, listening to the rain,
Either in pain or thus in sympathy
Helpless among the living and the dead,
Like a cold water among broken reeds,
Myriads of broken reeds all still and stiff,
Like me who have no love which this wild rain
Has not dissolved except the love of death,
If love it be towards what is perfect and
Cannot, the tempest tells me, disappoint.

Edward Thomas, 1916

Chapter One

I clutch the envelope tightly to my chest – so tightly, in fact, my nails tear into the crumpled paper, which has been softened by my sweaty palm and the relentless downpour. I release my grip slightly. It's too precious to damage, but I'm so scared of losing it. I feel like one of those mad scientists in a James Bond film who has developed a mini nuclear warhead and has to transport it somewhere with the utmost care to avoid detonating it at the wrong time. I'm not sure comparing myself to a villain is wholly accurate, though. Perhaps I should have laid it on a velvet pillow or something, like a prince carrying a glass slipper. Yes, that's better – a prince, not a villain. A princess? *I shouldn't be in charge of something like this.*

As I scurry down the high street, the eyes of passers-by rouse suspicion. *Do they know what I have? Are they after me?* I walk faster, heart pounding. It's difficult because my bloody shoes are killing me. Pleather. Man-made leather. Plastic-leather *pleather* sandals – a bargain at £12.99, but seriously, I've already spent double that on plasters for all the blisters they've given me.

The quicker I walk, the harder my bag-for-life bashes into my legs. Dented tins of peas, beans, stew and whatever else I'd salvaged from the 'whoops' shelf after work all unleash their fury on my

1

shins. It isn't uncommon for certain staff members to accidentally-on-purpose cause a few *whoopsies* themselves. Not me, of course; it's a sackable offence and I can't risk losing my job since I'm the sole breadwinner in our house and my baby boy has just gone off to university so I need every penny.

Thirty-seven years old and I've already packed my Kieran off to university while most of my friends are waving their kids off to high school. It makes me feel so *old*. When I looked that handsome six-foot-two beanpole in the eye and kissed him goodbye, I blubbed like a baby. He was still my little boy, even if I had to stand on my tiptoes to get close enough to grab his cheek. Of course, he'd just grunted and wiped the residue of tears, snot and my kisses off on his sleeve almost instantly. *Boys*. He's turning into his uncle Gary.

I'm still scurrying, every step causing me to wince in pain. Bag-for-life. *Bash*. Sandals. *Chafe*. And so continues the pattern as I dash through the town centre towards the bus station. Rain is forecast, thunderous downpours no less – an amber weather warning had been issued by that gorgeous weatherman, David Whatshisface, on the TV. He could make any weather seem bright and cheery. *I'd weather his storm.* I chuckle to myself, not even sure if that would even make sense to anyone other than me.

A deafening roar rips through the sky. *Uh-oh.* I try walking even quicker. *Bash, chafe, bash, chafe.* I don't have a brolly, though I know they're unwise in a thunderstorm anyway – David said so. I can see the bus station in the distance all lit up in the dusky evening like a heavenly portal to refuge. Just one busy road, several passers-by eyeing me (I'm still suspicious), and a plume of smoke from the smokers outside the pub to negotiate and I'll be home and dry, literally.

Just as I allow myself to dream of being home, the heavens open. Of course they do. They couldn't have waited just five more minutes – where would be the fun in that? The rain is so heavy it soaks through to my skin almost instantly. My denim jacket is leaden with liquid and the nylon of my uniform is soaked. I'm cold and sticky and my feet are squishing about in my sandals, squelching with every step. The envelope is getting quite soggy now so I stuff it into my handbag and tuck my bag tightly under my armpit for safety.

I slow my pace, unable to keep it up because my mascara and foundation have run straight into my eyes, partially blinding me. I wipe them with the back of my hand and notice it's streaky black when I pull it away. *I must look a sight.* I've reached the road and the cars are coming thick and fast. Headlights, taillights, headlights, taillights. *Gap.* I make a dash for it, landing in a huge puddle by the kerb as I do. Brown water droplets dribble down my American Tan tights. *Why didn't I wear trousers?* David promised rain!

I make it across the road and begin negotiating the shrunken smoke plume, which is now concentrated to the little canopy above the door. My task is made all the more difficult by the next torrent of foundation and mascara liquid streaming down my face. The smoke makes me cough and splutter and I'm flapping my arms about as best I can with a one-ton carrier bag on my arm and a stiff denim jacket shrink-wrapping my body.

As I near the edge of the smoking circle, I bat the air one last time – one time too many for my so-called bag-for-life, which bursts open, spewing bargain tins aplenty all over the pavement. As I scan the devastation, I notice that the pesky little pokey thing you never quite know how to work has fallen off the corned beef tin. *Typical.*

I never swear.

Ever.

But if I did, Hells Angels would blush at the words I'd choose right now.

'Cath, you idiot!' I mumble instead.

A tatty-haired man bends down and starts to pick up the tins and I follow. Warmth in my chest grows from the seed of his kindness. He has a lit cigarette in his mouth and the smoke from it is so close and raw that it's burning my nostrils, but he's kind enough to help so I do my best to ignore it.

'Thanks, love,' I say, my voice thick with implied gratitude. He just nods and hands me four of the five tins he's picked up. I look at him, confused, as he stuffs the corned beef in his pocket and shrugs. The rain is beating down still, pummelling into my bag, and I'm shaking with the cold. Or shock. Before I can organise my thoughts and string together a sentence of scorn, he's stubbed out his cigarette and vanished back into the pub taking my tea with him. As my eyes sink to the ground, I spot the glinting little silver twisty thing off the corned beef tin, and it's mildly satisfying to know he'll never get to enjoy my tin of deliciously processed meat.

Striking corned beef hash off the menu tonight would be one more thing for Gary to moan about. Still, I have the envelope and no amount of whinging from my freeloading brother would change that. Hearing those words in my head makes me feel a little guilty. I'm supposed to be helping him, supporting him, but instead, I'm slowly losing my patience with him. I make it to the bus station and can see my bus has pulled in at stop number sixteen, which is right at the other end of the station, of course. I start running. I'm holding my shopping in two arms, cradling it like a precious baby so I don't lose any more tins. *Gary will have to have the stew.*

Just as I approach stop fifteen, there is a miracle. My bus is still in! *Thank God!* I slow to a walking pace, panting – the smoke, the bus fumes and the fact I haven't done any exercise since my last year eleven PE lesson all contributory factors.

Juggling my groceries, I stuff a hand into my bag, fumbling for my purse, which I locate quickly, and glance down at it to find some bus fare. The rumbling sound of the bus engine coming to life alerts me to the fact it's about to leave. I have no choice but to barge past the people queuing at stop fifteen and pop my head and arm outside; I wouldn't make stop sixteen. I'm waving frantically, balancing my precious tin baby in the other arm. 'Please stop.' The headlights get closer, but they're gaining speed. *Please stop*. 'Stop!' I yell.

He doesn't stop.

The next bus comes an hour later.

Chapter Two

When I finally arrive at the end of my road, I'm trembling, battered, and bruised, and all I've done is commute home from work.

The off-licence near the bus stop is open, and I have an idea to salvage the evening. My spirits are still high; I still have the envelope and I'm almost home. I plonk a bottle of cava on the counter and rummage in my purse for six pounds.

'Celebrating tonight?' Jim, the owner, asks.

'Ooh, yes I am.' I can't help but grin. 'But I can't tell you why – I don't want to jinx it.' I smile and give a little shrug.

'Well, whatever it is, you enjoy it, love.' Jim smiles back. 'How's that brother of yours doing?'

I want to offload and explain how exasperated I've become with him, how he never helps around the house and has yet to find a job, but I find myself unable to. I don't know if it's embarrassment or loyalty, or a complete unwillingness to bore the lovely Jim to death with my woes.

'He's good,' I say instead.

'Glad things are working out.' He smiles. 'I told him he could have a few shifts here to tide him over, but he said he thought things were looking up.'

Oh, did he now? 'Yes, apparently so,' I say.

Jim smiles again and hands me my penny change, which I pop into the charity box by the till.

When I finally make it through the front door, relief embraces me, tighter than my shrink-wrapped jacket. I'd make tea, then pull out the envelope and ask Gary if he'd help me celebrate, we'd have the bubbly and then I'd run a nice hot bath, putting that awful journey home behind me. Perhaps I'd book a meal for us at the weekend, at that new pub in town. I could even ask Kieran to come over and make it a real family affair. It would cheer Gary up and I'd quite enjoy the company and change of scenery. I smile dreamily as Gary approaches me.

'I'm goin' down the pub,' he mumbles, barging past me and causing a few tins from my precariously balanced bag-for-life to tumble to the floor.

My heart sinks. Gary always goes out for an evening drink, so it was silly to feel so deflated when tonight is no different. I should have expected it, and it wasn't like he knew I had exciting news to share with him. I contemplate asking him to stay in but as I turn around, the front door slams shut in my face.

At least I could have a bath and then make tea in my own time; that was something. My feet sting as soon as the bloodied blisters hit the hot soapy water, but the rest of my body needs a soak just to warm up because apparently it would have killed Gary to pop the heating on. The house is like an igloo and will take a good few hours to warm up. As much as I love him, I could batter him with a cut-price baguette at times.

After my bath, I heat up the tin of stew and butter some bread, which has started to go a little hard. It isn't mouldy thankfully, but bread never does seem to go mouldy anymore, which is a little odd come to think of it; I wonder what on earth goes into it nowadays. Still, this piece is okay – it just isn't deliciously fresh. I could have brought some deliciously fresh bread home if Gary had managed to send a simple text message to let me know we needed some. I shake my head as I take a bite.

I'd taken pity on him after our mum died. It had hit us both hard as we never knew our father and she'd been both mum and dad to us. I was so close to Mum and she was always there for me and Kieran – so much so that I'd never felt like a single parent. Gary was close to her too and after she died, he'd sunk into depression. He'd already lost his girlfriend, and a year or so after Mum died he lost his job too, but two years have passed since she died and I shouldn't need to be looking after him anymore. I'd let him move in about six months ago while he got himself back on his feet, but so far he's not displayed any signs of getting a job and moving out, and he only uses his feet to walk to the pub.

I place my bowl and bread on the kitchen table and remember the bottle of cava in the fridge. Celebrating alone seems a little sad but what choice do I have? A little glass wouldn't hurt, would it? One now, and perhaps Gary would have a glass with me when he got back from the pub, I reason. Maybe we could even have a chat about him moving out if he comes home in good spirits. The bottle is disappointingly warm despite having sat in the fridge for a good few hours. The blooming thing has two settings: frozen and lukewarm. I've asked Gary a million times to look at it for me or call someone out, but evidently, it's been too much trouble for him.

Remembering how fast corks can pop, I take a tea towel from the drawer to catch it in; I'd seen someone do that before at a party. Placing the towel over the cork, I begin to push at it with my thumb as hard as I can. It isn't budging so I place my hand over it, trying to ease it out, but the thing is stuck fast. I try my other hand: more wiggling, more pulling and even a twist here and there, but it is no good. I even hold the bottle with my thighs and try with both thumbs but it's useless and my hands are red and sore. Resigned to the fact I won't be having a glass of bubbly,

I dump the bottle on the side and put the kettle on instead before sinking into the kitchen chair, where I cry.

I hate myself for it because I try so hard to be upbeat and positive, no matter how hard things get, but sometimes things pile up and the weight becomes too heavy to bear. It's not just the fact I've had an awful journey home or that I lost my corned beef. It's the fact that I've never complained about my life being samey and unadventurous in all the years that it has, but the one time I try to brave something new, the cork just won't pop. I can't help but wonder if it's a sign from the gods to quit trying and just accept my fate. I let out a small humourless laugh through the tears before wiping my face and finishing making my tea.

The house is still and quiet but I'm not in the mood for watching TV. I miss grumpy Kieran barging through the door, hungry, as he always is. Like most teenagers, he spent much of his time in his room, but just knowing he was up there was a comfort. I could always make an excuse to pop in and see him, to offer him a drink or collect his dirty laundry and if he was ever out, I always knew he'd be coming back. Now the emptiness of the house is a feeling rather than a state and it's odd. But that doesn't mean I want Gary to stay; he needs to rebuild his own life. It's just something I'm going to have to get used to. No son, no Mum, no Gary. Just me.

The stillness thickens and prickles my skin. I'm sure it's emphasised by the sad deflated attempt at a celebration. Needing to busy myself, I have an idea.

Kieran's lifetime collection of junk is still cluttering up his room. It's all stuff he hadn't deemed important enough to take to university but apparently felt was fine to leave in my house. I decide I'm going to have a good sort-out. What's that saying? Clean house, clean mind? I shake my head – that doesn't sound right at all; I've always had a clean mind and no amount of mess in Kieran's room could change that.

My emergency stash of cardboard boxes from work come in

handy once I've rebuilt them and filled them with Kieran's junk. Old school books, piles of posters kept under his bed, superhero figurines he hasn't played with in ten years and some board games that probably have most of the vital pieces missing.

My loft hatch is stiff, but the stick I keep for opening it still works if I really yank it, and the steps come down easily after that. *That's something at least.* I climb them, pulling the light cord when I reach the top. I clamber over the boxes I'd already stashed up there and feel a little bit of guilt at the fact I'm just as much of a hoarder as Kieran. I pick up a box to make some space and when the recognition of it registers, I have to sit down. For a moment, I just look at it.

After Mum died, I'd inherited this box. It contains all her little keepsakes: things that Gary would have never wanted in a million years. He was more interested in the sandwich toaster and the little retro DAB radio she had in the kitchen. I know what's in the box but I hadn't been able to bring myself to open it yet. I was too heartbroken and now I feel terrible because I'd forgotten all about it.

I cross my legs on the dusty boards and wipe the lid clean before lifting it. There's a photo of me and Gary lying on top, which was taken when I was about five and he was eight. I take in my plaited pigtails and brown corduroy dress and can vaguely remember the day. Gary is wearing brown velvet jeans and a red jumper and is looking at me with disdain. We'd been to a park and he'd pushed me over and I'd grazed my knee. He was angry because I'd snitched on him to Mum. God bless the Eighties.

My father had walked out about a year before that picture was taken and whilst I barely remember him, I do remember Mum's smile that year. It was always there, plastered on, oversized and exaggerated, but her eyes didn't crinkle in the corners. It wasn't until I got older I realised how hard it must have been to maintain that brave face for us and I wish we'd have behaved much better for her.

I continue to rummage. There is an old concert ticket for Boy George in the box, football match programmes from when she used to take Gary to watch Tottenham Hotspur, and my first pair of ballet slippers. Right at the bottom is an old wooden matchstick storage box that I don't remember ever seeing before. I pull it out and examine it curiously. It's quite intricate in its design, and I wonder why it hadn't been on display at home. It was the kind of thing Mum would have loved to show off on her mantelpiece.

I take off the lid and inside the red-velvet-lined box is a stack of ancient-looking notelets, each one yellowed and fragile. My heart is beating in my eardrums with anticipation. They are certainly old enough to have been from my dad all those years ago. *Perhaps I'll finally discover where he's been for all those years.*

Hesitantly, I take out the top one and carefully unfold it. The date at the top strikes me hard: *1916*. I have to double-check it before reading on, confused.

7th February 1916

My dearest Elizabeth,

This is the farthest I've ever been from home, and I can tell you, France is almost as beautiful as the Home Counties. Perhaps one day, when the war is over, I can bring you and Rose here. The war is going to last much longer than we'd hoped, I'm afraid. Who knows how long we'll be knee-deep in muck for.

I hope Rose is looking after you. I know how you worry, but I'll be fine. We're working quite closely with the French and I've even been learning a little of the language. I'll teach you both when I get home.

Avec amour (I hope that's correct)
Yours,
Will

My eyes begin to burn a little and a ball forms in my throat. This is a letter to my great-grandmother from my great-grandfather. I remember my mum telling me the story of how her grandfather volunteered to fight in the First World War. He'd been killed in Belgium I think. Her mother, my grandmother, was five years old at the time and hadn't really remembered him, something I could always relate to. Naturally, my mother didn't know too much about him other than that he was twenty-four when he died.

Kieran bursts into my mind. He's not much different in age to what my great-grandfather had been. I try to imagine him going out to war. The thought of it twists and knots my insides, and I can't fathom how the mothers of the WWI soldiers felt, waving their sons off to war.

Of course, Kieran wouldn't have survived the boot-polishing stage, never mind the trench-digging and gunfire. I love him to bits, but he's a bone-idle little so-and-so, a trait that must be from his father's side. I couldn't imagine why a twenty-four-year-old man with a wife and daughter and his whole life ahead of him would want to go to the front line for the king's shilling. It was so brutal and horrific, but I suppose back then people did it for their country.

I read the letter again; the part about him wanting to take my grandmother and great-grandmother to France stands out. My grandma never even had a passport, never mind visiting France. That makes me feel sad – that one of the only surviving pieces of communication from her father said that he wanted her to see France, and she never went. Granted, there was another war soon after the first, but my grandmother lived until the late Eighties and still never made the trip.

I take out the next letter, which is addressed directly to my grandmother. The date is too faded to read but I can just about make out the intricate penmanship.

My dearest Rose,

I hope your mother is well. I miss you. I hear you've grown somewhat. You'll be as tall as me when I come home. When I return, I'll have many stories to share with you. As I write this, I'm on leave looking out on luscious green fields with red poppies and blue cornflowers growing. It's quite the picture beneath the blue summer sky. You'll have to see this one day. It's 'un lieu de beauté' as the French say. I've picked up a bit of the language.

Some of my comrades have taken up poetry. It's not something I'm good at, but I'll send you a poem as soon as I get the chance.

Take care, my darling.

Yours,

Daddy

The letter squeezes my chest. Something about the upbeat tone suggests he really did think he'd return home – or he was putting on a brave tone for his daughter. Hindsight paints a tragic picture of a happy family destined for heartbreak.

There are a few more letters and, strangely, some are written in French. I place them all back inside the box carefully and make a note to ask someone to translate the others when I get a chance.

The letters play on my mind all evening. Knowing my grandma never went to France in the end saddens me somewhat. I'm a lot like she was: a homebody, unadventurous and happy in the safe familiarity of where I've always lived. But it was her destiny to travel to France, or at least it *should* have been, and that thought is still weaving through my mind when Gary returns, partially inebriated, from the pub.

'Have you been buying posh plonk?' he asks, picking up the bottle of cava and inspecting it as he walks in.

'I … err … yes,' I say, no longer in the mood to celebrate.

'Two glasses, eh?'

I remain silent.

'One was for me, wasn't it?' he says with a small laugh. Like it's so implausible that I'd have company round. 'You don't have twenty quid I can borrow since you're splashing out on fizz, do you? I've had a lot of outgoings this past fortnight and I need something to tide me over until my next JSA payment.' He pops the cork with ease and pours two glasses of fizz into large wine glasses since I don't own fancy flutes.

The hair on the back of my neck bristles and I take a deep breath to ensure what I say next comes out nonchalantly. The last thing I want is an argument. 'No news on the job front yet?'

He pauses, and his face reminds me of a Transformer as the different muscles pull together almost mechanically to arrange some kind of pained expression. "Fraid not. They don't seem to be able to find anything to match my skills. Twenty years I worked as an engineer and I'm not going to throw away that kind of experience sweeping school corridors or stacking shelves. No offence.'

I'm far from offended, but I'm very close to cross. 'Well, maybe you'll have to.' I maintain an even tone. 'You're spending more than you have coming in and it's a vicious cycle. Jim said he'd offered you a few shifts so you might have to take him up on it, or I can see if there's anything going at my place if you like?'

'Cath, look, I'm waiting for the right job.' There's agitation in his tone. 'If I take up a few shifts with Jim, my JSA will stop and I'll be worse off.'

'You can work at my place while you're waiting for the *right job*. You could work full-time there.'

'Oh yeah.' He lets out a dry, humourless laugh. 'And get stuck there like *you* did because there's no time to look for anything better once you've been suckered in. What is it you've been there now? Eighteen years?'

His words sting and I glare at him. It's true. I was bright at school, did well in most of my GCSEs and even got my A levels in English Literature, history and media, but after falling pregnant I needed money for the bills and the shift patterns worked well for me with a baby. 'I think you've had too much to drink,' I say eventually, standing up to leave.

'Aren't you drinking your plonk?' he says, oblivious to how he's made me feel.

'You have it, it's warm anyway,' I say before storming out of my own kitchen. Hot tears well in my eyes. Not through sadness, but through embarrassment. Embarrassment that he feels he's better than me despite spending the last half a year in a parasitic state. Embarrassment for thinking he'd be pleased for me when I showed him what I had in the envelope. And embarrassment for not standing up for myself.

16

I hate how he makes me feel as if he thinks everything I've done is insignificant – but I've raised a child, I've always paid my way, and I've saved him from the streets. I may not have an engineering degree, but I like to think that being a good person counts for something. I know it's his circumstances making him so bitter, but it's still hard to take. He's a good person underneath and I'm sure he'll find himself again.

I just don't want to be in the crossfire.

It's time for him to leave.

Chapter Three

'Look!' Kaitlynn squeals, waggling her newly taloned hands in front of my face as I walk into the staff room the next day.

'Oh, very nice,' I say politely, acknowledging her luminous pink, sparkly-tipped nails.

'Well, I had to treat myself with the annual bonus money, didn't I? It was a whopper this year! Can you believe how much we got?' Her voice is so high it penetrates my eardrums like a laser. '*And* I have a date on Saturday with this total *ten* I met on Tinder,' she gushes.

A total *ten*? Kaitlynn is about ten years younger than me, but somehow latched on to me when she first started at the supermarket, and we had developed a close working friendship ever since. Every so often, her reality-TV-inspired vernacular stumps me, and this is one of those times. The confusion must have manifested on my face.

'A total ten, as in a ten out of ten. A hottie, Cath. F-I-T.' She giggles.

'That's great, Kaitlynn.' I smile. In a way, she is probably closer in age and generation to my son, but since he communicates mostly through Morse grunts, I've learned nothing about popular culture through him. 'But ...' I pause.

'But what?' She pounces on me as if I've said something wrong.

'I was just about to ask why he's on a dating website if he's so good-looking. Surely he has women falling at his feet wherever he goes? Especially if he has a nice personality, which he should have if you're going to date him.'

Kaitlynn laughs and gives a simple, 'Oh, Cath.'

'What? I'm not so out of touch, you know. Good looks and a nice personality are relationship fundamentals – they don't go out of fashion.'

'Tinder is just a bit of fun, and not many people hang around long enough to find out the personality part.' She winks and pulls out her phone. 'Firstly, it's not a website, it's an app. Secondly, you can find all the hotties nearby within seconds, and you don't have to leave your house. Watch.' She starts flipping through pictures of men, muttering about who is 'fit' and who isn't. It's a bit like the Argos catalogue of blokes. Suddenly, she gasps. 'Cath, you should totally try it.'

I couldn't imagine what my tired old face would look like amidst the beautiful, taut-skinned twenty-year-olds. I'd be some kind of booby prize or worse. A dare. 'Oh no, no, no. That ship has sailed.'

'Of course it hasn't. You're never too old for a bit of male company, if you know what I mean.' I wince because I do, of course, know what she means. 'What are you spending your bonus on? You got more than me, Miss Employee of the Year! Splash out, lady, you're loaded,' she gushes. I feel heat flush my cheeks. Employee of the year is quite a big deal and whilst I'm not struggling to cope with the pay-out, I am with the recognition. 'We could get you some highlights and a few new tops: one for a selfie, one for a date, and you'd be good to go.'

'I'm not interested. I'm more than happy to watch a Noughties romcom with a glass of wine. At least that way, I always get the perfect guy.' I grin because I'm right and have never been disappointed.

'Fine. You stick to your old movies but don't come crying to me when you realise Matthew McConaughey isn't all that.' She folds her arms and looks disappointed. 'What are you planning on doing with your bonus then? Not giving it to that son of yours or helping *Gary* out even more, are you?' She spits out the word 'Gary' like an unwanted lemon pip.

Kaitlynn hates that Gary can't stand on his own two feet at 'his age'. She sadly lost her mother to the big 'C' a few years ago, which is partly what brought us together since that's what I lost my mum to and it all happened at a similar time. From what I can gather, they were incredibly close, and the fact Kieran isn't on the phone to me once a day and round visiting every Sunday really irritates her. I've tried explaining it's a son vs. daughter thing, but she doesn't buy it.

I shake my head. 'I haven't decided yet.'

'Well, make sure you spend it on yourself,' she warns.

Later on, during a checkout lull, I tell Kaitlynn all about the tragic letters I'd found in the loft. The thought of my great-grandfather saying goodbye to his wife and child for what turned out to be the last time, and my grandma never fulfilling his wishes all weigh heavily on my mind.

'That is so sad!' says Kaitlynn when I tell her how my gran never fulfilled my great-grandfather's dreams and left the country. 'It's like a John Green book or something. I actually want to cry.'

'I know,' I say sombrely; though I've never read a John Green book, I get what she means. I'm about to offer something philosophical when Kaitlynn gasps again.

'Why don't *you* go to France? You could see where your great-grandad is buried. I watched a TV programme about the centenary and apparently, you can trace your relatives and see exactly where they are commemorated.' She slips excitedly into her theme and throws her hands up dramatically. 'You should do the trip your gran should have done. It's perfect. Your bonus and prize money would cover it and you'd be fulfilling your great-grandfather's dream. Plus, Kieran and Gary won't get a penny of your hard-earned cash!'

'No. Not a chance am I going travelling to a foreign country alone! It's a ridiculous idea. That money will come in handy for something much more necessary. A new sofa perhaps.'

She lets out a 'hmph' sound. 'What, so Gary can leave an indent of his bottom on it? Stylish!'

'You're missing the point. I'm not frittering away the money.'

'Why not? You never go away, and you have all your holidays left to take from about 1995, so it wouldn't be a problem I'm sure. You never spend anything on yourself so it will just sit in an account until Gary wears you down and you end up loaning it to him. You won't see a penny.'

'Don't be silly, I can't just up—' I'm interrupted by the electronic gong of the tannoy.

'Attention. This is a staff announcement. Can Jamie come to checkout four, please? Jamie to checkout four.' I glance at Kaitlynn in horror but she just winks as she lets go of the button, and a rather fed-up-looking Jamie approaches us.

'Yes, Kaitlynn?' he asks impatiently.

'Jamie.' She smiles sweetly. 'As store manager and all-round supermarket don, can you please give Cath some time off for a holiday? She is the employee of the year you know. She deserves a break.' He looks from Kaitlynn to me and back to Kaitlynn again and shrugs.

'I don't see why not. She's entitled to them.' He turns to me. 'You accrue enough of them. Off anywhere nice?'

Heat rushes to my cheeks when I don't have an answer. 'Oh, no. I ...' I feel like a numpty and glare at Kaitlynn. 'Possibly France.' There's no way I'm going to France alone, but perhaps some time off wouldn't hurt. I could finally get the fridge fixed but I can hardly say that to Jamie.

'How long will you need?'

'I, er ...' I have no idea because up until forty seconds ago, time off wasn't even on my agenda, but I'd feel too foolish to say it's a mistake. 'A few days,' I say, feeling that would be reasonable for a fake trip to France. Now that I can afford one of those twenty-four-hour appliance repairmen it would still leave me a day or so of R&R.

'Weeks,' Kaitlynn interrupts, placing a forceful hand on my shoulder. 'She means weeks, a few weeks.'

'Okay. Pop in the office tomorrow and we'll look at dates.'

By the time I get home, I've managed to convince myself it would be fun to try and learn French. Being able to read my great-grandfather's letters would not only be a real feat, it would feel quite special too. While Kaitlynn had a point about fulfilling my grandmother's legacy, she still has the frivolous air of youth that leaves most people at some point during their thirties. I, on the other hand, am beyond that. By a pinch.

When I get home, the electricity is off. Luckily, I'd topped my card up because I knew it would have been way out of Gary's remit to go out and do it. He's asleep on the sofa in the eerie twilight when I enter the lounge. The mail is still sitting on the mat, pots are piled up on the side in the kitchen, and when I check upstairs, I see the bathroom mirror he promised to fix back to the wall is still propped up on the floor. Bubbles of rage start to rise and pop in my chest as I storm back downstairs. *I can't facilitate this festering blob any longer.*

'Gary. Wake up. Gary!' I prod him, and when he doesn't move straight away, I wonder if he's actually started to decompose on the sofa through sitting still for so long. That would be much worse than an indentation of his bottom.

'What is it, Cath?' He comes around slowly.

'The electricity is off.' I fold my arms and glare at him.

'I knew you'd be back with a card so it seemed daft to go and top the spare up.'

'I bet you were more than happy to use up all the emergency credit watching daytime telly, though. Hmm?'

22

'Cath, I—'

'And did you fix the mirror?'

'I needed string. I wanted to ring you to pick some up from work but I didn't have any credit on my phone.'

'And what's your excuse for not washing your own pots? Or picking the mail up off the mat?' I'm practically yelling at him now.

'Calm down, Cath, I was going to do all that; I just nodded off. I was down the Jobcentre today and they don't half wear you down with all their questions.'

'Do they? Do they wear you down? You poor, poor thing!'

Gary is sitting up now, looking at me with his eyes unusually wide. I've never spoken to him this way before. 'I'm going for a shower,' I say before something I'll regret pops out of my mouth.

When I come back down, I hear rustling in the kitchen and a pang of guilt hits me when I realise he must finally be fixing the fridge. Maybe that's what he needed all along: some tough love. I tiptoe towards the door. I don't want an awkward conversation about it, nor do I want to disturb him and give him reason to stop so I make a mental decision to just thank him when it's done by treating him with my windfall money. He used to like golf. Perhaps I could buy him some time at the driving range.

I hover in the doorway, watching his shoulders as he's hunched over something. I wonder if it's the broken part. I can't profess to know anything about fridges or their accoutrements, but something about the way he's holding himself seems odd – protective, like he's shielding what he's got in his hands. That's when I notice he isn't mending a fridge part at all; he's got a knife wedged beneath the lid of my money tin, and he's trying his hardest to unjam it.

The sound of it popping off makes me jump, and I gasp. Gary turns around and already in his hand is a twenty-pound note.

'What on earth do you think you're doing?' I ask, shock and anger adding a punch to my tone.

'Cath, I ... er ...' He holds both palms up towards me. 'It's just a loan. I was going to put it back, and I saw that three-grand cheque you got from work ... you can afford it.'

I don't know what to say. The fact we came from the same DNA suddenly seems quite unbelievable. It's as though every ounce of my goodness is mirrored by dishonesty in him. It hurts. 'You—' I jab a finger in his direction '—need to move out.'

His face pales and I notice his forehead is clammy. 'Move out? You're not serious. Cath, I'm sorry, I was going to put it back next week. You can't kick me out. Where would I go?' Desperation is etched in his features and his voice drops to a whisper. 'You wouldn't see your brother out on the streets, Cath, would you?' A tremor ruffles the last three words.

I walk into the lounge, sit on the sofa and sigh. No, I wouldn't, and he knows me too well. 'Gary, you were trying to *steal* from me.'

He slumps into the armchair. 'I was desperate. I wouldn't have done it if you weren't so flush, and I did ask last night if I could borrow some cash. It was just a loan, I swear.'

'It's the final straw, Gary.'

His eyes drop to the floor.

'I just can't trust you now. Not until you sort yourself out.'

'If you kick me out now, I'll end up on the streets.' He throws his head into his hands.

'You've been here six months now and haven't made any progress on the job front, and I've allowed you to coast along. I'm as much to blame as you are.' I gesture to his slobby, track-suited self. 'It's time for you to get out of this funk and then we can both have our lives back. But right now, I can't stand to be around you.' I want to say the words again: *Get out*. But I can't do it. I can't see him on the streets. 'What you did is going to take me a while to come to terms with, and at this moment in time I just can't be near you, never mind share a house with you. You've betrayed me in the worst possible way.' He nods sombrely, committed to his fate, and despite my better judgement, I feel sorry for him.

'I'm going away, and I want you gone when I get back.' The words leave my mouth before I can think about them, and I'm not exactly sure where I'm going, but the idea of a break of some kind suddenly seems so appealing.

'Pah. You're going away? By yourself?' He sneers as he speaks.

I fold my arms defiantly. 'Yes.'

'Where to? An exotic cruise? An Amazon trek? A camel ride across the Gobi Desert? Or is it just a soggy weekend in Brighton?' His tone is mocking, each word fuelling a new burst of anger inside me.

I pause, and without anything better to say or any other ideas I blurt, 'F ... France.'

'France?' He laughs. 'Seems a bit cultural for you. You can't even speak French and you dropped it for GCSE. What the hell are you going to do in France?'

I'm in no mood to explain myself, and I can't bear the thought of listening to him mock me, so instead of answering him, I bore into him with my eyes.

'It's none of your business. I want you gone when I get back.'

He glares back until his nerve falters and he starts to back down. He knows I mean it.

'How long have I got?' he asks.

I think back to Kaitlynn's interjection. *Am I brave enough to go to France alone?* 'Two weeks.'

'Two weeks?' He looks aghast.

'Better start job-hunting now then.' I smile tightly.

25

Chapter Four

On board the ferry from Portsmouth, I take a solitary seat at the bar under strict instructions from Kaitlynn to have a glass of fizz to kick-start my holiday. I think 'calm my nerves' is more appropriate. I still can't believe I'm doing this, going to France on my own. *Well, bonjour madame indeed.* I order a glass of champagne, my newly highlighted chunky lob bouncing around my shoulders as I speak. Some music starts to play and children gather around a small stage as some interestingly dressed entertainer comes out waving his arms around much to their glee.

Despite eventually showing Gary the letters, I'd not managed to change Gary's opinions about me going to France. I'd explained why I was making the trip and how it was the Darlington family destiny, hoping to generate a spark of emotion, but he just didn't get it. Under different circumstances, it could have been a family pilgrimage of sorts: me, Kieran and Gary tracing the rich history of our ancestor. Instead, he'd just quizzed me about what I was hoping to see or achieve since everyone involved is dead and would be unlikely to care. That stung because our mum would have cared. I don't know why she never showed me the letters but I do know she would have cared.

I wipe the moist corner of my eye with the sleeve of my ill-fitting blazer that I'd got for eight pounds in the sale at H&M because I thought it looked smart.

In the end, I booked four weeks off work, because my manager asked me if I wouldn't mind taking all my annual holiday in one go. It was very unusual to be granted so much leave all at once, but he said it was a quiet time of year and it was better from a staff planning point of view if I did. I think he was worried about union action if word got out that the 'employee of the year' didn't take holidays. It probably sets a bad example. Plus, as Jamie said, I'd never get around to taking the remaining two weeks if I didn't do it now. He was right, of course, and it gave Gary a decent length of time to pull his finger out.

And now here I am, sitting drinking champagne at breakfast time. I giggle and immediately look around self-consciously, but nobody seems to have noticed.

I'd briefly studied WWI poetry for my A levels, and I'd left a library copy of Wilfred Owen's *The War Poems* for Gary to read, along with instructions for returning the book. He may not have any sympathy for our grandmother and the loss of her father, but he could blooming well educate himself on the horrors of the Great War and learn a little about our great-grandfather's sacrifice.

Suddenly overwhelmed at the thought of losing my treasured letters, I check my tote bag in a panic. It's there, exactly where I'd left it. I pull it out, handling it like a lottery ticket with all the right numbers on.

A sleek leather wallet filled with my fragile pieces of history.

I'd sorted the letters chronologically and placed each one in a plastic wallet for safekeeping. I'm not sure what I'll do with them after the trip but I know I want them with me as I retrace my great-grandfather's Great War journey.

Another Kaitlynn idea – to treat myself. It seemed fitting to have something special to transport them in, and I'd got a pretty good deal, otherwise I wouldn't have splashed out, but all that excitement is now wavering because the financial implications of four weeks abroad isn't to be sniffed at. I'd be needing my entire prize money, my annual bonus, and there is a good chance I'll need to dip into my modest savings too.

As if on cue, the waiter slips the bill in front of me, and when I spy the charge I baulk. *Surely he's charged me wrong?* I pick up the wine list and double-check the price – something I should have done before I'd ordered 'a nice glass of champers', but I got caught in the moment. Sure enough, it *is* fifteen euros a glass. I leave the cash on the plate, mentally calculating how many tins of corned beef I could've bought with that, before I decide to head up to the sundeck.

Fighting the wind, I make my way to the railing and take out the first plastic wallet, clutching it tightly.

The letters don't cover his whole story and he never discloses his location so I had to use the internet to research the journey of his regiment and match up the dates. He'd been an early enlistee, one of the so-called 'Kitchener's Mob' and he'd sailed from Southampton to Le Havre in December 1915 after almost thirteen months of training, prolonged partly by a lack of training equipment and uniforms. Most soldiers arriving after him had nowhere near that length of training.

The first letter my great-grandfather sent was just after he'd landed in France during the winter of 1915.

12th December 1915

My dearest Elizabeth,

It was a choppy trip across the old 'salt water' and the paddle steamer was bursting at the seams. I've not seen so many sick men before. We've travelled a bit by train and foot since. The combination of new boots and woollen socks hasn't been fantastic but otherwise, I'm getting on all right. There are some pretty villages around and the locals I've met have been very hospitable, but we've not really been allowed to explore.

Give my love to Rose.

Forever yours,

Will

I glance out, over the railing, taking in the formidable grey rolls beyond. The same 'old salt water' my great-grandfather crossed on his first trip to France, no doubt feeling a sense of apprehension incomparable to my own. Though you wouldn't know it from the letter. It's hard to decipher his tone from so few words but I'm sure I've conveyed more terror in the three text messages I've sent to Kaitlynn already this morning:

This is a bad idea. I should cancel. C x

I honestly think I'll get lost and I can't speak French! What am I doing?

Kaitlynn????

I certainly didn't have the calm demeanour to use words like 'choppy' and 'salt water' colloquially.

I tuck the letter back into the wallet and look across the waves, allowing my eyes to close whilst I feel the roll of the boat. My mind wonders to the men. Boys? For most of them it would have been their first time on a boat and their first time leaving their parents, never mind their country. If they could go off to France then I should stop being silly and put my big girl pants on.

After some time on deck and a leisurely lunch, I can see land from the lounge and cannot fathom how five hours have passed already.

My phone shrills to life. We must be close enough to land to catch a signal.

Mum, I'm coming home this weekend. K

I'd specifically phoned to tell him I was going to France and was met with the usual grunted response. I tap out a quick reply.

I won't be there, but your uncle Gary will be. Mum xxx

His reply is instant.

What do you mean you won't be there?

Chapter Five

I arrive in Le Havre warm, sticky and tired but, luckily, my budget hotel is only a short taxi ride away. The taxi driver doesn't speak a word of English and my French is just about on par with that, so I hop in and thrust my printout from Expedia his way and hope for the best. I glance out of the window, eager to catch my first glimpse of Le Havre but the blocky, grey, modern buildings are something of a disappointment. I'd hoped for rustic and charming not modern and unusual but as my mother used to say, 'The world doesn't revolve around you, Cath.' Besides, I'd read up on the place and knew it had been obliterated in the Second World War so I should hardly be surprised.

The lady at the hotel reception speaks to me in French and my cheeks flame as I sheepishly pass her the printout detailing my one-night stay. After dumping my bag, I decide to wander out for some food, and am relieved to spot a McDonald's restaurant where I order a familiar Big Mac using the touchscreen menus and sit down, placing my receipt on the table so that the order number is clear and nobody should need to ask me a question.

The last person I spoke to was the bartender on the ferry and that was hours ago and now I feel as though my voice has shrivelled up and died. That's probably an over-reaction but I'm used to talking a lot more because of the job I do and it's surprising how isolated and alone you feel when you're unable to communicate. I feel like a mute, which would no doubt please Gary if the condition was permanent.

As I stroke the condensation beads on the side of my cola cup it dawns on me that, actually, I don't feel like a mute. I feel ignorant and stupid. I should have tried to learn a little bit of French before I came to France but I didn't exactly make the decision rationally.

I finish my food and go straight back to my room and flop on the bed. Four weeks is a long time to be trapped in this solitary bubble and I don't think I can do it. My stomach hasn't stopped churning since I arrived. I don't know what possessed me to come. Kaitlynn had filled my head with silly ideas and Gary pushed me over the edge. No matter, I'll put this right and draw a line under it. Tomorrow, I'll go and get a ferry home.

Chapter Six

After a fitful night's sleep, I pack my case and head down for the serve-yourself breakfast. Sunlight floods the room from two floor-length windows and in its warmth, I'm put at ease. I should at least see the town today. I help myself to a banana and a yoghurt and sit down to look over the first letter from my great-grand-father once more. Something about being in the place where he wrote it fills me with a sense of warmth and excitement, like I'm connecting with him.

When I read it again, I notice there is no sense of fear despite what he came here for. I'm obviously reading between the lines but I get the impression of a jolly old chap tootling off to war, not a scared young man heading towards life-or-death danger. It puts my own discomfort and fear of unfamiliarity to shame and if he could leave his homeland to fight a war for his king and country, I can bloomin' well spend a bit of time touring the place he died protecting. Can't I?

I wander the streets aimlessly. The kind English-speaking lady in the tourist information place gave me some leaflets and I learnt about the rebuilding of the town after the Second World War and how they used concrete because they didn't have access to stone or any money to transport it here. The results are quite unique even if I'm not quite getting what I'd hoped for. As I browse the patisseries and boutiques, I wonder what my great-grandfather saw. I'm sure the place was bursting with military activity then, not shoppers and couples strolling by the water.

After collecting my wheelie case from the hotel, I make my way to the train station before I have a chance to change my mind about continuing my journey, only this time I walk to take in as much of the city as I can.

On the train, I see some of the stunning views I imagine my great-grandfather saw. The green and yellow colours of the vast rapeseed and corn fields. The gentle roll of the terrain with beautiful rustic farmhouses and churches dotted about like decorations. *This is more like it.*

Right! I need to make an effort with the language. I can't stay silent for weeks. If my great-grandfather could do it, I have to at least try.

I fumble in the front pocket of my wheelie case and take out my phrase book.

Please.

Thank you.

What time is it?

Where is the nearest payphone?

The trouble with these phrases is that even if by some godly miracle I managed to pronounce them correctly, I wouldn't understand the reply. I skip ahead to the 'Ordering food and drink' section and practise ordering some simple items aloud, which earns me the odd sideways glance from other passengers, so I end up stuffing the book away and staring out of the window.

When I arrive at Paris, I have an hour to kill before my train to Arras. It's a town I chose by looking at the map for somewhere quite central to the places I want to visit, and which was large enough to have a train station. The reality is, I don't know what to expect.

Sitting down in a small café I run over the phrase in my head

– *Un cappuccino, s'il vous plaît* – but when the waiter comes over, he speaks so quickly that I don't have a clue if he wants to take my order or wants me to move, leave, pay, or is complimenting me on my bargain blazer. *Okay, that last one was a stretch.* I freeze. Scrambling for the words, I manage to spurt out the sentence I'd been so sure of just seconds before, but it's barely audible, even to me and doesn't sound anything close to how it had in my head.

'One cappuccino coming up,' he says in perfect English before walking off. It is safe to say I won't be masquerading as a French person any time soon – I feel such a fool. I've planned a few nights in Paris at the end of my trip before I take the Eurostar home and hope that by the time I come back, I'll be better equipped to at least order a drink.

The train ride to Arras is okay, mostly because I don't have to speak to anyone other than the ticket inspector and I do understand the word '*billet*', mostly because the ticket inspector repeats it several times whilst jabbing a finger at the ticket I've left out on the table. Thankfully, finding my hotel on arrival is a simple task since it's right opposite the station.

I stand outside and take a breath. *It's only four weeks; it will fly by.*

A horn honks as I step off the kerb and I jump back.

I can do this. I definitely can.

Chapter Seven

I walk past a red coach towards the revolving doors of the hotel, nervously running the phrase I need through my head: *J'ai une réservation pour Darlington*. If I'm going to be in France for four weeks, then I'll have to at least make an effort with the language even if I'm ruling out practising aloud on trains. *Reservashon or reservacion?* I run over it again as I step into the narrow cylinder, only remembering my wheelie case trailing behind me when it wedges in the doorway, jamming the entire mechanism. I yank the handle but it's stuck fast, and within seconds a small handful of people have accumulated, waiting to get in. I yank again. Nothing. '*Pardon*,' I say to nobody in particular.

I glance at the reception, but the man at the counter has his head down, seemingly unaware of my predicament. I bang the glass with the heel of my hand but he's oblivious. Becoming frantic, I search for a stop button or an alarm or something but there is nothing. *Surely this happens all the time?*

A man from outside starts to try and prise the door open. He's dressed in a red T-shirt that looks like a uniform of some sort, and I wonder if he's here to fix the doors – surely they shouldn't trap people like this. There was probably an 'out of order' sign somewhere. I tug the handle of my case while he heaves the two sides open with strong arms. Eventually, it springs free, throwing me back against the glass. That's when my eyes meet his, deep and blue. The moment I catch them, I look away, but not before I notice his striking resemblance to David the weatherman. A fresh, citrussy smell hits me when I stumble out and my cheeks flame.

'Thank you. *Merci*,' I say hurriedly, before adding a half-bow for good measure. An action that I'll dwell on later when I replay the whole embarrassing ordeal in my head. I scuttle towards reception without awaiting a reply.

'No problem,' the man shouts after me in perfect English. His deep voice has just a hint of a French accent.

'Good afternoon and welcome.' The cheerful man on reception greets me with a smile, instantly putting me at ease.

I draw a breath to reboot my system. 'Good afternoon. You speak English?' I smile, relieved. My rehearsed French has vacated my brain; likely it ran away with embarrassment. 'I have a room booked under "Darlington".'

He clicks away at the keyboard. 'I have it right here. It's ten nights with breakfast?' I hadn't booked more than that because of the expense, and I wasn't sure if I'd want to stay somewhere else and see a new place once I'd completed my great-grandfather's journey, though I'd no idea where. My plan is to use the Airbnb app that Kaitlynn told me about to find something cheap, but I'll cross that bridge when I come to it.

I nod, and he hands me a key before he passes on some information about breakfast times and how to find my room. I'm about to head to the lift when I hear some American accents coming from the small bar area. There are two older couples drinking beer and, strangely comforted by their familiar language, I drag my case to the bar where they're sitting, just to listen for a while.

'*Une petite bière—*' deep breath '*—s'il vous plaît*,' I say slowly but confidently as I perch on a stool at the bar.

The barman, whose name is Kevin according to his badge, looks up at me and smiles. 'A small beer coming up.'

'Thanks,' I reply, once again deflated by the fact my French was so painful he couldn't bear to humour me. Still, I'm only half a day into learning French. I can only get better, right?

'You're English, huh?' One of the older American ladies turns to me with a broad beaming smile. She's tall and slim with a sleek silver bob and is wearing a green matching pants suit.

'Yes, English,' I give a half-wave, 'Just over on holiday to visit the war memorials and museums.'

'Us too. We're fascinated by the history of it all. My husband, Harry, over there, was a vet.' She points to a crinkly, affable-looking man in a navy baseball cap. 'Not in the First World War, though, obviously. I mean, I know he's old but ...' She winks, and I warm to her recognisable Southern-belle charm straight away. 'He had a British uncle killed in the First World War and he's wanted to take this trip for so long.'

'Me too. My great-grandfather was killed in the war. In Belgium actually, but he was posted in France too. He was close to Arras when he fought in the Battle of the Somme. I'm here retracing his footsteps. Sort of.'

She gives a sympathetic smile. 'So, are you here with your family?'

'Oh no, it's just me. My son is away at university and my brother wasn't really interested in coming with me,' I say, not entirely untruthfully.

'No husband?' she asks, with unmasked surprise.

'I don't have a partner.' Kevin places my beer in front of me and I take a big glug of it.

'Oh, well that's too bad, a pretty girl like you. Harry and I are fifty years in, and he drives me mad some days, but he's my Harry and I wouldn't have him any other way.' Her eyes twinkle with affection as she gazes over at him and I mumble a 'congratulations' that I'm not sure she hears.

'I'm Martha, by the way.' She holds out a papery-skinned hand to shake and her pale blue eyes rest on mine.

'Cath,' I reply, taking her hand.

Martha proceeds to introduce me to the other couple, Roland and Cynthia, who say a cheerful 'Hi, Cath'. Cynthia's voice is hoarse like a smoker's and sounds almost as though someone is stood behind her cranking it out. I give a shy wave. Roland is in a sports jacket and chinos and he has a maroon baseball cap on. Cynthia is a little shorter than Martha with a fuller frame. Her hair is chin-length, snow-white and wavy.

'If you're alone, you should come and get dinner with us – we'd love for you to join us. We've found a pub in the square that sells decent hamburgers so we're heading there soon.'

Eating alone was something that had always daunted me a little and some company would be nice. They seem like a friendly bunch and the familiarity of burgers is welcome, so I say 'yes'. We agree to meet in the lobby half an hour later, which gives me time to dump my bags and freshen up with a quick shower.

When I return to the bar, the four of them are already waiting for me. A man is stood talking to them. As I near the group, my chest thumps with recognition. The man who freed me from the revolving doors is stood drinking a glass of water and he has them all engrossed in whatever he's saying. As he catches sight of me he grins and takes a bow with an elaborate hand-twirling gesture in reference to my earlier faux pas. Heat immediately floods my cheeks.

Unfortunately, Martha spots me before I have the chance to dart back into the lift or hide behind a pillar or do some kind of tribal dance in the hope the ground might open up and swallow me whole. 'Cath, this is Olivier. He's our tour guide and we've badgered him to join us for dinner.'

'Pleased to meet you. Again,' he says, his gravelly voice beautifully iced with that rich French accent.

I glance at him, looking away at the exact same moment our eyes connect. My cheeks are still on fire. Realising I'm being rude, I mumble a quick hello and thank him again for freeing me earlier before turning back to Martha to make polite conversation about hamburgers.

'Ahh, about those. I was just telling Olivier how I'm a bit of a connoisseur of French cuisine. Ever since Julia Child released *Mastering the Art of French Cooking* back in the Sixties I've dabbled in French cuisine and I've gotten pretty good even if I do say so myself. Olivier said there is a place near here I'd love. You don't mind, do you Cath?'

'Not at all.' My mouth is dry and the words feel thick and chewy. A burger had sounded safe, both to the palate and to the purse, whereas fine French dining doesn't sound safe or affordable at all. It sounds terrifying. Excuses not to go whirl through my brain and whilst I surprise myself with my creativity at such short notice (I'm someone's 'phone a friend' on the *Who Wants to be a Millionaire?* reboot; I've discovered I'm highly allergic to the French air and must stay inside indefinitely; I'm OCD and *have* to eat a burger on a Sunday; eating French food in France seems so cliché) I don't actually get any words out in time.

'So, it seems you two have already met?' she says, looking from me to Olivier.

Olivier nods. 'I bumped into Cath as she was checking in,' he says, with his eyes fixed on mine. He's being polite by not telling the story, and I appreciate that but decide to come clean anyway because laughing at myself has gotten me through some of life's toughest challenges.

'Actually, I got my bag stuck in the revolving door and Olivier here kindly freed me.'

'Ahh, so you were her knight in shining armour,' Cynthia says, and I wince a little with discomfort.

'It happens all the time,' Olivier says, playing it down and I'm thankful.

'Well, I do like a girl who can make an entrance,' Martha says with a glint in her eye.

We're all chatting about food as we come to a stop before the road outside the hotel, and, instinctively, I glance right and put a foot forward. Something firm comes out of nowhere and pelts me in the stomach. I look down, surprised to see Olivier's tanned arm stretched out in front of me. The contact causes me an unfamiliar flutter in my lower abdomen.

'I'm sorry,' he says. 'It's a force of habit. I'm so used to getting British people on my tours who forget to look left.' The tips of my ears burn and I'm not sure if it's in response to the fact I can't manage to cross the road or the fact I had *unusual feelings* for a stranger's arm.

We walk for about ten minutes before entering the huge square, the Place des Héros, which is much bigger than I'd expected it would be and much more impressive with its Flemish-Spanish baroque-style buildings. The restaurant is a similar bistro style to the others in the square and given the fair weather, we decide to sit outside.

'You sit there, honey.' Martha directs me to the seat next to her, which is opposite Olivier. Obviously, I don't know her very well, or at all actually, but I suspect she's done it on purpose even if it is just because Olivier and I are similar in age. I take the menu from the waiter and study it to look busy. There's a drought in my mouth once more as I scan the unfathomable offerings. There are a few recognisable words such as '*fromage*' and '*poulet*' to the more obvious '*crabe*' and '*porc*' but I've no idea what they come with. Whilst I'm not a fussy eater as such, something awful like tarragon sneaking into one of the sauces could come as a nasty surprise.

My hands are clammy on the menu and I glance up for some respite only to rest my eyes on Olivier who isn't looking and I get that strangely pleasurable flicker in my lower stomach again. He has messy light brown hair that is sort of styled in a floppy

'Hugh Grant' style circa 2003 (after the curtains but before the grey). It's in great condition too, and the light from underneath the parasol glints off it like it does off the hair in those shampoo adverts.

I try to refocus on the menu. It's definitely unusual, but what is also unusual is the depth of blue to Olivier's eyes. They're hypnotic. I don't think even David the weatherman could lose the entire British navy fleet in his oceanic eyes.

I become vaguely prickly, aware of someone watching me, so I glance up from the menu. Sure enough, Olivier is looking at me. So are Martha and the others and then I notice a presence looming to my left: the waiter, who is looking at me expectantly in his smart black and white attire protected by a chequered apron. Suddenly, the thought of messing up my order or ordering something weird ('oh, Cath, that's a palate cleanser') panics me but I'm out of time.

'Oh, *pardon*, I'm sorry.' My voice croaks. I skim the entrees one last time. 'The *porc* please.' I daren't even try to pronounce the full title 'Filet de porc sauce Normande' even though it seems fairly simple. I can't help but wonder what Normande sauce is. Is it garnished with fibres from the Bayeux tapestry? Seasoned with the ground bones of William the Conqueror perhaps? *That would certainly explain the price.* The others have gone for the filet mignon but at thirty-three euros a pop, I decide to give that a miss since I could buy two evening meals in a more low-key place for that.

I don't even feel that hungry since a thousand butterflies have taken up residence in my stomach, filling the cavity entirely.

Taking a deep breath to try and neutralise them, I turn to Olivier, who looks relaxed, sitting back in his chair easily, resting his head on one hand. The underside of his forearm is turned outward and I can see the veins in his wrist like a map of his body leading back to his heart. In an attempt to look relaxed too, I mimic his position but something about having my arm exposed

44

like that makes me feel naked so I turn it inward and eventually place in my lap. I must look noticeably odd, as Olivier asks if I'm okay. I nod but I'm uncomfortable, and I don't really know why because I was fine earlier. Olivier's presence has changed the dynamic somehow.

Martha and the others have entered into conversation about something they're all 'in on' from back home, and since I'm sitting on the end, I don't even attempt to join in because I'm worried that if I say something and they don't hear me, I'll look foolish.

Olivier doesn't seem to suffer the affliction of inner turmoil as he looks around, soaking up the vibrant atmosphere of the square. I once again attempt to follow suit, glancing around, trying to appear nonchalant and comfortable, but I can't shake the feeling of Olivier's presence. My senses are heightened and I'm on edge, like I've entered an electric field or a flagship Primark store in the mid-afternoon.

'Cath?' Martha's questioning tone brings me around, but I can't tell whether or not she's asked a question because sometimes Americans add that questioning infliction to anything they say, don't they?

'Sorry, I was miles away.' I smile. Trying to appear normal exhausts me, and a part of me starts wishing I was back home in Berrybridge where I am normal and so is everything around me.

'We were talking about our tour tomorrow, dear. The coach is going to Thiepval and Albert and we wondered if you wanted to tag along. If that's okay with you?' She looks pointedly at Olivier.

'Of course,' he says to Martha before looking me directly in the eyes. 'There's space on the coach so I don't see why not.' A tingle spreads across my back. Although Thiepval isn't part of my great-grandfather's documented journey, it's in the heart of the Somme Valley and I'd perhaps see some of what he'd seen. I want to go but I haven't looked into the costs yet. Having to fork out for this expensive dinner and a coach trip wasn't budgeted for. My money is vanishing quicker than the frozen turkeys do at Christmas.

'How much is the trip?' I can't look anyone in the eyes as I ask as casually as I can but inside my stomach is rolling with waves of embarrassment.

Olivier bats the air with his hands. 'Nothing. Like Martha said, there are spare seats and we're going anyway.'

'Thank you but I'm more than happy to pay the going rate.' I hope nobody else notices the subtle rise in the pitch of my voice.

'Please, be our guest,' he says in a way that feels final and a warmth fills my chest.

'So how long have you been a tour guide?' I ask, feeling braver.

'I've done this for almost twenty years now. I wanted to utilise my English and most of the people who use our tours are either British or American. Plus, I love history and travel and since the company is Europe-wide, I get to see more than just northern France.' He takes a sip of his beer.

'I've always loved history too, and seeing different places has to be a bonus.'

His features lift a little. 'Definitely.' He nods. 'So do you travel much?'

I shake my head. 'Hardly ever. I wasn't brought up in a family of ambitious travelling types and we never really had much money. My mother was a single parent and just a regular hard-working, working-class person who enjoyed relaxing at home on her days off. She took me and my brother on minibreaks to Wales and for days out and was great in the sense that she could create adventures for us without even leaving the house.'

I smile. 'One time, she turned the lounge into Loch Ness. She covered the floor with blue flannel sheets from my brother's bed, and our big brown sofa was a sailing boat. She used a snake puppet as the Loch Ness Monster.' I stop talking, remembering how my mother used to make us close our eyes and imagine the gentle swaying of the boat. I can still feel it now if I really concentrate and it wasn't too dissimilar to the ferry crossing to Le Havre considering there wasn't any water or a boat in sight. 'Sorry, you probably have no idea about what I'm blabbering on about.'

He looks bemused by my expression but smiles warmly. 'Everyone knows of the Loch Ness monster. Not too many have seen him though, hey?' His eyes glint mischievously before a more sympathetic smile forms on his lips. 'Your mother sounds like a wonderful woman.'

'She was.'

'Oh, I'm sorry.' He holds his eyes on mine for a moment too long, and I fight the urge to move my hair off my face. I'd read in some 'women's' magazine in the staffroom at work, that doing that can be seen as a sign you're attracted to someone, and I certainly don't want to give off those types of signals, thank you very much.

'Were you just talking about Loch Ness?' Cynthia's gravelly voice cuts through the tension that I'm ninety-five per cent sure I'm imagining.

'We were. Have you ever been?' I rest my chin on my hand and look at her, glad to have someone else to focus on.

'Yes, Roland and I went about twenty years ago. It's such a beautiful place, isn't it?'

'I wouldn't know, I've not actually been. My brother and I used to pretend our living room floor was Loch Ness.' I don't feel like sharing the story again; it seems strangely intimate all of a sudden.

'Well, you must go. It's one of the most beautiful parts of the world, and you live so near.'

'I'm sure I will,' I say politely, though our opinions of what constitutes 'near' seem to differ somewhat.

The food arrives and the conversation mostly centres around travel. Since I've very little to contribute, I listen with genuine

47

interest and make a mental note to travel more whilst I push the food around my plate. Now Kieran is grown up, I *should* travel more. It makes sense to see the world. My annual bonuses will cover the cost of a trip once a year and even though I've only just arrived in Arras, I feel like I'm doing okay if you discount the door fiasco and the fancy menu. Travelling alone doesn't seem so bad.

'Are you going to eat that?' Olivier asks. The sauce is a pale green colour and it smells sort of fruity with a tinge of alcohol but there's no indication of delicate embroidery fragments or the DNA of an ancient monarch so I take a forkful and raise it to my lips with trepidation.

'Yes.'

He leans across the table and whispers, 'It's an apple and brandy sauce.'

I give a small smile in response but feel ridiculous inside even though there was nothing mocking in the way he said it and I don't think he was trying to embarrass me.

I take a bite and it's a delicious explosion of flavour with the apple complementing the pork and the brandy flavour cutting through perfectly. Mum had always thought fruit and meat to be an odd combination, so much so she'd laugh at the cranberry sauce display at Christmas and shake her head with utterings of 'bonkers, fruit is for pudding!' As a result, I'd never thought to combine fruit and meat but this works so well. I stuff the next forkful in and it seals the deal. Cranberry sauce next Christmas it is!

Back at the hotel, I bid the others goodnight and head up to my room where I fall asleep, wrapped in the warmth of the evening, the aromas and flavours of France, and, strangely, thoughts of Olivier. There's something about him that's quite unlike anything I've seen in anyone before.

Chapter Eight

'Good morning!' my new travel buddies call as I walk in to breakfast the next day.

'Did you sleep well?' Martha asks. She's dressed smartly in pink capri pants and a matching blazer with a white T-shirt underneath.

'Good morning,' I reply. 'Yes, very well in fact.' I think the travelling had worn me out because once I dropped off, I had the deepest sleep I've had in ages.

'Did you sleep in?' Cynthia asks.

I nod, unable to confess the real reason I was late. Ridiculously, I couldn't decide what to wear. I'd eventually settled on a thin white T-shirt and denim shorts and left the room before I could change my mind. I head to the buffet and take a tray, piling it up with coffee, orange juice, a croissant, jam, yoghurt and some fruit. 'I'd never normally eat this much at home.' I chuckle as I sit down at the next table.

'You'll need your strength. Lots of walking today, girl,' Harry bellows, punctuating each word with his spoon.

'Oh, Harry, I'm sure Cath can manage a bit of walking, can't you, Cath?'

'I—'

'Olivier has us doing *a lot* of walking,' Roland interrupts before I can reply. 'I think he does it on purpose to tire us out so we nod off on the coach home and don't bombard him with questions.'

Cynthia pats his arm. 'Oh, Rolly, you're such a conspiracy theorist. He's just making sure we don't miss anything.'

'Anyway ...' Martha holds her hands up. 'Before this gets all domestic, let us summarise and move on. Lots of walking. Hard for us old folks, okay for Cath. No conspiracy. Got it?' She places her hands down firmly on the table and leans over to me. 'If we don't nip these things in the bud early on, those two will be at each other's throats before we set foot on that coach.'

I stifle a giggle.

'Good morning, my cheerful travellers,' an accented voice booms above us. Turning, I see Olivier stood behind me. He's in a crisp red T-shirt and navy chino shorts, and smells of that familiar, deliciously fresh scent, like a bottle of Original Source shower gel. Crisp, citrussy and minty. His messy hair has been arranged in some semblance of style with a dry product of some kind. Not that awful gunky stuff Kieran uses. I swallow as everyone else choruses 'Good morning'.

'We'll be leaving in ten minutes. Please make sure you have everything you need. Your money, cameras, teeth and so on. I will be at the coach out front.' I giggle as he turns and goes off to a few of the other tables. I doubt many people could get away with that kind of cheek with Martha, but she giggles too. Everyone excuses themselves to go and gather items, take medication, or pay a visit, and I arrange to meet them at the coach.

After finishing my oversized breakfast, I make my way outside. I'm the first to arrive so lean against the wall at the entrance and rummage in my bag for no other reason than to look busy, but I do benefit from the reassurance that everything I need is in there. 'You can get on board if you want.' Olivier walks from around the far side of the coach as a few other people start to trickle out of the hotel.

'Yes, thank you. I will.'

I follow behind as the small group climb the steps and make their way down the aisle. About halfway down, I take a seat and shuffle up to the window enjoying the quiet for a moment.

'They're a nice bunch – your new American friends.'

Surprised, I turn to see Olivier perch himself on the armrest of the chair across the aisle.

'Oh, yes. Yes, they are. Considering I've only just met them, it's so kind of them to invite me today. And you, thank you for letting me come along – I haven't got my head around travelling alone and getting from A to B in a strange country yet. Not that France is strange, it's normal just with the cars on the wrong side of the road and ...' My cheeks prickle.

'It's no problem,' he says easily. His calmness is the perfect cure for my flustered babble and I start to relax. 'Why are you here? In Arras alone, I mean.'

I give him the shortened version of my story – that I've come to see my great-grandfather's name inscribed on the Menin Gate – and I try not to sound like Sad Sack from the Raggy Dolls when I explain why I've had to come alone.

'Ahh that's a shame. We've already been to Ypres on this tour, in fact we're almost done with the war trips for now.' I'm relieved his attention is focused on the trip, and not the alone part.

'It's okay. Without wanting to sound ungrateful, I think it's somewhere I should probably visit by myself.' He nods knowingly as more people start filing onto the bus.

Our first stop is the museum at Albert. While Cynthia and Martha natter the whole way around about what they might buy from the gift shop, Roland and Harry are as engrossed in the fascinating exhibits as I am as we follow the journey of a real soldier from a card we were handed at the reception. The gas

51

masks, the weaponry, the life and fears of everyday people are all completely unimaginable.

The tour ends with a sound and light display, giving me a taste of what life might have been like during the night-time shelling that decimated the trenches on the front line. With each ear-splitting explosive bang, I flinch. It's hard to imagine how my great-grandfather and millions of other men lived this way, not knowing if the next one would hit him or a fellow comrade. I close my eyes. I'm sheltering as the bombs drop and the guns fire whilst praying for survival. I become aware of my heart racing.

'Are you all right Cath?' Harry puts his hand on my shoulder and I nod.

'I'll catch you up,' I say as they make their way outside.

I rub my thumb across the card I'd been given at reception. I bet being out there was quite lonely really. Despite the camaraderie and brotherhood within the regiments, these men were expecting to die and death itself is the most solitary event in a person's life because once your eyes close and you start to fade away, it's just you versus the unknown. Complete loneliness.

I imagine the smell of death, the sight of it, and the fear of it would be lonely too, because the feelings are so visceral, how could they be put into words? Something that deep is more a state of being and that's a loneliness like no other. It's not just having nobody to chat over breakfast with. It puts my first day in Le Havre into perspective, that's for sure.

The exit takes me out into a garden, the equanimity of which contrasts starkly with the underground depiction of hell I've just emerged from. In a way, it's symbolic really because tranquillity and peace were built upon the sacrifices and horror of war shown below. Yin and Yang.

I stop to sit on a wall and admire a statue in the garden. 'It's a cliché but life really is short,' Martha says, sitting down next to me.

'I know. Deep down, that's probably one of the reasons I took this trip,' I say honestly. It hadn't escaped me that my life had become stuck in a bit of a rut for the last ten years or so and the fact it took Gary of all people to push me to do something different is quite sad really.

'I don't have much advice to offer the younger folk these days, but all that seize the day stuff is spot on. Life really does pass you by if you're not careful. Anyway, I'm a bumbling old fool and I need to go pee.' She uses my shoulder for support as she eases her way back up to her feet and then she's off again, leaving just her words and the scent of lavender lingering behind.

We have an hour to explore the town. While the others disappear off to the café, gift shop, or to walk around the town, I just sit for a moment, looking out over the river. I take out the second letter I have from my great-grandfather.

17th December 1915

My dearest Elizabeth,

We've reached the camp safely. It's enormous! We could see it as soon as we stepped off the train as it covers the whole hillside. We've been shown kit and read the regulations. On the walk over to the training ground yesterday I saw the sand and sea, though it's freezing. I'm developing a taste for bully beef stew.

All my love to you and Rose.

Will

I wasn't able to find out where the training camp was with such little to go off and that saddens me somewhat. Putting the letter away, I notice my phone screen is lit up.

There's a message from Gary.

Read some of those poems. Bit sombre eh? The leccy metre has run out. Do you have any money on your card?

'Grrr.' I grit my teeth. *Can't he put some money on it for a change?*

I'd emptied the tin in the kitchen so he can't raid that, but I do contemplate telling him about my secret emergency stash of pound coins under my bed. I think better of it.

No, sorry. You'll have to dip into your beer money x

I smirk a little bit as I hit send. *There's a first time for everything.*

Another message pops in from Kaitlynn. I must have just picked up a signal or something.

How is it? Are you okay? Is the hotel nice? Did you find your GG's grave yet? Work is hell – can we move to France? I'd rather eat frogs' legs than work here xxxxx

Always the drama queen.

Martha and Harry are sitting on a bench outside the front of the museum, eating chocolate éclairs. The heat from the sun burns through my T-shirt, which feels odd because I hadn't expected it to be quite so warm in France.

'Those look good,' I say when I'm close enough.

'Mmm.' Martha nods while licking her lips. 'I can definitely recommend them.'

'Go and get one – the patisserie is right there,' Harry says, pointing to a shop with a big blue canopy on the corner.

'Hmm, well, if you insist,' I say playfully.

I return a short while later with my own in a paper bag. 'Here, saved you a seat,' Harry says, patting the bench beside him as I approach. I sit down, unable to speak because I've just taken a delicious bite. 'Now I'm the envy of the town, what with two beautiful ladies by my side.' He chuckles while Martha just shakes her head.

'You old fool,' she says, and then smiles at him. I can't help but notice her eyes sparkle a little as they lock on his, and my tummy knots a bit, taking me by surprise. I don't suppose I've ever witnessed real-life love like this before. I've been alone a long time, and it doesn't bother me at all, but since Kieran left and Gary moved in, I suppose I've subconsciously wondered if this is all life has in store for me. Working to make ends meet and coming home to start all over again for someone who doesn't really appreciate me. I suppose, soon, it will be just me and I'm not sure if that will be better or worse.

I notice Martha leaning forward so that she can see me around Harry, and I hope I haven't zoned out again, missing what she had to say. I relax when I notice her mouth is full of the last piece of her éclair.

'You and Olivier seemed to hit it off quite well last night,' she says after she swallows.

'He seems like a very nice man,' I reply diplomatically.

'Oh, he is.' Her face illuminates. 'He has been so good to us on this trip. I'm going to miss him.' She allows her soft features to drop.

'Hey, do I need to have words with that young man?' Harry interrupts in a mock-stern tone.

'Oh, be quiet, you old fool,' she replies, brushing him off, before turning her attention back to me. 'I saw you chatting on the coach earlier.'

'Yes,' I reply, unsure as to why this is becoming a 'thing'.

'He hasn't really done that with anyone else. Usually, he hangs around by the door to answer questions and when everyone is on board, he gets on and sits at the front.'

'Oh Martha, come on, she's the only woman on the coach who

doesn't need a Zimmer frame, incontinence pads and Super Poligrip! Of course they have something in common.'

'Speak for yourself! I need none of those things.' Martha hits Harry's arm playfully, causing him to chuckle.

'She doesn't realise she's an octogenarian,' he leans over to whisper to me.

'My hearing is fine too,' she says.

'Harry is right,' I say, before the senior citizen banter escalates to World War Three proportions. 'Olivier and I are just similar in age and there's nothing to suggest he's single anyway.' I curse myself for getting drawn into the debacle.

'Well, he must be, the hours he works … I guess I'm just an old romantic. When I see two wonderful people alone I just want them to be happy together.'

'It's not really how real life goes,' I say softly, hoping not to offend her.

'You're here a while. There's still time.' Her eyes twinkle again, and I start to feel uncomfortable. Not least because she's way off the mark and Olivier would probably be horrified if he knew.

'Martha,' Harry says, placing a gentle hand on her knee, 'did you come here to matchmake, or did you come here to sightsee and learn about the Great War?'

She frowned. 'Trick question. You forgot to say: raid the gift shops.'

'Well, that goes without saying.' Harry shrugs.

'Do you want to come and look around the shops with us? The others went to get a late lunch and I'm not sure they'll be finished yet.'

I smile. 'No, I want to just sit for a while. It's been a lot to take in but thank you. You go ahead. I'll catch up with you later.' They were kind to offer and I know they genuinely don't mind me tagging along, but to them, this is a once in a lifetime trip, and having me hanging around wasn't a part of their original itinerary.

Once they've gone, I lift my face to the sky, allowing the warmth of the sun to heat my skin, freeing all the happy endorphins. When I lower my head and open my eyes, Olivier is standing in front of me. My heart bangs in my chest.

'Oh, hi,' I say, hoping I hadn't just looked like a complete idiot.

'Sorry to disturb you. I'm just checking to make sure everyone is okay and seeing if you wanted any advice about the town or anything?' He shuffles on his feet a little, and for the first time since meeting him, he looks a little vulnerable.

'Thank you, that's really kind, but I'm okay. I've treated myself to this delicious éclair—' I gesture to the last partially melted bite that I'm clutching with my pincers '—and was just going to get a coffee and look around the shops. I'm easily pleased.' *Easily pleased? Cringe.* Does that sound like I'm insinuating something? I'm definitely not.

'Would you like some company?' he asks. Perhaps I'm imagining it because of Martha filling my head with nonsense, but I think there's a look of hopefulness on his face.

'Yes, if you like,' I say, trying to hold back my apprehension. It's one thing chatting on the coach, but to go for an actual coffee seems a bit nerve-racking. I try not to panic thinking about it.

'Great, I know a wonderful café just across the road.' He points to a place with outdoor seating beneath a black and cream canopy that's only about one hundred and fifty metres away.

'Perfect.' I stand up and we walk silently towards the place. My stomach starts to feel all twisty and I regret saying yes, wishing instead that I'd come up with an excuse and not mentioned the coffee. *Shopping, I could have said shopping – men hate shopping!* my brain screams, remembering how Kieran used to go pale and clammy at the very thought of it.

When we arrive at the café, we spot a table outside, and as we approach it, he pulls out a chair but doesn't sit down. 'For madame,' he says, making my chest feel all light and tingly at the unfamiliar gentlemanliness.

I thank him and sit down, instinctively picking up the menu to avoid having to find something to say.

'They do wonderful scallop and prawn skewers here.' he says.

'Oh, I'm not hungry. That was the biggest éclair I've ever seen and I ate it all. I'm sure it was meant for two people.' I let out a small laugh and put the menu back into the holder.

He laughs. 'No way! They're standard one-person sized éclairs. The ones I make are twice the size.'

'You can make éclairs?'

'I prefer to make savoury dishes like casseroles but yes, I can make éclairs.'

Olivier beckons the waiter over and orders coffees for us both. *Blimey.* 'So, you can cook then?' I ask, failing to hide the surprise in my tone but in fairness, Gary is my only real male comparison and I think he'd starve to death if he had to so much as open a tin of beans himself.

'I wash the dishes too.' He grins playfully. 'I learned quite young,' he says, glancing down at the table. When he doesn't say any more I get the feeling there's more to the story but I don't ask. We sit in silence for a few moments.

'The Basilica is a beautiful building,' I say, struggling for conversation. At work we're trained to ask the customers pre-set questions at the checkout to make them feel welcome and to avoid awkward silences but I think asking Olivier if he wants a five-pence carrier bag may strike him as a little odd.

'It is.' He perks back up. 'It was hit by a German shell in 1915. See that golden virgin statue at the top?' He points but he needn't have. It's huge. 'It bent to a near horizontal position after the shelling. Legend has it, the Germans believed that the side to cause the golden virgin to finally tumble, would be the side to lose the war.'

'Really? Did it tumble?' I ask, intrigued by the story.

'Yes, however, it was bombed purposely by the British in 1918 to stop the Germans using it as a lookout tower after they occupied the town. Needless to say, the Germans' belief was proven wrong.'

'That's an interesting story,' I say, finding myself wanting to absorb as much knowledge of the time as I can to build a picture of what life was like. 'It's hard to imagine it as a pile of rubble now,' I add as the waiter sets two coffees down in front of us. Once the waiter has gone, I ask Olivier how he knows so much about history.

'I was a bit of a history nerd at school.' He grins. 'A geek, I think they say?' He's still grinning as he speaks so it can't bother him that much. 'I didn't care, though. There's a rich history in the region where I'm from and it's interesting to me. How about you? You're here – were you the same?'

'What, a geek?' I say with a dramatic hand on my chest.

He studies me and the hair follicles on the back of my neck tingle. 'Somehow, I can't see it.'

I glance away self-consciously and think back to my comprehensive education in a failing school on the outskirts of London. Somehow, I can't make it fit with the perfect image I have of him, reading history books studiously on an evening whereas I was probably chatting on the phone with my friend about which boys we fancied, whilst my mum yelled at me to revise.

'History is something I've become more interested in recently,' I say instead, before filling him in on the letters that I'd found. He nods animatedly as I explain all about them.

'That's fantastic. To have a piece of history that you get to keep for yourself. I'd love to read them … if they're not too personal, of course.' His interest is welcome and warm in contrast to Gary's indifference.

'No, they're not personal, not anymore at least. I'd love you to look at them. It seems my great-grandfather was trying to learn French when he was stationed here and three of the letters are written in French.' I bite my bottom lip, unsure as to whether I should continue. In the end, I dare myself to go on. 'It would be great if you could translate them for me.'

'I'd love to. I'd be honoured if you'd allow me to.'

Once we've finished our coffee, we part ways. Olivier has some paperwork to take care of for the tour company and I've been desperate to browse the little shops. I have half an hour left to do it.

***

On the coach, I take in more of the scenery. Olivier is sat in the adjacent seat. 'You can't drive very far without coming across a cemetery or memorial, can you?' I ask as we pass another small garden filled with white headstones.

'No. It wasn't always possible to remove the bodies from the front line. Search and rescue teams were sometimes killed trying to retrieve the dead. In many cases, the solution was to bury men close to where they fell. What it shows us now, though, is how death was all around. It was everywhere. No living man on the battlefield escaped witnessing the horrors of the Great War.'

I swallow hard and fall back into my seat, gazing out of the window and trying to understand how and why it even happened. Soon after, I catch a glimpse of a giant archway.

'What's that?' I ask.

'That's the Thiepval Memorial to the Missing. That's where Harry will find his uncle's name.'

'Wow. I wasn't expecting it to be so big.' I don't really know what I *was* expecting.

'It has to be big. There are over seventy-two thousand names of missing men inscribed on it. It's the biggest Commonwealth memorial to the missing in the world.'

'You're like a walking, talking encyclopaedia,' I quip and he grins.

'I know, who needs Google, hey?' I like how he matches my tone.

'How can that many men have been lost in these fields?' I say aloud, casting my eye back to the window and across the concealing beauty of the farmland beyond.

'It was complex. Not just a case of a man killed, carried to a grave and buried. Some men were blown to pieces and others buried by bomb blasts. Some men who'd been buried by their comrades in the field were later excavated by further bomb blasts. Soldiers' remains are being found to this day, usually when building works take place. But, as you can see, it's a slow process as there is little building work going on here.' The reality of what he's describing is so far from what we see here today it's hard to imagine.

The coach churns up crunchy gravel before finding a place to stop before two grassy mounds with a path through the middle.

Olivier stands up and taps the microphone twice. 'We've arrived at Thiepval. That modern building over there houses the museum and visitors' centre. There is a gift shop too and a couple of vending machines for refreshments. If you follow the path to the left it takes you up to the memorial. I'll be wandering around if you need me.' With that, he heads down the steps and begins helping the more infirm passengers off the coach, greeting everyone personally even if not by name.

'Did you send that postcard?'

'Have you found your glasses case?'

'Is that a new handbag, Beryl? Someone went crazy in Albert!'

I can't help but notice how genuine he seems, and I find myself smiling.

The sky is the brightest blue, the weather warm, and the grass a luscious green. It's a beautiful day in the Somme Valley, and the forecast shows no sign of it changing. It's as though the views and weather here are acting as some kind of consolation for what happened in the early twentieth century. It's like nature's own memorial to the sacrifices made. I fill my lungs with fresh country air and follow the path until I see the red-brick and white-stone structure. The path ends and the last part of the walk is across a well-manicured grassy area.

I slow down, breaking away from Martha and the others. Harry had gone all quiet when we stepped off the coach and I sense this is a more emotional part of the trip for him. He needs to be with his wife and friends and won't want some stranger tagging along. I wander into the vast space of headstones beyond the memorial, and I'm taken aback by the abundance of pristine, white crosses, each representing a fallen soldier. I glance at the inscription on one:

A SOLDIER OF THE GREAT WAR
KNOWN UNTO GOD

They don't even know his name. My stomach lurches. The headstones, each decorated with flowers, are aligned in four quadrants, symmetrical and all facing a larger, white-stone cross at the front. It seems like a beautiful testament to the heroics of these men.

I sit on the steps of the archway, taking out a leaflet I'd picked up at the museum in Albert. It's written in French. I'd paid no attention to the language when I picked it up, just the pictures, which are grainy, black and white images capturing the men in the trenches.

Sometimes I feel like my life is hard. The thankless task of looking after Kieran and Gary, working a dreary job just to make ends meet and having no real friends to confide in, other than my teenybopper colleague at work. Most of my old friends drifted away when I had Kieran. There are only so many times you can say you can't get a babysitter and go to the nightclub before people stop asking you. But I didn't blame them then and nor did I care. And I don't now.

If this trip has taught me anything so far, it's that I'm lucky. I live in a safer world, I'm with my loved ones and I have everything that I need. These men had it hard and how they got up and fought is beyond me, but they did.

I glance across the archway, and in the corner, I can see Harry's distinctive cornflower blue rain jacket. Martha has her arm around him as Roland and Cynthia hover behind them. It's an emotional scene and whilst I feel almost voyeuristic, I can't help but look on. Harry has these three people who've travelled thousands of miles to be by his side for this moment and it's one of the most special things I've ever witnessed. As I dab the corner of my eye, I sense a presence behind me.

'It is very moving being here, isn't it?' Olivier comes to stand by my side.

'Yes. So many men lost. It's hard to comprehend that each one of those names inscribed on the memorial and each of those crosses was a living person.'

'And as you saw before, there are countless cemeteries just like this one. That's what is the most staggering. Not just the number of graves in the cemetery, but the number of cemeteries.' He sits on the step beside me.

'What I find especially sad are the graves of the unknown soldiers. Their families won't have had the opportunity to visit their graves to pay their last respects,' I say, wishing I could do something about it.

'Not many family members had the financial means to come and visit back then.'

'I suppose, and we do have memorials back home. Every town and village has one.'

'Yes, I know, we do tours to the UK too.' This interests me more than it should.

'So, you go to England sometimes?' I ask.

'Yes, about once a month. I love it over there. Especially when we visit London.' The thought of Olivier being so close to where I live sends little sparks of excitement through my chest.

'What do you do in London?'

'You mean after I have lunch with the Queen, see my buddies in parliament and meet up with the Beckhams?'

'Hmm?' I twist the corner of my mouth in bemusement.

'Okay, we have a picnic outside Buckingham Palace, walk past Big Ben and go to Kensington Gardens. It just sounds more exciting my way.'

'So you do the touristy stuff?'

'I suppose – we cover some of the points of interest surrounding the world wars too of course.'

'So, you must know a lot about the Great War.'

'I do. It's interesting, but I also like to think me spreading the word about how horrific it was helps to make sure it doesn't happen again.'

'Only it did happen again,' I say sombrely.

'Ahh, yes, but I wasn't born then, and my predecessor must have lacked my charismatic charm.' He smiles, and we fall into a surprisingly companionable silence, watching the Americans laying a poppy wreath before a stone fascia.

'Hello,' the lady in the gift shop says cheerfully as we enter. She has a southern English accent, broader than mine, but is wearing the same T-shirt as the other staff members. Olivier introduces her as Jenny.

'Olivier has been filling me in. It seems you're on quite a sentimental trip?'

I nod. 'Yes. My great-grandfather fought in the area. He was out here for almost two years before he was killed in Ypres.'

She gives me a knowing look. 'There's lots of information in the museum if you want to know more about the battles in the region?' she says. 'There is the free exhibition too, just to your left.'

'That would be great.' I look at Olivier, unsure if he'd prefer to leave me to it.

'I'll join you.' He smiles warmly. We walk in silence, reading the accounts and studying the pictures, some graphic, depicting the haunting faces of the fallen; others depicting more triumphant moments.

'Some of these men are my son's age.' The thought is incredibly hard to bear.

Olivier nods and I notice his face is sombre.

There is a film to view too, and once we've seen everything, Olivier suggests paying to go into the museum, which I happily agree to.

As we walk the halls, I watch Olivier reading the information intently. He must have read it dozens of times, yet he is still engrossed, reading it like it's new. A few of the people off the coach tour are dotted about and Olivier makes polite conversation as we pass.

We approach a replica German fighter plane and he turns to me. 'Do you know the exact journey your great-grandfather made?'

'Almost. All I'm missing is where he trained. He wrote a letter from the training camp he went to after landing in France but I've been unable to find out where it actually was.'

'Perhaps Jenny can help. She's worked here years and is as interested in the war as I am. Almost.' He winks.

When we head back out to the shop, Olivier explains what we're after and Jenny asks me for all the information I have.

I give her his regiment and battalion information and find myself nattering away. 'He was just twenty-four.'

She tuts and shakes her head. 'So young.'

'It's staggering how many were,' Olivier adds.

'He enlisted himself. Given the dates he served, he was one of the first out there and he was married too.'

'The propaganda was very compelling back then. Many men

signed up out of pride for their country. I don't think the reality always hit them until it was too late. Not the Kitchener's Mob anyway.

'Right, so it was the training camp you were after?' Jenny asks, squinting at the screen.

'That's right.'

'This page here should have everything you need.' She stands up and gestures for me to sit down. I read the in-depth log of where the regiment were from day one until the end. Most of the information ties up to what I'd found.

'Étaples.' I say. 'That's where he trained.'

'I thought that was probably the case, but I wanted to be sure,' Olivier says.

'Is it possible to get there from Arras?' I ask.

'Yes, it's about an hour and a half away by car, give or take.'

I feel like a weight has been lifted now the missing piece of the puzzle has been filled.

'I'm really glad I did this today. Olivier, thank you so much for bringing me, and Jenny, thank you for all your help.'

'Don't be silly, we enjoy it,' Jenny says.

The coach journey back to Arras is quiet. Many people on board had a relative killed in the war, and seeing so many names on the memorial was such a moving sight. Others are perhaps worn out after such a long day. I sense that the thick silence is that of appreciation for the efforts to maintain such a fitting tribute. I glance around and most people are sitting gazing out of the window; a few have even nodded off in the eerie, dusky light you sometimes get on a summer's evening.

It isn't long before my mind wanders to Olivier. Not because he's good-looking – I can admit to myself that he is now – but because I saw a soft side to him that I didn't expect. He seemed so confident in himself last night, which I suppose, being a tour guide, he has to be; but I didn't get the impression he was quite so sensitive. But seeing him obviously touched by emotion earlier just made me want to hug him. I scold myself for being so silly. He could be a married man for all I know, and if he isn't he would never be interested in me: a doughy checkout girl held together by Aldi's own 'I can't believe they're not Spanx'.

What am I even thinking? I scold myself. I don't even want a man; I'm happy with the way things are and a man would complicate things. Besides that, I'm sure millions of soldiers didn't give their lives so that I could lust after attractive Frenchmen. I think my existence should be more meaningful than that. Then I think about what my existence actually *is* and can't imagine millions of men would have given their lives for that either. A routine of work, bargain-hunting, romcoms and David the weatherman. *But I have brought up a son, who has got into university*, a small voice in my head says.

'You know, during the Second World War, soldiers passed the Thiepval memorial and paid their respect to their fallen fathers.' Olivier has slipped into the empty seat beside me.

'Gosh, it's unimaginable. What they were going through, and to see that on top. I don't know …' I reply, no longer surprised by Olivier's sharing of random contemplations.

'I'm sorry, I know I keep bothering you with my war trivia but I don't always get much interaction from the tourists. Some, not all, seem to want to *say* they've seen the sights rather than actually absorbing the history. They want an Ypres fridge magnet or the Thiepval shopping tote but not always the knowledge, you know? That is sad to me.'

I nod in silent agreement. His passion for war history intrigues me. I've not met many men with such rich interests. Since being in school, most of the men I'd met were into the same things: football, computer games, and pictures of topless women, with regular trips of enrichment to the pub thrown in of course. Cardboard cut-out-and-keep activities for a limited range of stereotypically masculine interests.

Different was drawing me in.

Chapter Nine

The following morning, at Martha's insistence, I tag along on a short trip to the beautifully kept British cemetery in Arras, which is followed by free time in the town centre of Arras in the afternoon. It's slightly off-piste but I have plenty of time in France and part of the reason why I'm here is to do the journey my grandmother should have done and experience France. After the heaviness of yesterday, something light and breezy ticks all the right boxes so when the ladies decide to go shopping while the men catch a game of football I'm quite excited.

We deposit the men, along with their mumblings of soccer being a 'girls' game', in the pub and hit the high street. Martha and Cynthia are like magpies, drawn to the jewellery shops, whereas the great weather is giving me a penchant for some pretty cork-wedged shoes. If I play my cards right I'd need never wear my torturous pleather sandals again. By late afternoon, I still haven't bought any but I have enjoyed ogling all the different ones in their pastels and metallic hues. The others, meanwhile, have all managed to secure some yellow gold items. A ring for Martha's granddaughter and a necklace for Cynthia's daughter, plus a few items for themselves, I notice.

'Well, it's a beautiful day and there's outdoor seating at the cafés in the square. How about some alfresco lunch?' Martha asks.

'That sounds good to me,' Cynthia replies.

'Thank goodness.' I sigh. 'I was beginning to get embarrassed by my lack of shopping stamina in comparison to yours.'

'We've just had more practice.' Martha winks.

We find a table in the shade on the edge of the square and order three ham and cheese toasties and a bottle of white wine, and before long, we're tucking in.

'France is such a happy place,' Cynthia says with a wistful sigh, before draining the last of her small tipple of wine.

'Happiness comes from within and from the people you're connected to, not from a place,' Martha says between mouthfuls.

'I know that, but the people here seem so relaxed.' Cynthia gestures to couples ambling through the square and people sipping wine in the bars, chatting leisurely. 'It's the weather – it's warm and sunny but not stifling like the summers back home in Georgia,' she concludes, and I think back to my dreary bus commute home and mentally agree.

'Well, I think it's the company too,' I say, raising my glass to a chorus of 'I'll second that's.

Cynthia rests her head on her fists dreamily. 'We do love our men, but having a "girls only" day is just what the doc ordered.'

'So, these men you're both sporting, are they your first husbands?' I ask, spurred by my wine-induced confidence.

Martha smiles fondly and nods. 'Yes, Harry is the only man I've ever been with. Sixty-two years we've been married. Don't get me wrong, I could throttle him sometimes, especially now he's older as he can be such a cantankerous so-and-so.' She pauses and then smiles again. 'But I wouldn't be without him really.'

'Same for Roland and me,' says Cynthia. 'Fifty-nine years.'

'How about you, Cath? Have you ever been married?' Martha asks.

Still chewing my toastie, I shake my head. 'No. My son came

along as a result of a few alcopops and a bag of Walkers prawn cocktail crisps.' This draws a few blank expressions. 'His father was an older boy who I'd idolised since year eleven. When I told him I was pregnant, he didn't want to know. I heard he'd moved away not long after that and then, well …' I realise I'm droning on, telling a story that's probably the same one that thousands of women could tell.

Cynthia looks puzzled. 'So, what happened?'

'Nothing and there wasn't anyone after him. With a young son to care for I can't say I ever looked my best.' I giggle at the memory of being complimented on the unusual pattern on my top that was actually dried formula that I hadn't noticed had slopped down my side. 'There isn't much time for man-hunting with a little one. I don't have any regrets though; I wouldn't swap Kieran for a different life. How could I? He's such a smart boy, off at university now.'

Cynthia places a warm hand on mine. 'But now your son has grown up, don't you feel it could be the time to start looking for that special someone?'

I feel heat flush my face, and it isn't from the sun. 'No.' What I actually want to say is 'that ship has sailed', but I don't want to seem like I'm fishing for sympathy.

'No?' Martha repeats. 'Why in heavens not?'

'I don't feel like I need a partner to be happy. Besides, my lazy good-for-nothing brother, Gary, has moved in temporarily so I can hardly invite a man in for coffee.' I feel like this is a good point to steer the conversation away from dating. 'Before I came here, I was basically Gary's live-in butler.' I pause.

'How long has he been living with you?' Cynthia asks.

'He's been there six months but now I've told him he's to find a job and a flat while I'm in France. Mostly because I'm sick of waiting on him hand and foot.'

'You should never let a man walk all over you.' Martha jabs a knobbly finger in my direction.

'He should be waiting on you!' says Cynthia.

I smile. 'And pigs might fly! In a way, he's been good company since Kieran left. But now he's driving me mad. Do you see why I need to be single? Men annoy me.' I direct my last comment at Martha but grin a little so she knows I'm joking.

'I'm not painting a very good picture of Gary here, am I? He's not that bad. He used to work hard as an engineer and got laid off and basically hit rock bottom, which is why I took him in. I didn't mind doing all the housekeeping at first because I was used to it, but he was at home all day so I did expect him to chip in whilst I was at work. He didn't. Eventually, he started spending more time at the pub and doing less and less at home, so I've given him his marching orders.'

'And what did he say?' asks Cynthia.

'Okay then.' I shrug. 'He didn't have a choice.' I don't want to tell them the real reason for the final straw.

'Young men just don't have the fight in them anymore,' Martha says, shaking her head. She's right; I can't imagine Gary signing up to protect our country like our great-grandfather did. God knows what he'd do if conscription was ever deemed necessary again, because I don't think 'lazyitis' would be suitable grounds for an exemption.

'So there really hasn't been anyone since Kieran's father? It's a long time to be by yourself,' Cynthia says.

'No, I've not really been interested. As Kieran started to grow up, I felt too frumpy to go on dates. I felt, well … I didn't think anyone would be interested in me. Nobody was, really. Then I learned how to be happy alone and have been ever since.'

Martha points her glass at me. 'Baloney. You're a beautiful young woman. What I wouldn't give for skin that doesn't sag and hair that's not all wiry and colourless.'

I smile because Martha doesn't strike me as someone who gives a hoot about her physical appearance as long as her clothes are smart, but I'm grateful for the confidence boost.

'A lot of happiness can come from marriage, but there's no harm in a vacation romance either.' She chuckles. I can't help but laugh too, purely because of the contrast between her modern views and her deeply lined and frail face.

'Somehow, I don't think this is the right type of holiday for a romance, but I am enjoying getting to know you ladies,' I say, hoping that's the end of it.

'So, on to a completely different subject – Olivier is very handsome, isn't he?' Martha says, ignoring my comment with a wicked grin. Cynthia murmurs her agreement and I purposely remain silent. 'If only I were a few decades younger.' Her eyes are full of mirth.

'It's kinda sexy when a man is so knowledgeable,' Cynthia says while I sit, gobsmacked at these seemingly respectful, delightful elderly women discussing Olivier like a group of year elevens would talk about their school crush.

'A girl can dream,' Martha adds wistfully.

I give Martha a mock-stern look. 'I know what you're doing here and it's not going to happen. Poor Olivier, he has no idea you lot have his life planned out for him.'

'Not his life, exactly, just perhaps, the next four weeks or so.' She grins.

'Okay, Martha, leave the girl alone now,' Cynthia cuts in before turning to me. 'You know when she gets her teeth into something she just won't let go. She's an old romantic really.'

'I am too, but I prefer the movie kind of romance, not the real-life version.'

'No harm in some real-life romance. Roland used to escort me to work at the clothing factory every morning. He lived on the next road to ours, and although I never asked him to, he was always waiting for me each day,' Cynthia says.

'They call that stalking nowadays – and when it goes on for that long it's a felony,' Martha interrupts, causing Cynthia and me to howl.

'Oh, nonsense.' Cynthia brushes her off. 'He'd hold out his arm for me and say, "May I escort you, ma'am?" and we'd chat about the weather and movies and things until one day, he asked me out for a milkshake and he paid. There was none of this "split the bill" business you kids are fond of. That was our first official date and we've been together ever since.'

'Ahh,' I coo. 'That is a lovely story and very romantic.'

'Stalker,' Martha chimes in again, and we all giggle.

'I just couldn't see anything like that happening nowadays – in the UK at least; I can't speak for American men. Do you know, the last British man I made eye contact with stole a tin of corned beef from me.' I fold my arms.

'What the …?' Martha says. 'I knew there were some cultural differences, but I thought that was just because you had all the Colin Firths and we had the crazy *uncoupled* Scientologists.' I smile at her celebrity mash-up.

'That's why I prefer to live vicariously through the movies.'

'There hasn't been a good romcom out in a while,' Cynthia says, and we all nod in agreement. 'There was that one with the handsome young man in it – what was it called? *Stupid, Crazy, Love.*'

'*Crazy, Stupid, Love,*' I correct. 'That's one of my favourites and yes, the boyfriend, Ryan Gosling, phwoar!' I giggle.

'The boyfriend? Not that young whippersnapper. I meant the father. Steve Whatshisface.'

I stifle a smile.

'You old cougar, you.' Martha nudges Cynthia playfully before the conversation finally moves on. I can't help but think even the cougar ship has sailed for these ladies but I admire their optimism.

'So, one more day before we head back to the States,' Cynthia says, sharing out the last dribble of wine with a slightly shaky hand.

'I've loved France, but I'll be glad to get back to my big bed,' Martha says. Though I've only known these women a few days, they've become a sort of safety blanket of warmth. I haven't had to eat alone and joining their tour meant I've not had to really make an effort to do anything for myself. It's been a lot easier than my time in Le Havre. I'm both nervous and excited for the days ahead, but I'll miss my cosy nest of elderly companions.

'What are your plans for tomorrow, honey? Are you sure you don't want to join us in gay Paris?' Martha asks while we wait for the cheque.

I pause before answering. 'Actually, Olivier has offered to translate some old letters of mine, which my great-grandfather wrote to my grandmother. Some have been written in French and I'm desperate to know what they say.'

She doesn't reply, but the look she gives me says it all.

Chapter Ten

Outside the hotel is a car park forming a sort of square-shaped roundabout with a couple of restaurants beyond it, one of which is where I'm meeting Olivier in just a few moments.

I spot him as soon as I walk in. He's reading a book which I recognise. The title is in French, but the cover image and the word '*Lumière*' in the title give away the fact it's the popular book I'd seen on the bestseller shelf at work: *All The Light We Cannot See*. I smile because his interest in history is even present in fiction. I can see why he was perhaps treated as a bit 'different' at school, and that makes me feel sad on his behalf. People like him should be our role models.

'I see you're interested in the Second World War too?' I ask as I sit down opposite him. From his startled expression, I guess he'd been too engrossed in the book to notice me come in.

'Hi, Cath.' A smile breaks on his face once the reading spell is broken. 'I'm interested in most history. And most fiction.' He waves the book. 'The beauty of living in the now is that we can look back on all our mistakes and change things for the better. The beauty of fiction is that we can lose ourselves a little.'

'I'd like to think so.' I let his words linger a moment because they're true.

'So—' he claps his hands together '—we shall order some food and drink and take a look at these letters.' Sometimes his accent and grasp of English leave things open to interpretation, and I'm not sure if that was a question or instruction. Either way, I like the confidence he has to take charge.

'Great. I'll have an omelette and a black coffee,' I say.

When the waitress comes to take our order, she engages Olivier in conversation as I sit uncomfortably, unable to recognise even one word. Every now and then her knee kinks and she giggles, pulling on the sleeve of her jersey top. From his body language and tone, it seems Olivier is oblivious to any attraction the waitress may feel. Perhaps it stems from his childhood, or maybe he's married. I glance at his hand but don't see a ring.

'My apologies,' he says after she's gone. 'I come in here a lot and we chat about the tours and things. She was just asking how the latest tour had gone and I was telling her we're about to translate some letters written during the First World War.'

'Not a problem,' I say. 'It's me who should be apologising. I should at least try to speak some French. I've tried to learn a little bit, but the practice versus reality is a whole other issue. No offence, but you all seem to speak so quickly, it's hard to pick out the words I should recognise, never mind understand the ones I don't.'

He gives me a sympathetic glance. 'To be able to speak English, I basically sat with headphones on every afternoon during my school years. Then I pushed myself to use it at every opportunity and now get plenty of practice on the tourists. Fortunately, there is no shortage of English-speaking people in this region. So don't be too hard on yourself.'

'I suppose. I don't think I've ever met a French person in the UK, though I meet plenty of people who speak English with a foreign accent, so who knows.' I shrug.

'When Anais comes back, you should thank her – just a very simple *merci* to start with.'

I can do that. Just as I convince myself I spot her flouncing back with the coffees.

'*Merci*,' I say as she places them down on the table. She smiles and nods before scuttling back towards the kitchen.

'See. Easy-peasy,' Olivier says and I smile at how he makes such a childish phrase sound so sophisticated with his French accent.

'That was okay, and I'm comfortable asking for other things, as long as they are croissants, coffee, omelettes, or ham in quantities of one, two or three.' I laugh.

He stifles a grin. 'What more do you want? You've covered the main food groups. But now I see why you may need my help with the letters.' He pours some milk into his coffee and stirs the dark liquid. 'Unless, of course, your great-grandfather wrote from the battlefields to talk only about his breakfast?' I look up to see the corner of his mouth twitch, and realise I'm seeing a sliver of his less serious side.

'If you're not careful, you might not find out!' I grin, and he does too.

'In that case, I'm very sorry. Please forgive me.' He throws me an over-animated pleading look and I narrow my eyes in jest.

'Hmm, last chance, buster.'

He salutes me before moving on. 'Have you already tried to use an online translation tool?'

'I thought about it, but I wasn't sure it would be accurate enough, and I'd really like the true translation, the one that will help me get a deeper understanding of my great-grandfather's personality. I have the letters he wrote in English to my great-grandmother, so these may not give anything else away. I just thought his tone might be different in these because he wrote them as a father and not a husband. Of course, his French could be terrible, in which case, that may explain a few things – perhaps it's hereditary. Who knows?'

'Me, hopefully.' He smiles. 'Shall we take a look?'

I take my leather wallet and carefully slide out the fragile, yellowed papers.

He gasps before handling them as if they are delicate bubbles that could pop and disappear into oblivion at any second. 'These are very rare, you know.' He doesn't take his eyes off the letters. 'The mail was censored during the war, and I don't recall seeing any British letters written in French before. I'd have to look into it, but my guess is that these three skipped censorship. If the officers couldn't understand the language, they may not have trusted the content. Perhaps he was trusted and did a self-declaration ...' He trails off and I stare at him blankly, not really following what he means.

'Sorry, I got carried away. Soldiers could use a green envelope and declare the content as relating only to private, family matters as a way of bypassing censorship,' he clarifies.

My eyes fall to the letter and he starts reading it aloud in a quiet voice.

Ma chère Rose,

J'ai converser avec un français allié qui m'a aider à apprendre le français. Il passe le temps et est une distraction bienvenue du grondement des ennemis obus et du tintement des balles. Je sais que tu ne liras pas ça avant d'être plus grande. Ta mère veillera à ça. Je voulais t'écrire une série des lettres en français pour t'encourager à apprendre la langue quand tu seras plus âgée. Je pense qu'il serait important à l'avenir de parler une autre langue.

Gros baisers

Papa

I catch him wide-eyed and engrossed as his eyes dart left to right across the page. 'This is wonderful,' he says eventually, before noticing my puzzled expression. 'Sorry, I've just never seen anything like it. He is telling your grandmother, Rose, that he is learning French from one of his Allied comrades to pass the time and that it is a welcome distraction from the shellings. He also says that he has written to her in French because he wants her to learn the language when she is older because he thinks it will be important in the future.

I feel a pang in my chest. 'Insightful,' is all I can manage to squeeze past the ball in my throat.

'It's amazing he found the time to learn anything more than a few phrases. The troops actually invented their own language at one point to tackle the language barrier issue.'

'Is it fairly accurate then?' I ask, in awe of how my great-grandfather managed to learn a language on the battlefields when I couldn't even manage to do it in the safety of my high school with a qualified French teacher at my disposal.

He tilts his hand left and right to indicate it is so-so. 'There are some common grammatical mistakes, just tense and the adjective positions here and there, but given the conditions and time he had to learn, I'd say he did a fantastic job.'

Emotion wells up inside me, and I barricade the sob in my throat. 'It's a lot to absorb,' I say, my voice squeezing through a barrier of emotion. 'He was out there, not knowing if he would live or die or ever see his family again, and his one wish was for a better future for his daughter.'

As a parent, I could understand that, but in a life or death scenario, could I learn a language just so I could write to Kieran in the hope it would spur him on to better himself? I don't think so. There were days I couldn't even bear to make him pick his dirty socks up off the bathroom floor and all I've ever battled is everyday life. My stomach feels hollow at the thought of my grandma not fulfilling her father's wishes. I know it would have been impossible for her, and I certainly don't blame her, but the situation is just so profoundly sad.

'Did your grandmother ever manage to read the letters?' he asks softly, seeming to sense my melancholy.

I tilt my head. 'I presume so, but I don't really know. I'd never seen these letters until I found them in a box of my mother's old things after she'd passed away. She died unexpectedly, and we lost my grandmother years ago.

'I'm sorry about your mother. Losing a parent is hard.' He swallows, and something flickers across his face before his brow furrows in the middle. I appreciate his sympathy.

I draw a deep breath to keep my voice steady. 'What does the next one say?'

Ma chère Rose,

Dans la dernière lettre de ta mère, elle m'a dit que tu étais son rayon de soleil, la distrayant d'inquiétude. C'était un réconfort à lire. Presque aussi réconfortant que la belle campagne ici en France. Un jour, nous vaincrons les Allemands et serons en paix. Ensuite, vous viendrez et verrez par vous-même.

Les jours sont longs et je vis pour les lettres de ta mère.

Tu es sa force.

Gros baisers

Papa

'Here he is talking about how Rose is her mother's strength, and how hearing about her keeps him going. He's trying to be brave but in this one line – "*Les jours sont longs et je vis pour les lettres de ta mère*" – he is saying the days are getting longer and he lives for the letters from your great-grandmother. It seems he's reached a point where he's finding it hard, understandably, of course. He also says that he'd like for your grandmother to see the French countryside.'

'Ah yes, he'd written that in one of the English letters too … but she never came.' My stomach lurches and a sob escapes on my last word. Olivier puts his hand on mine; the heat from it creeps up my arm, and my eyes linger on it before he snatches it back.

I don't know what to say or do other than pretend it didn't happen. He felt sorry for me. That was all. 'I'm sorry, it was so long ago, and obviously I never even knew him, but it's sad that she never came to fulfil his dying wish.'

'Not many people had the means,' he replies sympathetically. 'But you're here now.'

Our eyes connect and though I can't speak, I hope my gratitude shows.

'What regiment was he in?' he asks after a sip of coffee.

I rummage in the envelope for the piece of paper it was written on. 'The sixteenth Battalion. The Welsh Regiment but that doesn't sound right. None of my family were from Wales.'

'So many men responded to the call to arms, it wasn't always possible to place them in their local regiment. We can look up some history on them if you like?' I nod. 'Shall we read the last one?'

I nod again. 'Yes please.'

25 Juin 1916

Ma chère Rose,

    Je ne peux qu'espérer que cette lettre te parviendra. Nous avons eu beaucoup de fortes pluies et les conditions ici s'aggravent, mais je ne vous châtierai pas comme je l'ai fait avec votre mère.

    Je reçois le vent d'une offensive imminente dont je ne peux pas discuter. Tout ce que je peux dire, c'est que cela arrivera bientôt.

    Je t'aime de tout mon coeur,

    Papa

'This one is before the Battle of the Somme. He's alluding to a big offensive looming but there's no indication he knew how big.'

'His letters changed after that,' I whisper. 'They were more sombre, less full of hope.'

'The Battle of the Somme changed many men. Nobody expected the devastating losses,' Olivier says matter-of-factly. 'The British Army had been shelling the Germans in the run-up to the attack and believed their trenches would be empty. Some British soldiers were so confident they'd find nothing but bodies they were even reported to have kicked footballs across no man's land that day, like carefree boys on their way to school.'

My eyes drop to the table just as the waitress appears with our food, but I no longer feel hungry. I thank her and the solemn moment passes.

'I know you're tracing your great-grandfather's footsteps but where will your journey take you?'

'I know he landed in Le Havre in December, so I've been there already. Then I know he was in the trenches near Neuve-Chapelle until June 1916. He fought at the Somme, in the Battle of Mametz Wood, before taking part in the third battle of Ypres, where he was killed.'

Olivier nods sombrely and for a moment, we both stare at the letters.

'If you like, I can write down the word-for-word translations for you?' he says, more upbeat.

'That would be really kind. Thank you so much Olivier.' I'm already pulling out my notebook and pen. We spend the next hour chatting as he explains the wording, how to pronounce the phrases, and what they mean. I enjoy watching him and his animated enthusiasm as much as I enjoy his knowledgeable explanations.

He talks a lot with his hands and cracks jokes. It doesn't take me long to realise I'm enjoying his company more than I'd expected to. Actually, it's more than that: I'm tuned in to him. The whole of me is. Perhaps more than I should be.

'Wow, it's almost dinner time,' I say, checking my watch during a lull in the conversation.

'You're in France now. Often our meals take a few hours and all merge into one.' He smiles.

'Still, you've been very kind, and I've taken up most of your day off. I should let you go and relax,' I say, taking out my purse.

He places his hand on mine, and that familiar warmth returns. 'Please, I can get this. To see those letters has been a real treat for geeky old me, and I'd like to thank you for sharing them with me.'

'But you've just spent an hour translating them – I'd like to pay to thank *you*,' I protest. 'And for all the interesting stuff you told me about the war.'

'Please, it was nothing. I enjoyed it.' He holds up a hand as though his words are final, and I relax into a smile, defeated.

'Okay, thank you.' It has been a long time since a man has bought me lunch and accepting graciously doesn't come easy. I hover awkwardly, not knowing the etiquette for walking away from overly helpful, practical strangers who've just paid for lunch.

'I imagine you will be seeing off your American friends tomorrow?' he says, helping me out.

'Yes, noon they leave, don't they?'

'That's right. Then the day after that, I'm off and if you'd like, I can drive you to Neuve-Chapelle.'

My chest eases up before I'd even noticed it was tense. I think I'm relieved to have him come with me, purely because he's so knowledgeable and it will be like having my own personal tour guide. Or at least that's what I tell myself.

As I turn to leave, Olivier's phone rings. I hear him answer in French, cheerful at first, then his tone becomes more serious. Reminding myself it's none of my business, I carry on towards the door.

'Cath. Wait,' Olivier calls after me. I turn around, surprised.

His face has paled. 'There's been an accident.'

Chapter Eleven

We've almost arrived in Paris. The two-hour journey has been spent mostly in silence – Olivier intent on the road; me, worried sick. Martha had a fall a few hours ago and has been taken to a hospital in Paris. The phone call Olivier took in the café was the coach driver filling him in. When Olivier told me, I'd panicked and insisted on accompanying him to the hospital. But for the last half an hour or so, I've been sitting here chewing the corner of my nail, wondering if diving into the car with him was a massive over-reaction. Martha might be embarrassed; she might wonder why a practical stranger has travelled for two hours to visit her. Olivier *has* to go, he works for the company she was on a tour with, but me? I'm just a hanger-on. *Is there such thing as an old folks' travel groupie?*

When we park at the hospital, Olivier already knows where to head. I assume the coach driver told him where she'd be before setting off to take the rest of the passengers back to Arras.

The corridor opens out into a waiting area and I spot Cynthia and Roland sitting on the edge of some pink padded chairs with a pale-yellow wall as their backdrop.

Cynthia, who has her fist pressed against her lips, jumps up to her feet when she sees us arrive. 'Oh Cath, Olivier!' Worry is etched into her features as she takes us in an embrace, me first and then Olivier. Roland stands up to shake our hands.

'What happened?' Olivier and I both say in unison.

Cynthia looks between us both. 'She tripped and fell backward down some steps. I don't know how it happened. It was awful.' She clasps her hand to her mouth, and Roland places a comforting arm around her.

'She's a tough old bird, she'll be okay,' he says, patting her.

I'm about to ask what her injuries are when a man in a white overcoat approaches us. I can just about decipher his words when he asks if anyone can speak French.

Olivier steps forward and the two enter into a brief conversation while the three of us look on.

'He says her injuries aren't too bad, but she has broken her leg. We can see her now.'

Cynthia's whole body sags with relief, and we all follow the doctor into the small room where Martha is sitting up in bed, chatting away to a nurse. Harry is beside her, holding her hand.

'You had us worried!' I say when she catches my eye.

'Oh, I'm fine. The doctors and nurses have been looking after me, haven't they, Harry?'

'I think they're frightened to death of you,' he replies, and we all laugh a little, not just at the joke, but at the relief that she's her usual self.

'Just a hairline fracture of the fib-u-la.' She sounds out the word in her Southern accent and the sound dances in my ears. 'I've seen the X-ray. Doesn't even look like you need a darn fibula if you ask me,' she says, and I can't quite tell if she's being serious.

'Of course you need it! Why else would God give you one?' Cynthia says. I catch Olivier giving me a sideways glance, his smirk mirroring my own.

'Well, there's a much bigger, sturdier-looking bone right next to it, and I'm glad that one is still intact is all I'm saying,' Martha replies to Cynthia, as though that's the end of the matter.

'So, come on then, what happened?' I ask, before a full-on row about the human anatomy breaks out.

'Well,' Harry says, placing a hand on Martha's good leg. 'She was having a selfie at the top of some steps, would you believe?'

I choke back a snort of laughter.

'I was not *having a selfie.*' Martha places a hand on her hip while the look on Cynthia's face suggests her mind may too have involuntarily slipped into the gutter. 'I asked *you* to take a picture of me with the Eiffel Tower in the background.'

'*You* wanted a picture of *yourself.* Your-self,' he repeats. 'A selfie! I am all up on the lingo.' He throws his hands up as though he's won – game, set and match.

'That isn't a selfie, you old fool,' she replies. I notice Olivier turn away as Martha explains to Harry what a selfie is. The slight jiggling of Olivier's shoulders suggests he's finding this whole conversation as hilarious as I am.

This is confirmed when he whispers, 'I am beginning to wonder if Harry pushed Martha down the steps.' And I giggle before he adds, 'I'm also wondering if I'd blame him.'

'I was on the steps of the Trocadéro with the Eiffel Tower in the background, and I'd asked old Instagrandad over here to take a photo.' She glares at Harry. 'A selfie of myself,' she mocks. 'A simple photo of me and the tower like thousands of people probably take each day. Take a step back, he said. I can't get you in.'

'Oh my.' I clasp a hand to my mouth.

'It happened so quickly. Rolly and I didn't see a thing,' Cynthia says, eyebrows pressed together. 'One minute she's posing, the next she's in a crumpled heap screaming in agony.' She looks worriedly at me and Olivier.

Olivier holds up his hands. 'It's okay, I'm not the police.' He lets out a small laugh, and it breaks the tension that has mounted from the drama.

As dusk draws in, we decide to make our way back to Arras.

Martha is being kept in overnight because of concerns over her high blood pressure, which means she'll miss her flight back to the US tomorrow. Olivier has told her not to worry and that he'd sort it out. Cynthia and Roland have decided to stay in France too in case Harry needs anything, which I think is very sweet.

Harry stays with Martha in the hospital while Olivier takes me, Cynthia and Roland back to the car. Cynthia bundles several fancy shopping bags in the boot before getting in.

Once we're on our way, the mood is understandably sombre. Everyone is weary and processing the events of the day.

'So,' Olivier pipes up cheerfully, 'did you get to see the sights of Paris? Before the accident, obviously.'

'Oh, yes. It's such a beautiful city, the architecture, the history, the Eiffel Tower,' Cynthia says dreamily. 'It's the most romantic city I've ever seen.'

Roland clears his throat uncomfortably and Olivier flashes me a sideways glance and a knowing grin.

'I haven't ever been,' I say.

'So *that* just then was your first visit?' Cynthia gasps. 'Well, that wasn't romantic at all.'

Her words hang in the close air of the car as I sit there for a moment, pretending to be indifferent to her inference, if there even was any.

'Well, I didn't come to France for the romance,' I remind her.

'I know.' Thankfully, she agrees.

'What?' Olivier says in mock horror. 'France is the country of love!'

I giggle and feel immediately silly.

'How about you, Roland? Did you like Paris?' Olivier asks, and I'm thankful he's moving the conversation on.

'It was nice and all, but expensive,' he says. Olivier lets out a small laugh in agreement. 'The ladies had us shopping on the Champs-Élysées. They should call it the *Chumps*-Élysées because that's what all the husbands walking up there are. Chumps.'

'Oh, Rolly, you sound just like Harry now. I swear he's made that joke at least fifteen times.'

'You women almost bankrupted us. I swear, high rollers in Vegas have lost less money than Harry and I did today.'

'But I got a gorgeous new scarf,' Cynthia adds.

I fight heavy eyelids as the darkness settles and silence absorbs us. Olivier's eyes are fixed on the road ahead and when I glance to the back, Cynthia has her head resting on Roland's shoulder. They've both nodded off.

An almighty bang rattles the car violently, and we swerve to the left and then sharply to the right before coming to a stop on the hard shoulder of the A1 autoroute.

'What was that?' My voice trembles and my heart races as I look around the car to make sure everyone is okay.

'I don't know. I think the tyre has blown.' Olivier is already climbing out of the car to investigate before any of us can gather enough of our marbles to respond.

'Are you two okay?' I ask Cynthia and Roland. They both nod but Roland has his hands wrapped tightly around Cynthia's. The sight ignites a little ember in my chest.

'It's a flat,' Olivier says with a sigh as he slumps back into his seat.

'Ah, okay. Do you want me to help change it?' I offer – it can't be that difficult after all.

'The car doesn't have a spare.'

'Can you call the French AA or something?' I ask trying to be pragmatic.

'Alcoholics Anonymous?' He looks at me quizzically.

'No, a breakdown helpline or something. I don't know.'

'I don't have anything like that. I can make it to the next town if I drive steadily but we're over an hour away from Arras. I can't get us back there tonight,' he says, and I know what is coming. I'm tempted to suggest napping in the car until we can get help in the morning but one more look at Roland's white knuckles wrapped around Cynthia's hand suggests that's not an option.

'Can we find a hotel nearby?' I say, despite my dwindling funds. Olivier, one step ahead, is already searching on his phone.

'There are a few options nearby in Compiègne. I'll make some calls.' He gets out of the car and disappears in the darkness. The silence is only interrupted by passing cars and snippets of muffled French dialogue.

'Okay, I found us a room,' Olivier says getting back in the car. 'Two rooms.' His Adam's apple bobs in the moonlight as sighs of relief drift from the back.

Two rooms. I swallow hard.

After checking in, Cynthia and Roland head straight to bed. They've had a big day so I can't blame them.

'Fancy a drink?' I say, knowing I'd need some Dutch courage to get me into that room.

Olivier's reply comes far too quickly. 'Yes.'

He's got us a twin room but even so. I'm imagining the characters from the film *Inside Out* are in my head, except my characters aren't balanced by one another. They're all 'fear' and they're each having some kind of meltdown. I have nothing to sleep in and my underwear is the comfy 'old faithful' sort, not the sort Hollywood would have men believe is 'everyday lingerie'. In fact, everyday lingerie is an oxymoron. There's no such thing but men don't know that.

Why am I even thinking about underwear? What has gotten into me? There are bigger fish to fry. I should be more worried about snoring or trumping in my sleep. *Oh God!* Now I've thought of those things, I *am* worrying about them.

I take a huge gulp of my wine as soon as Olivier places it down in front of me.

'It's been quite a day,' he says mistaking my gulp of wine for Martha-related worry, rather than bodily-function worry.

'It certainly has. I'm glad Martha is okay.'

'I think she appreciated our visit. It was very kind of you to give up a whole day of your holiday to go.'

I brush the remark off with my hand. 'I had to make sure she was okay.'

'I know. I just don't think many people would have dropped everything like that to take a two-hour trip for a lady they'd only recently met.'

I feel heat rush to my cheeks. 'It's how I've always been.' I reach for my wine and take another sip. 'How much do I owe you for the room?'

'Nothing. The tour company has a business account with this hotel so it's all covered.'

That's a relief.

I wonder if it's just me who feels the conversation that flowed so naturally earlier now feels stilted in light of our sleeping arrangements.

We chat mostly about Martha and the others whilst we finish our drinks. I'm soaked with apprehension about going to the room, but Olivier seems more relaxed.

'I suppose we should go to the room,' I say not wanting another drink for fear it could make the aforementioned snoring more inevitable.

He smiles. 'I'm sorry I couldn't get separate rooms,' he says, obviously picking up on my less-than-gleeful tone.

'I'm just worried I might snore or something and keep you awake. I sometimes sleep-talk and I've been told I can get a bit shouty. I might wake you up whilst I'm yelling at a green and yellow rabid cat or something.'

Olivier laughs softly and I feel a little more at ease.

'You're a funny lady,' he says, catching me a little off-guard. Secretly, I'm flattered.

'I just blurt things out when I'm nervous,' I say honestly.

'You've nothing to be nervous about. I'll be the perfect gentleman.' A shiver runs up my spine. Even though I know there was no hidden meaning and he's just saying he won't walk in when I'm on the loo or something, my body responds to the comment. I swallow whatever words try to bubble to the surface.

'How about a walk?' he asks, taking me by surprise. 'Roland and Cynthia will want to get back to the hotel tomorrow I'm sure, but isn't "seeing France" part of the reason you're here?'

I nod. 'I suppose it is.'

We step outside into the sooty darkness. Everything is silent, and the dynamic between us shifts without the subtle background noise of the bar. We walk in silence through the deserted streets until eventually, Olivier speaks. 'It's actually quite a fitting coincidence we've ended up here.'

'Why's that?'

'It was here where the armistice was agreed. On the eleventh of November, 1918. Your poppy day.'

'Remembrance Day,' I whisper. My eyes tear up for no fathomable reason. I'd not really thought much beyond the third battle of Ypres and my great-grandfather's journey but this, being here, is so significant.

We walk past the beautifully lit palace, which feels illicit since we have the view of it all to ourselves. We then walk to the stunning gothic town hall, with its impressive façade, in relative silence until Olivier points out a statue commemorating a battle in which Joan of Arc played a part in defending the town. Just walking past the old, pretty building, lit by street lamps and moonlight helps me realise that this is what my great-grandfather wanted his daughter to experience. I can't quite believe I'm here, doing what she should have done. I wonder if Olivier can sense that too. Perhaps that's why he's so quiet: he's allowing me time to process.

'It feels like we have the whole town to ourselves, doesn't it?' he says after a while. It does; it feels as though the town has been built just for us.

'Yes, it does.' My words come out as a whisper as he slows to a stop and turns to face me.

'It's my favourite time to go out walking, when everything is still and quiet.' He takes a step forward and my whole body is alert with his proximity. I swallow as he reaches up and sweeps my hair from across my face, sending strange sensations through my body.

For a moment, we stand there, looking into one another's eyes as a gentle breeze whips around us.

'We should get back,' I say.

When we enter the hotel room, the air changes between us again and I feel awkward with the thickness of it. Olivier throws down his satchel on the desk chair and takes off his shoes. 'Which bed would you like?' he asks.

I glance at the two beds and reason that the one closest to the bathroom would probably be the best. 'This one.'

He flings himself on the other and sprawls out. *How can he not be fazed by this?*

'Mind if I use the bathroom first?' I ask, and he shakes his head.

Once inside I slump on the toilet seat and let out a huge sigh. I'm a grown woman; I should be able to spend a platonic night with a man in a hotel room without crumbling to pieces. I don't know if it's Olivier's presence in particular that's making me feel so self-aware or the fact that having a man in my bedroom is such new territory.

I switch on the shower and have a wee once the water comes through loud enough to mask the sound and it's a good job I did because it's been a while and I've stored water in camel-like quantities. Then I hop in the shower and rinse off the day. Once I've patted myself dry, I put my underwear back on, which feels disgusting against my clean skin. I look in the mirror.

My comfy nude-coloured pants are from a multipack from the clothing department at work and the mismatched bra is a plain black jersey style. It isn't even underwired. I could be a poster girl for 'Agent Preventer', the lesser-known underwear-brand-slash-birth-control guaranteed to put off even the most amorous of men.

On the plus side, everything sits quite well in this old-faithful pairing and there are no obvious unsightly bulges.

In the absence of toothpaste, I rinse my mouth vigorously with water and that's about the best I can manage. Wrapping the tiny hotel towel around me for modesty, I open the door and peek around it.

'I'm not looking,' Olivier says. His arm is thrown lazily across his eyes and I appreciate the gesture. Quickly, I slip out of the bathroom and hop into bed. Pulling the covers up to my chin, I drag the towel out, placing it on the floor beside me for in the morning.

Now all I have to do is get to sleep.

Easier said than done.

When Olivier returns from the bathroom, I cover my eyes in a gesture to mirror his and once he's in bed, he asks if it's okay to turn out the lights, which I agree to of course. I couldn't wait for the darkness. Now it's pitch black I can feel his energy. He's just a metre or so away and I can hear the steady rise and fall of his chest.

'Cath?' Maybe he feels it too. I wanted to speak to break the tension but I couldn't find the words.

'Yes?'

'I'm sorry I won't be able to drive you to Neuve-Chapelle tomorrow now.'

'It can't be helped,' I say. I can't and shouldn't rely on him to take me anyway.

'*Bonne nuit*, Cath.'

I smile in the darkness. 'Goodnight, Olivier.'

Chapter Twelve

A high-pitched clanging sound wakes me with a start and the unfamiliar pale blue walls don't immediately register.

'Olivier?' I sit up, tucking the quilt tightly under my armpits.

'Welcome to this morning,' he says with cheer. I can't tell if he's teasing me for sleeping in or it's an odd turn of phrase because of our language differences.

'It's good to see you in the land of the living.' Okay, so he *was* teasing.

'Good morning,' I croak as he hands me a cup of coffee. *I could get used to this.*

'I've found a local man who can fix my tyre today so I'm going to pop into town for an hour or so. It's still early so you can relax here and have breakfast if you like.'

'Actually, could I come? It would be nice to see some of the town by daylight.'

His face lifts slightly and I can't help but feel like he's pleased, although I'm about as good as reading men as I am at reading French.

'That would be nice,' he says. His hair is ruffled, and T-shirt crumpled but somehow, it suits him. I, on the other hand, can't imagine the circumstances have been as kind to me.

Under the fluorescent lighting of the bathroom, things are worse than expected. My face is dry and blotchy and my hair wayward. But, on the bright side, getting ready without so much as a hairbrush takes no time at all and I freshen up as best I can with water and the plasticky hotel soap.

The weak morning sun isn't quite enough to take the chill off my bare arms but it feels refreshing as I walk by Olivier's side. We have an hour before we collect the car and the town hasn't woken yet. He talks animatedly about the history of the place and I listen with interest, whilst simultaneously keeping a safe 'morning breath' buffer between us.

'How about you, Cath, what are your interests?' he asks as we stop to look at the Château de Compiègne.

'It's just as beautiful by day,' I say, avoiding the question. It shouldn't matter that I have no real hobbies, and I shouldn't be embarrassed to say so but I am.

My tactic works and he starts talking about the chateau, leaving me a little bit in awe. I could talk for ages about the differences between own-brand products and premium ones but I doubt that would be of interest to anyone.

'So anyway, I talk too much. Tell me about you?'

My heart sinks a little. 'I work long hours in a supermarket and run a home – there isn't much time for anything else. Not very exciting, hey? But if you'd like me to tell you all about subliminal marketing and why you pick up those three-for-two deals you don't need from the supermarket then I'm your gal.' I realise I'm gesticulating wildly and hook my thumbs through the belt loops of my jeans to minimise the risk of taking off.

The corner of his mouth lifts. 'You're more interesting than you give yourself credit for.'

'That's very nice of you to say but I'm okay with leading a simple life. It's what I know, it's ... safe.' My eyes meet his for a second too long and for a moment, I don't feel safe at all. I feel unfamiliar in every sense: in this place, in his company, in my own body.

'You came to France on a journey, by yourself. That's pretty brave.'

My skin prickles at the compliment. The decision to come was impulsive, manipulated to some extent, but it wasn't brave. I check my watch.

'The car should be ready.'

'It can wait.' His words are firm and take me by surprise. 'We're not leaving here until you admit that coming to France was brave and exciting.'

His arms are folded, and his stance suggests we could be here all day if I don't comply. I glance around at the pretty town with spurs of winding lanes packed with shops and café bars and feel sparks of excitement. It *is* such a wonderful place steeped in such rich history, not just here, but Albert and Arras too. A smile cracks on my face. 'You're right, this place is so beautiful, so exciting, the buildings, the patisseries and the fact there are random flower pots everywhere … I just want to absorb it all. The act of getting myself on a ferry was quite something but I'm so glad I did.' I realise I'm talking to myself as much as I am to Olivier and when I look at him he's frowning, and I hope he doesn't think I was being sarcastic.

'So why do you want to rush and get the car then?' He breaks into a smile. 'Let's look at the flowers and get pains au chocolat from the bakery.'

This fits with my newly Brasso-ed dullness so I throw caution to the wind and grin. 'After you.'

We head to the patisserie nearby and soon after, we're nibbling delicious fresh pastry and looking out over the river.

'Oh, my goodness, this is practically melting in my mouth,' I say, biting through the buttery pastry and dark chocolate filling.

'They're delicious, aren't they?'

My mouth is full, so I nod before turning back to the pretty view across the river as a boat passes through the arch of an old stone bridge.

'I never do anything like this,' I say. 'Back home there's always something better to do. Actually, *better* is the wrong word – there's always something more important to do. Life never just stops still to give me a chance to catch up and just … be.'

'I suppose the way of living is different here. We allow ourselves time to relish what we're doing, enjoy our surroundings, our food, our company.' He glances at me and I look away, unable to take the full force of his gaze. 'Of course, if anyone asks, we work hard too.'

'You really love your work, don't you?' I say, thinking back to how personable he can be with the tourists and how passionate about his subject he is.

'If you find the right job, it shouldn't feel like work. It should feel like the place you want to be each morning.' He dusts his hands and screws his empty paper bag into a tight ball before tossing it into a nearby bin. I mull his words over.

'I haven't found that. Don't get me wrong, my job is fine, but I couldn't honestly say that I skip there happily each morning. I can't complain because I get by and the people there are nice. You've been lucky to find your passion.'

His eyebrows knit and his lips part like he's about to speak but he rubs his chin instead.

'Maybe I will do something different one day,' I say, knowing I probably won't.

'You'll never regret trying to achieve your dream, even if it all fails, but you'd spend your years regretting not having a go.'

'Wise words … The trouble is, I don't really have any dreams, other than winning the EuroMillions that is.'

'And do you always play?'

'Religiously.'

'So, you try, and fail, without regret? Now imagine that one week you don't play, and your numbers come up.'

I laugh. 'It would be just my luck.'

'Ahh, but that is what you're doing every day that passes where you're not striving to achieve your dreams. You just need a dream with better odds.' He winks and starts to walk beside the river. I jog after him.

'So, you're telling me that becoming a tour guide was your dream?'

'Not at all. I fell into this and found I love it. Dreams don't need to be work-based, they could be to travel, learn a craft, eat your body weight in cheese, I don't know.'

I think for a moment. 'This trip is already opening my eyes to new experiences. Maybe things will become clearer when I go home but it won't be to eat my body weight in cheese, maybe just half my body weight. I have to leave room for chocolate.'

'Ahh, yes, good thinking.'

We walk in silence before heading back towards the town centre. 'Cynthia and Roland must be wondering where we are,' I say.

Once we have the car, we drive back to the hotel and head inside to find them sat in the small lobby with their coats and bags, all ready to go.

When she spots us together, Cynthia raises an inquisitive eyebrow. 'The car is as good as new,' I say firmly, hoping there will be no need for any other questions. Back at the hotel in Arras, Olivier asks if anyone would like a coffee, but Cynthia and Roland want to head straight for their room to make some calls back to the US to let family know what's happened and that they'll be back a day later than planned.

Once they've left, Olivier and I hover around the lift.

'I should go too,' I say. We'd driven to see the Armistice memorial before setting off back and it's now late afternoon, but I know his offer wasn't intended for me, really; he probably just wants to go home and rest.

'Oh. Okay.' I can't be sure if I'm imagining it, but the muscles in his face slacken a little. It's subtle but I sense a bit of disappointment. Perhaps he feels as wound up as I do after the drama of the day. I think we all need a good night's sleep.

***

We wait anxiously for Martha's return. Olivier had popped in as we were finishing breakfast to let us know she'd been discharged, and then he set off to collect her and Harry. Cynthia and Roland didn't want to leave the hotel, so I stayed in the bar with them after a brief stroll out for some fresh air. Olivier had managed to get the four of them on a flight home for tomorrow and so it looks as though everything is going to work out.

'Ta-dah!' Martha bursts out of the revolving door. I'd expected her to be in a wheelchair but she's hobbling on crutches, and Roland's words from yesterday ring true in my ears. *She's a tough old bird.*

'Oh, Martha, it's so good to have you back.' Cynthia makes her way over to hug her.

The two embrace for a moment before Martha pulls away and looks to the rest of us. 'So, I'm thirsty, who's buying?'

We sit around in some comfy chairs while Harry goes to the bar. He wants to buy a round of drinks to thank everyone for pulling together, though I'm not really sure what part I played in helping. After the drinks arrive, the group start chatting away. Olivier throws himself into the midst of the conversation while I retreat into myself a little, allowing the chatter to circulate around me for a while. When I come around, Martha is explaining to the others about how her cast is split so she's allowed to fly but how she'll have to get it 'fixed up properly' when she's home.

Olivier excuses himself shortly afterwards and makes a joke about how he now has another airport trip to make tomorrow. The time has flown, and once he has left we decide to order some bar food. While we're waiting for it to arrive, Martha looks at me for a moment too long, and I think I know what's coming.

'It was so nice of you to come to the hospital,' she says, confirming my suspicions.

'I wanted to make sure you were okay,' I say, sounding casual.

'So, did you just happen to be with Olivier when he got the news?' Mischief dances in her eyes, and I can feel the corners of my mouth defying me by curling upwards. 'You were!' she says before I have time to answer.

'You already knew we were meeting to go over my great-grandfather's letters,' I say, not playing into her hands.

'Ahh,' interrupts Cynthia. 'We've had some progression.'

'We?' I glance at her before shaking my head. '*We* haven't had anything.'

Cynthia proceeds to tell a much more exciting story of the night before, until I butt in and downplay it all.

'We went for a walk and chatted a bit. He's a lovely person, but mostly we were worried about *you*.' I flip the conversation around.

Martha sighs. 'Okay, it just would have been nice if something good came out of this whole tomfoolery.'

'It has. We've all learned a valuable lesson,' I say pointedly, attracting the attention of the men too. 'That we should never ask Harry to take a *selfie* of us.'

Chapter Thirteen

'It's been a wonderful few days. Thank you so much for taking me under your wing and arranging for me to gate-crash your tour,' I say, bringing Martha in for a hug.

She wobbles a little on her crutches as I embrace her. 'Not a problem, honey. Now, you'll write me on the Facebook, won't you?'

I smile. 'Of course.'

She reaches up to straighten my twisted vest strap but lets her hand linger on my shoulder after. 'And you look after yourself, or at least let that nice young man look after you while you're here.' She raises an expectant eyebrow and I nod to appease her. 'Good.'

The truth is, I've been wondering whether I'll see much of Olivier once the Americans have gone. There will be no real reason to. He's already on the coach as he had to take a phone call, so other than a quick hello at breakfast when he popped in to confirm the Americans' travel plans, I haven't spoken to him today.

'Martha, I know I've spent the best part of sixty years waiting around for you, but American Airlines won't extend the same courtesy!' Harry places an arm around her waist and leans in

106

slightly towards me, holding out a hand to shake. 'It's been lovely to meet you, Cath, and I wish you all the best with your trip.'

'Thanks, Harry. Martha, he's right, you should get going.'

She sighs and rolls her eyes like an adolescent. 'Like being stuck in France would be so terrible!'

'Martha!' Harry barks.

'All right! Goodbye, honey.' She hugs me again and whispers, 'I see the sympathy has already worn off.'

'Bye, you two,' I say as they make their way on board the coach. I say my goodbyes to Cynthia and Roland and it's decided that a Facebook 'chitchat' group would be set up for 'us women'. I smile to myself, with no idea if it will actually happen and if it did, what we'd chitchat about, but I like the idea of keeping in touch.

I wave the coach off and as soon as it's gone, the dense feeling of being alone starts to shroud me. The hotel foyer is still and quiet when I walk back inside. The bar is empty and unmanned and just the receptionist sits at the desk, tapping away on his keyboard. He gives a polite smile and nod as I slump into one of the chairs. The next place I know my great-grandfather went was Neuve-Chapelle. I log into the hotel Wi-Fi to try and figure out how to get there. As far as I can tell, I'll need a train and a taxi, and the first train would be leaving Arras in twelve minutes. If I hurry, I can make it.

Checking myself over, I realise I have my jacket and bag and don't need anything else. I get a rush of excitement as I change direction and walk back past the reception towards the main doors of the hotel. The receptionist gives me another polite nod, only this time his brow forms a slight 'V' shape.

Once on the train, I relax into my seat, relieved I'd managed to figure out the departures okay. The beautiful French country-side whizzes past in a tumble of greens and yellows. My mind wanders back to my great-grandfather's letters, where he'd referred to its beauty and hoped my grandmother would visit one day. I don't believe in life after death and I'm not particularly religious, but if he is somehow aware of my trip, I hope it's enough to make up for my grandmother not making the journey. I hope somehow it would make his death mean something more.

I'd left most of the letters in my hotel room for safekeeping, but I do have the one he'd written in Neuve-Chapelle and the English translations Olivier had written in my notebook. I've kept them with me since he gave them to me and keeping them close feels like I'm keeping a piece of my great-grandfather close too.

I take the notebook out of my bag and scan over Olivier's neat, cursive handwriting that slants slightly to the right. The letters don't really say much about the war or what it was like to be there at the time. I suppose sometimes the things people keep from us tell us the most about their character. The fact he sheltered the women in his life suggests he wasn't just brave, but considerate too. My chest swells as I close the book back up.

The train soon pulls in to the station at Béthune and I swallow hard before climbing into a taxi and uttering '*Neuve-Chapelle s'il vous plaît*' nervously in the absence of a thrust-worthy piece of paper. I'm not even sure that's the proper way to direct a taxi driver but he sets off so all I can do is hope for the best.

The taxi pulls up outside a memorial. I can only assume he knows why I'm here.

'Do you want me to wait?' he asks, and I'm relieved he can speak English because I'd been panicking about sorting out the payment.

'No, thank you.' He looks at me like I'm odd but points to the charge on the meter anyway. I pay him and get out. The memorial is to commemorate almost five thousand Indian soldiers lost in battle. I head inside the circular enclosure and take a seat on a stone bench and remove the next letter from my great-grand-father.

12th January 1916

My dearest Elizabeth,

Just a few lines to let you know I'm in good health. We're in the dugouts and the weather is awful. It has poured for days and we're knee-deep in water. The conditions are terrible and I've seen rats bigger than cats. Do thank the church for the parcel they put together for me – the socks have been a particular blessing. It's good to hear that Rose is settled in at school now. I send you both all my love and please don't worry. We can do nothing but see this thing through.

All my love,
Will

Sitting here in the cemetery reading this makes me wonder about the other men. Each one had a family, a story, and nevertheless faced the indiscriminate threat of the shells and bullets as they rained down without mercy. The sadness I feel for them is profound, and if I let it, it could consume me.

I decide to go for a walk and head towards the houses to see the town that they fought for.

I wander the streets, and for the most part, I'm happy on my own, but part of me already misses the humour and life that the Americans brought to the tours and the random but interesting knowledge Olivier shares. Still, I must get used to my own company; it's only a matter of time before I'll be back home and living by myself.

I have to be able to be alone. I have to accept it as a permanent state.

The sight of an old lady on a bench catches my eye. She looks older than Martha and co, judging by her weathered skin and pale cloudy eyes, and to be honest, something about the picture she paints makes me feel sorry for her. A shopping bag sits by her feet and she grinds her whiskered jaw as she watches passers-by. I don't need to rest but I sit next to her. I'm unsure why. Because I didn't like to see her alone, I think. She casts me a hollow, indifferent look before slowly turning her head back to the quiet road ahead.

Why is it I pity this lady while sitting here convincing myself I'll be okay with living alone? It can't just be because she's old, because I will be too one day. Perhaps I should let Kaitlynn set me up on one of those dating websites when I get back home. What harm could it do?

My phone frightens the life out of me as Beyoncé's notes scream from the ringer and the old lady huffs and slowly rises to her feet before hobbling off. 'Hello?' I answer quietly to compensate for disturbing the peace. I hadn't even checked the screen to see who it is.

'It's me.' Gary sounds despondent.

'Hi, Gary, how are things? Any news on the job front?' I keep my tone upbeat.

He sucks his teeth, resulting in an irritating smacking sound. 'Nothing yet. I've told you before, it's hopeless. Don't worry, though, I'm going down to the housing office and I'm going to tell them I'm homeless.'

I exhale, allowing the air to leave my lungs completely. 'You are not homeless. Don't be so dramatic, and don't you dare take accommodation from someone who is genuinely in need.'

'But you said—'

'Don't you twist my words,' I scold. 'I said you've to get a job and start standing on your own two feet again.'

'You told me to find a place.'

'Gary, I won't see you on the streets, you know that, but you do need to revert back to being a grown-up! Find a job and then get a flat. You have three and a half weeks to get your backside into gear.' I press the end-call button without even a goodbye. If ever I needed a timely reminder that being alone was in fact a good idea, this was it.

Spurred into action, I rise from the bench and decide to find the town centre. I get all the way to the town hall before I realise I'm actually heading back out of the town rather than into it. I continue towards the farmland and look out across the fields, wondering where those wet and muddy trenches were and where the obliterated front line ended and the beautiful countryside began.

Now, there is no sign of them, not from my vantage point at least but just being here helps me feel closer to a man I've never met. I stay a while just imagining. I remember the words from a poem I studied back at sixth form: 'Dreamers', by Sassoon.

My own interpretation of that poem was that all soldiers were in a moral grey area where killing and death had become a normal part of life. Now I see it more like the men were in emotional and physical limbo, not knowing whether they would live or die. Either way they didn't bank on having a 'tomorrow'. As I cast my eyes across the farmland before me it's the image of peace and colour, and I wish the people who fought for this could know that. *I hope they somehow know the grey land has gone.* I dab the moist corner of my eye.

Since there isn't much else to see, I head back towards the town hall and try a different direction, and another but it doesn't take long to realise that the town is so tiny it doesn't warrant a taxi rank or bus station. *There isn't even a hotel.* What the hell am I going to do? It takes everything I've got not to go into full-on panic mode, but I can feel frozen terror popping at the surface, ready to burst out. I'm keeping it at bay with a series of deep breaths and the wispy notion that I can't possibly be stranded. It just can't happen. *There has to be a way back to Arras.* I know I'm in rural France but it's still 2018.

Then I have a brainwave. Kaitlynn put an app on my phone last year when we were on our Christmas do. She said a taxi will come and find me and take me home from wherever I am and I wouldn't need cash. Plus, the app will text her and tell her where I am just in case the taxi driver happens to be a machete-brandishing maniac, not that she'd come rushing to France if he was but she would probably call the police. She said it worked all over the world. I'm giddy with hope as I pull out my phone and tap the app to open it. It's spooling or whatever the equivalent term is today. I smile at a man walking past for no other reason than he's the first person I've seen for a while, and then I look back at my phone.

Request has timed out.

I close the app and reopen it. That usually does the trick, doesn't it?

Still nothing happens. I look at the signal on my phone and it has that annoying 'E' symbol where 4G should be and I have no bars so even if I knew anyone here to call, I couldn't. My eyes dart left and right with despair, as if I'll find the answer by physically looking for it. With no other choice, I let the panic erupt but it comes out in short, sharp breaths because I'm so exasperated with myself for not anticipating this that I can't even cry tears. It feels like a punishment.

I wander aimlessly and not a car passes me by. There's a church up ahead. Would they take me in for the night? Do they even do that anymore? Did they ever? What would I even say? I don't know the French term for: 'I'm a lost and stranded idiot who needs to get back to Arras.' Maybe in the future getting lost and stranded will be called 'doing a Cath'. 'Oh, hi (insert name of loving relative here), I've done a Cath – can you come and get me?' Maybe it will even be funny to look back on in years to come.

My runaway thoughts are helping in no way, shape or form. I need a plan before it goes dark and I have to sleep in a field and no, the sad irony isn't lost on me that my great-grand-father did just that (except he was literally inside the field in a crevice of mud) and I am here to follow in his footsteps, after all. Maybe I *should* sleep in a field. *No, Cath!* My morning hair would guarantee I'd be mistaken for a shaggy dog and get shot at by an over-zealous farmer protecting his flock. God, being shot at, that really would be authentic. I scold myself for the poor taste of the last thought even though it came from panic.

Right, sleeping here is not an option. Walking anywhere seems improbable unless I want to lose my lower leg to a pack of rabid wolves – who knows what lurks in those fields and forests? Rats as big as cats apparently! *I'd rather take my chances with the rabid wolves.*

As I scour the immaculate pavement for some cast-aside cardboard to make an 'Arras' sign with, in case I need to hitchhike, I spot something in the distance and it's my only hope.

Chapter Fourteen

An elderly lady is cleaning the counter of the boulangerie as I walk in. When I go to speak, my mind draws a blank, as it's done on so many occasions since I've been here, so to avoid looking odd, I pick up a baguette and place it on the counter.

'I'm sorry, I don't speak French but I'm in a bit of a pickle and wonder if you could help me,' I say. My voice sounds rusty from lack of use. She looks me up and down and frowns. I know how ignorant it is of me to not speak French whilst assuming she can speak English, but this is a bit of an emergency. 'André,' she shouts, pointing her face towards a side door without taking her eyes off me.

André is a young boy of around twelve. A conversation ensues that I'm not privy to and I think she knows it. 'Yes, madame,' André says. *Ahh, he's the translator.*

I relay the story to him, and when he acknowledges me, my eyes fill with stingy moisture as he, in turn, fills the older lady in.

'She says not to worry, we can help you.' Despite the lack of emotion in his tone, the gratitude erupts inside of me and the tears I wanted to shed so desperately before come flooding out. The boy raises his eyebrows at me and if I'm honest, looks a bit disgusted at me for my outburst but I thank him anyway before repeating the word '*Merci*' over and over to the old woman.

'She said to come this way.' He doesn't wait for me to reply before heading back through the side door and gesturing to a floral sofa. 'You can sit here.' I do as instructed, all the while wondering if I've made a huge mistake.

A short while later, the old woman hands me a cup of tea and says something I don't understand before placing a bowl of fruit on the table beside me. I thank her again and sip the hot, sweet tea, instantly put at ease by its familiar taste and the old lady's kindness. My great-grandfather mentioned he found the French people to be welcoming. Perhaps I'm experiencing some of the same French hospitality he did. I like the idea of that.

'My uncle has a taxi in a nearby town. He will come and collect you in about thirty minutes.' André reappears. 'Do you have any cash to pay?'

I nod eagerly, and he disappears again. I'm left alone in the small living area, which I think is very trusting, but I probably do have an honest face. I did used to get away with the tiniest of fibs when I was younger, much to Gary's disgust.

'My uncle is here.' André is standing in the doorway. As I make my way into the brightly lit shop I stop at the counter to pay for my bread. The lady smiles and waves a hand, dismissing the charge. I want to protest but I physically can't, so I thank her again and turn to André.

'Thank you so much for helping me out today. I honestly don't know how I'd have gotten back to my hotel if you hadn't called your uncle.' André shrugs. 'Your grandmother is a special woman – you should look after her.' His eyes drop to the floor and he twists his mouth guiltily. 'Please tell her that, and tell her how grateful I am for the tea, and the sofa and the bread.' He nods.

By the time I reach the hotel, I'm sticky and I swear that what is left of my make-up is floating atop a millimetre of grease. The

116

taxi ride to the train station and the train ride home both felt twice as long as on the way there, but I'm back now and just need a shower and a good night's sleep. As I scurry through reception, I catch a glimpse of myself in one of the mirrors and it's worse than I imagined. My hair looks like it's been to Blackpool on a windy day without me, and my make-up is tear-stained and punctuated with two grey-black sacks beneath my eyes. *Thank God I'm back.*

'Cath?' *No, no no.* I could just carry on and pretend I haven't heard his caramel-smooth voice. I could invent an ailment next time I see him. Glue ear? He'd never know. As I ponder, I feel a warm, heavy hand on my shoulder and have no choice but to turn around.

'Cath? What's happened? Are you all right?' he says, concern etched in his features.

His warmth causes my knees to buckle slightly and I clutch his arm to steady myself.

'Come and sit down. I'll get you a drink.' I sit in one of the bucket chairs, realising I was wide-eyed at the sight of him a moment ago. He probably thinks I've been mugged, not hypnotised.

'Here.' He hands me a small glass with brown liquid in. The ice cubes tinkle as I raise it to my lips.

Eugh. I pull a face. 'What is it?'

'It's brandy. You looked like you needed it.'

'Well, it's enough to make me forget my own name, never mind my terrible day.' I'm half-joking but the crevice between his eyebrows suggests he hasn't picked up on it. 'Sorry, I don't mean to sound ungrateful. I'm just not used to spirits. Not unless they're inside those liqueur chocolates you get at Christmas – I can manage those.' The 'V' doesn't budge so I take another sip, trying hard to keep my face in neutral. 'Mmm, but now I'm really getting the flavour.' He wraps his hand gently around mine and guides the glass to the table.

'I just thought you needed a strong drink. Please, don't drink it if you don't like it. You'll make yourself ill.'

Note to self: My neutral face is not so neutral.

'Thank you.' My insides soften.

'Want to tell me about it?'

I nod and fill him in, and actually, when I strip it all back, taking out the bits that didn't happen, like the farmers, the wolves and the confusion at church, it wasn't even so bad. I couldn't find a taxi and a kindly shop assistant found me one. The End.

'Cath, I could have picked you up,' he says. I don't bother going into the whole phone signal debacle.

He's reaching in his pocket and pulls out a card. 'This is my number. I want you to call me if you're ever stuck again.'

'It won't happen again but thank you. I just hadn't anticipated how small the town was, especially because there was such a big battle there. I'd planned the trip based on a website and it said to catch a train and taxi. So, I'd naïvely assumed it would be a simple process.'

'Was the trip what you expected otherwise?'

I think back to reading my great-grandfather's letter in the open countryside and experiencing the same French hospitality that I think he did and, oh my God: 'Yes, it was!' Then I'm reaching into my bag and showing Olivier the letter and telling him all about how moving the Indian memorial was.

'So where is next on your journey?'

'He went straight to the Somme Valley after Neuve-Chapelle. Mametz Wood.'

'I could take you there if you like? And before you refuse, it would allow me to make up for not taking you to Neuve-Chapelle today, or even warning you how difficult it is to get to. I have another day off tomorrow in lieu of working today and I'd be honoured to, if you don't mind me tagging along. I know your journey is a personal one.'

I think for a moment. A wood sounds even more remote than

118

the village I went to today. My only other option is to hire a car but I don't have a car in England and I haven't driven for years. The thought terrifies me and if I'm completely honest with myself, there's something inside of me leaping around at the thought of Olivier's company.

'Only if it isn't an inconvenience?'

'Not at all, and if you want time alone, I can call to see my friends at Thiepval.'

'Then it's a date.' I wince. 'I didn't mean ...' He places a hand on mine, sending frissons through my own.

'I know what you meant.'

Perhaps it was a Freudian slip.

Chapter Fifteen

I wait anxiously at the main entrance to the hotel. There is every chance that Olivier could have forgotten about his offer to drive me to Mametz Wood and I'll be left waiting like a fool. He has a busy schedule, after all, and chats with so many tourists each day that it would be perfectly understandable if he *did* forget. After a busy day at work, I once forgot it was my own birthday until I got home and found a card from Kieran.

Olivier pulls up at two minutes to and I exhale with relief.

'Good morning, madame,' he says cheerfully through the open window of his tiny red Citroën C2.

I walk around to the passenger side and climb in. 'Morning, Olivier. Thank you so much for offering to take me today.' I've already decided to offer petrol money to alleviate some of the guilt I feel.

'It's no problem. It's a nice drive out, and I haven't been there for a while.'

He puts the car into gear and we are on our way.

'So, you're a week into your trip. Are you getting homesick?' he asks as we weave through the town.

'I don't really know. A lot has happened in such a short space of time that I haven't given home much thought. Maybe next week I will.' I let out a small laugh.

'I'm sure the hotel staff are looking after you.'

'Oh, definitely,' I say. 'Though I'm starting to get cravings for Galaxy chocolate and I can't find it in the local shops. I doubt the hotel staff will want to help with that. I've never gone without it for this long before so who knows what could happen.' He picks up on my humour and smiles, but I'm only half-joking. The symptoms of withdrawal are already starting to present themselves. Hallucinations, cravings and the unsatisfactory consumption of alternative-brand chocolate.

We don't talk much more once we've left the town; instead, he concentrates on the roads and I take in the views of endless farmland.

'We're almost there,' he announces as we turn onto a lonely dirt track, but I don't see anything. He glances my way and must read my blank expression.

'We're close. There's just this one last road.'

There's nothing else around. It's quite remote.

'You're not going to murder me, are you?' I laugh nervously, and Olivier looks taken aback.

'It was a joke,' I say but glancing at the lane and trees ahead, I'm not quite sure if it was now.

'This is the only way to reach it.' He holds his hands up. 'And I promise, I won't murder you.'

I frown at him. 'Good.' I suppose if he wanted to, he could have done it already.

He shakes his head and continues down the path until he pulls the car up and turns off the engine.

'Just a few steps to climb.' He points to a metal staircase climbing a hill.

'That's more than a few.' Roland wasn't joking when he'd said Olivier made them walk a lot.

'Come on. It's good for you,' he says, climbing out of the car.

We make it to the top and it's a few moments before I can

catch my breath. I take the time to read the inscription on the statue.

'*Mametz Wood, 1916*'.

I glance at the clearing and woods surrounding the hill we'd climbed. 'The fighting here was quite nasty. Apparently, there was a lot of hand-to-hand combat during this battle and the men actually looked their enemies in the eyes as they fought. Can you imagine that?' I say.

Olivier raises an eyebrow. 'You're full of surprises.'

'I studied war poetry many moons ago. I don't know as much as you but a few of the poets I studied fought here. My great-grandfather mentioned in one of his letters that some of his fellow comrades had started to write poetry and who knows, some of those men could even be the well-known poets that I studied. I haven't read any war poetry since my A levels but being here is bringing odd lines back to me. It's surprising what sticks in your memory.'

I look back at the monument. The red dragon tribute to Wales on top is clutching a fistful of barbed wire. Its relevance here is painful.

'I'm going to sit and read the next letter,' I say and Olivier nods knowingly.

'I'll go and have a walk across the clearing.' He heads for the staircase and I sit on the grass overlooking what would have been the battlefield.

My dearest Elizabeth,

We've had our first big piece of action. No doubt word has reached home about the big offensive so I wanted to write to let you know I'm all right. We've had the task of clearing the bodies. Grown men weep unashamedly as they carry their dead brothers from the churned-up, pitted land. I long to come home and see you and Rose, if just for a second, for I'm not sure if it would be my last. After what I've seen, I hold life and love dear.

I love you always.

Will

I choke back a sob as I carefully place the letter back in its wallet and make my way down the steps to where Olivier is wandering the grassed area before the woods.

'Are you okay?' he asks.

I nod and force a weak smile.

He gives me a knowing look before changing the subject. 'Look what I found.' He hands me a piece of twisted metal.

'What is it?'

'It's a piece of shrapnel. If you look carefully enough, they can be found all around here.'

'That's crazy,' I say, studying the century-old piece of death-inducing metal.

'And if you look over there, you can see where the land bears the scars of the trenches.'

'They're so close together.' I can almost picture being there at the time. Looking at the enemy. It was such a personal war in many ways.

'I don't know about you, but I could do with a beer. What do you say?' He changes the subject at just the right time, before things get too maudlin.

'I'd really like that.' More than Olivier probably knew. I'm glad he hadn't suggested food because I don't think I could eat a morsel, but a drink is something I can definitely manage.

We pull up outside a stone-built pub and Olivier greets the barman with a simple '*Bonjour*.'

I sit down, and he joins me shortly after with two small beers, pulled from the tap.

'Olivier, I feel like we've spoken a lot but I don't know much about you. Do *you* have any hobbies?'

'Being a tour guide is a bit like being a superhero, Cath: I'm always ready to help out a tourist in need.' His eyes are on me, heating my face.

'I think you're over-egging your career a little,' I tease. 'If that's the case I'm a senior trades executive providing goods for cash. I even run a packaging scheme.'

He laughs. 'See, there's nothing wrong with *over-egging*.'

'I know why you came to be a tourist guide and that you like history, but how did you become so interested in the war in particular?'

He sits opposite me and rests his elbows on the dark wooden table. 'That's a good question. It just sort of happened. I live in the Somme Valley so, of course, it is an important part of our history, and the people here are still very fond of the British because of their alliance. It's something that has been passed on through the generations.'

He takes a sip of his beer, which leaves a small white frothy line on his top lip, and I giggle. He leaves it there on purpose and pretends he's confused, and I laugh again before he wipes it with the back of his hand. 'I was very interested in the wars at school. I think it started when my father looked into our family history …' He tails off before taking a deep breath. 'Then when I became a tour guide, I discovered so much more. Of course, it is partly by design that I became so knowledgeable because that is why the tourists come here. But I do get to go to England, Belgium, Germany and so on, and I cover a number of Second World War tours too.'

'I'd like to learn more about the Second World War. But that might be for another trip.' I smile.

'It's a lot to take in.' He draws another sip of beer. 'So.' He clasps his hands together. 'You were saying that you want to learn French?'

'I do. I feel so unsophisticated being here and not knowing any of the language. Not that I'm at all sophisticated back in

125

England, but you know what I mean.' His puzzled expression suggests he doesn't.

'So what French do you know already?' he asks.

'Well, MFL ...' He looks even more confused. 'Modern Foreign Languages,' I explain, 'wasn't compulsory when I was at school so I only learned a bit of French up until the age of fourteen, and since I had no exams to sit, it was a bit of a doss.'

'A doss?' He looks even more bemused.

'People didn't take it seriously.'

'But you didn't want to learn? How did you expect to go to other countries and not speak the language?' A crevice forms between his eyebrows and suddenly I feel a little foolish. I don't think British teenage culture is coming off too well so I brush over his comment.

'I remember some basics. *Je m'appelle Cath.*'

'Very good. But do you know anything more? Because going around telling everyone just your name may seem a little self-centred.' I tense, feeling scolded, but a smile cracks on his face and I relax when I realise he was joking.

'That's a valid point.' I smile back. 'I do know some colours and a few food items – I've brought a phrase book with me and I read bits of it when I go to bed each night.'

'Well, that's a start. Perhaps I can help you during your stay? It would be nice for me to stop talking about history for a while.'

'It's very kind of you to offer but it's okay, I'll manage. You've done enough for me,' I say, hiding the reluctance in my tone. Spending time with Olivier is fast becoming one of my favourite pastimes.

Chapter Sixteen

The first thing I see on my phone when I wake up is a message from Martha on Messenger. I sit up to read it and smile instantly when I read the first line.

CHITCHAT GROUP

The capitals hurt my eyes, but in the message, she explains how she can't turn them off, nor can she find the punctuation on the 'darn eyepad'. She goes on to say that they all arrived home safely and that they're suffering from jet lag. Martha has an appointment at the hospital and Cynthia has enjoyed sleeping in her own bed. I tap out a quick reply so they know I got the message and fill them in on my trip to Mametz Wood before heading for a shower.

I'm eating breakfast in the lower-ground-floor restaurant when Olivier approaches me with a steaming cup of coffee in his hand. Seeing him first thing in the morning has become something I look forward to.

'We're going to the Lochnagar Crater today. It's a group of Belgian people but the coach isn't full so you're welcome to join us if you'd like to come along?' I'm not sure if I'm imagining the hopefulness in his tone. 'It's the only crater of its kind to be open to the public.' He almost sings the last sentence, like it's an offer I can't refuse.

I draw a deep breath, desperately wanting to say yes, but it doesn't seem right taking advantage of all the free tours, and I'm not even sure if it could put his job at risk. 'Olivier, that sounds like it would be really interesting, but won't you get in trouble if you keep offering me a free seat on your bus?'

'It's fine.' He bats a hand in the air.

'Can I at least pay for the trip?' I ask, hoping the financial reimbursement will ease my guilt.

'I'm afraid not. I cannot take cash, and this trip was booked through a tour operator. If I take your money it complicates things. The accountant will start asking questions about where all the cash is coming from … It's better you just come along as my guest. We can bend the rules a little, like Bonnie and Clyde,' he jokes but it doesn't ease my guilt.

I consider his offer for a moment. The thought of not going gives me a sinking feeling in my chest. 'Okay, as long as you're sure it will be all right? And you do know that Bonnie and Clyde did a bit more than bend the rules a little, don't you?'

'*Comme ci comme ça.*' He grins. 'It will be fine. It's an afternoon trip and the coach leaves at eleven-thirty from outside the hotel. I have some paperwork to do this morning, but I'll see you later?' His left eyebrow rises slightly in a way that makes him look vulnerable.

'I'll be there.' I smile.

The weather is forecast to be warm again, so I change into some grey cotton shorts and a pastel peach vest top, which hangs loose and hides the traces of twenty years' worth of milk chocolate addiction. Then I spend longer than usual twisting and turning in front of the mirror to make sure I look okay from several different angles. I even put on a tiny bit of make-up. It makes a change from towel-drying my hair and dashing out of the door without so much as glancing in a mirror and I look quite well if I do say so myself. I pack my ancient tan leather messenger bag with my phone, a small

Vaseline lip tin, and a travel-sized hairbrush just in case. I'm ready.

'You're looking fresh and bright,' Olivier says as I approach the coach; he's leaning by the doorway as carefree as ever.

'Thank you.' My insides squeeze a little with the fact he noticed.

'They're a tough crowd,' he says, pointing to the Belgian tourists on board. 'I don't think they liked the joke I just made. Maybe they don't have very good English.' He shrugs.

'Your joke?'

'Yes, I told a joke to break the ice.' He frowns as though it's obvious.

'I think I'm going to regret asking, but what was the joke?'

'I said …' He pauses to clear his throat. 'Please forgive my English. I try my best but I don't yet know what Armageddon means, but that is not the end of the world, is it?' He chuckles.

'Oh dear.' I groan.

'Not you too! Jeez, I thought you were my ally. Now I think I have changed my mind about you coming along. When I tell it on the American and British tours they howl with laughter!'

I raise my eyebrows. 'They howl, do they?'

'Okay, giggle. A little. Perhaps with pity. Like I say, my English is not so strong.' He holds out his hands and lifts his shoulders for emphasis.

'Your English is fine! It's your jokes that are not so strong.' I chuckle and step on board.

The drive out to the crater is another picturesque treat. There is so much green land in this part of France, it's hard to imagine where all the people live. It contrasts with the busy town of Berrybridge somewhat.

The coach pulls over on the side of a narrow road, which we're instructed to cross. We've been given an hour to look around and Olivier is going to do a short talk about the history of the crater.

The warm air feels delicious when it hits me as I step off the air-conditioned coach. The blue sky pops against the green coun-

129

tryside backdrop and is as beautiful as any exotic beach scene. I wasn't sure what to expect when I booked to come to France, but my expectations have been exceeded.

I walk the gravelly incline to the brim of the crater, where most of the people from the coach have already gathered. Olivier is just settling everyone down and is about to start. I can tell because his face has turned all serious.

'The Lochnagar Crater website cites this as being "the largest crater ever made by man in anger".' He pauses to allow his words to sink in then continues to talk about how a series of mines beneath the German trenches were detonated, forming the crater. I was particularly surprised to hear the blast was said to have been heard in London. He takes a battered navy-coloured notebook from his knapsack and opens it on a pre-marked page. My stomach flips. There's something so attractive about him, confident and in his element.

'Henry Edwards—' he waves the notebook, punctuating his words '—was here that day. He wrote a diary entry detailing his experience.' He pauses and it has quite a dramatic effect. 'I want to read you what he wrote because this is one of the only surviving accounts of the blast.' He clears his throat and begins to read. '"Two minutes to zero hour. We stood in our dugout almost drunk with thirst and hunger. The earth ahead packed to the brim with TNT, lay deceptive to the unwitting man. The chambers of its heart filled, spilling into its arteries. Then, the earth shuddered as the ground split asunder, roared with a deafening fiery rage, shooting its black death into the sky."'

He closes his book and puts it back into his bag before talking about how the explosion failed to neutralise the German defences and the Allied forces suffered heavy losses. 'The Lochnagar Crater now serves as a memorial to the fallen. As you walk around, you will see tributes in all shapes and sizes that have been added over time. The path runs all the way around but there are some uneven surfaces so do take care.'

130

When Olivier finishes, the crowd disperses, but I hover, waiting to catch him. 'That was impressive and interesting too. Well done!' I say, unsure if it is the right thing to say to a tour guide who is just doing his job.

'Thank you. I like it here, you know,' he says, wistfully. 'It has both history and nature combined. Look at these wild flowers.' He points to the grass inside of the crater. I hadn't noticed them before, but there are red and blue flowers dotted around.

'Poppies and cornflowers?' I say. Sure enough, amidst the foliage, and other wild flowers, poppies and cornflowers have sprouted sporadically. I pick a poppy and slip it into my bag.

'Would you like to take a walk around?' Olivier asks. I stare across the vast indentation in the ground, which looks like nothing I've ever seen before, and the beautiful landscape beyond, and I nod.

Even if there wasn't a rich, morbid history, it would still be a wonderful place to take a walk, especially with a kind, handsome, interesting man by my side, and as we walk, I allow myself to wonder if it would be this nice to always have a man by my side.

Later, we pull up at a café in the town of La Boisselle, which had been pre-booked as part of the tour. It's rather a novelty in some respects, kitted out with war paraphernalia and posters from the Great War era. The coach tour includes a bowl of soup and bread, which Olivier kindly presents me with once I sit down.

'This smells delicious,' I say, inhaling the delicious aroma of grilled Comté cheese atop the tangy homemade onion soup, which smells so traditionally French and homely I know it will stick with me as one of my fondest memories of the trip.

Olivier blows on a spoonful of soup. 'The food here is very good. We always book a light lunch here for our coach tours to the crater.'

And I can see why. The first spoonful is an explosion of flavour; the bitter onion and creamy cheese together is delightful and given that it is served with proper fresh bread, I'm in my element.

'Mmm. I must learn how to speak French, otherwise I'm going to really struggle when I move here because after tasting this soup, I'm definitely moving here,' I say, gesturing to the soup with my spoon enthusiastically.

'And we, people of France, would love to have you,' he says, making me smile. 'You know, if you really do want to learn the language, I meant what I said: I'd be happy to help you. You're here for a while longer and it's a decent amount of time to learn some basic conversation. Look at what your grandfather achieved in a short space of time.' Olivier tilts his head slightly to the side, allowing a stream of sunlight to strike his face, lighting up his eyes. He smiles easily in a way that I imagine is supposed to authenticate his offer but it just makes him look gorgeous and my chest flutters before I remember myself.

It's not just a polite gesture or flippant remark, but I can't impose on him. I've already taken so much of his time up, and the free tours I'd been welcomed onto were beyond generous.

'Thank you so much for the offer, but I really do feel like that would be an imposition too far. I have a phrase book and there are apparently some language apps I can get on my phone.' Something flicks across his face. *Disappointment?* But he doesn't argue; instead, he just shrugs and continues to eat his soup.

Perhaps I'm the one feeling disappointed.

Chapter Seventeen

I'm sitting in the reception area scanning through a pile of tourism leaflets when I catch sight of the familiar red and white coach pulling outside. My insides leap, alert and ready for my daily dose of Olivier. If I was a puppy, my ears would be pricked. The coach is empty, so I assume it's here to collect a group from the hotel. The doors open and I watch in anticipation for the daily glimpse of Olivier I've grown accustomed to.

When an unfamiliar blonde woman emerges, wearing the familiar red jacket that bears the tour company logo, my insides turn to lead. She enters the hotel, walking right past me, and heads straight to the reception, where she chats to the man behind the counter. She leans on the surface, resting her head on her hand, and they laugh at a joke I don't understand. Their unintentional tête-à-tête unsettles me slightly, and because I know it is ridiculous to feel this way, I acknowledge the feeling to be my own isolation, like when I was in Le Havre. Meeting the Americans on arrival and having Olivier around in their absence had meant that I was part of something. I'd almost forgotten that feeling of being here alone.

How ridiculous. A grown woman like me feeling alone, on a trip I chose to come on. *Alone.* I shake my head, earning a curious glance from the man at reception, who quickly reverts his attention back to the female tour guide.

Seeing his familiar face, even though he obviously thinks I'm odd, reminds me that I have to leave the hotel on Sunday and my chances of meeting up with people after that will be even slimmer. Before I went to bed last night, I even checked my funds to see if I could afford more time at the hotel, but unless I get lucky on the EuroMillions, it just isn't feasible.

I glance at the leaflets in front of me. One is showing the trench remains at Newfoundland Memorial park near Beaumont-Hamel, which looks interesting. I'll go there. By myself. I stuff the leaflet into my bag and go to stand up, just as a swarm of people explode into the reception area from the stairwell. I slide back into my seat, doing a terrible job of convincing myself I'm waiting for them to pass, and not waiting to see if Olivier emerges with them. He doesn't.

After talking myself into renting a car and waiting an hour for the concierge to arrange one, I'm on my way. The satnav is programmed so there shouldn't be a repeat of Neuve-Chapelle – I shan't be 'doing a Cath' today.

I read the John Oxenham poem carved into a bronze cast by the entrance, telling us to 'tread softly' and 'grasp the future gain in this sore loss'. Now is the future, we have grasped it. I find myself hoping once again that our achievements and ways of life are enough.

I walk the wooden zigzag of the deep Allied trench until I reach a shallow scar in the ground. A trench dug after the Battle of the Somme. I sit in one of the unnatural ripples in the grass, allowing my body to curve into what was once a dug-out trench. A man-made hellhole. Laying my head back I squint at the bright sky. It's overcast today but still a bright grey-white. Perhaps the soldiers took in the same sky and pretended they were anywhere but on the front line. I run my hand through the grass that was once thick, soul-sucking mud. It reminds me of a line from another poem by Rupert Brooke:

> If I should die, think only this of me:
> That there's some corner of a foreign field
> That is forever England.

I take the poppy I picked yesterday out of my bag and lay it on the ground. For the men in this foreign field that is forever England.

Walking back, I pretend to myself that I don't miss Olivier's take on things: his interesting nuggets of trivia, his emotion or his company. I try not to think about how they may have sounded in his accent with his short vowels and stressed syllables. And wonderful passion.

Later, I find myself back in Albert, which is the nearest town. There are a few cafés and bars across the small square by the museum and I decide to get myself some lunch, choosing a place with outdoor seating. Recognising very little on the menu, I opt for the *salade niçoise*, as there is a pre-packed version from work that I've enjoyed on occasion so I know what's in it.

I do feel foolish not even being able to understand a menu, and wonder if taking Olivier up on his offer of help would be so bad? It could work out well and having the freedom to come and enjoy lunch in one of the pretty local towns without worrying about language would be the icing on the cake. He's patient and kind, after all. *Or it could be disastrous.* There's a good chance I'll be useless and either embarrass myself or frustrate him to the point of implosion. Neither of which are outcomes I could live with.

As the waitress places down my salad and the small beer that I'd ordered because it was the only thing I could think of on the spot, I regret not ordering water. It's a warm day and I'm parched, but got bogged down in the pronunciation. I know it's *eau*. I can recognise it on the menu, but how do you say it? 'Ooh' or 'oh' or 'you'? Do I say 'un oh' for one water, like the game Uno? Or is that Spanish? I twist myself in knots again and sip my beer, making a mental note to go into a shop to purchase a bottle of water later. I'll ask Olivier when I next see him – with any luck that will happen before someone finds my painfully dehydrated corpse.

Now I'm thinking about Olivier again. Something deep inside is niggling at me but I don't want to admit what it is. I sip more beer. Perhaps if I say it quickly in my head, I won't have to register it – I can get it out of the way and move on. I realise I'm chewing my salad quite frantically. If anyone has noticed, I'm sure I look quite a sight. On the plus side, I'm chewing my food properly, just as my mother always taught me, so I won't suffer from digestion problems.

Okay.

I brace myself.

I'm bothered because Olivier didn't tell me he wouldn't be at the hotel this morning and I've missed him.

There! I've admitted it.

In my head.

I sit triumphantly for a moment with my mind finally clear and enjoy my delicious salad until my head fills up with questions again. *Why should he? Why am I even bothered?* When I was going out with Kieran's father, before the pregnancy and all, he'd vanish to the pub for hours on end and not tell me where he was. Kieran and Gary are always off God only knows where all the time too, so men not being around is what I've come to expect. Besides that, Olivier doesn't have to answer to me. I'm not his wife or mother. Heck, I'm not even his friend – not really. I'm just the annoying tourist he's taken pity on.

I finish my lunch and wave a twenty-euro note in the air to catch the eye of the waitress because I've no idea of how to ask for the bill. I'm shrunken in my chair as she places it down with a friendly smile and simply says, 'Madame.'

I definitely don't know how to ask for change and feel too embarrassed to sit here any longer, so instead opt for leaving a generous tip.

The city of Albert is as beautiful as it was the first time, and I take my time window-shopping and seeing the sights in defiant proof to myself that I don't need to depend on Olivier. I visit the Basilique Notre-Dame properly this time, and I finally buy a bottle of water, which I gulp down greedily.

My phone vibrates in my pocket just as I'm draining the last few drops. It's Kaitlynn.

How's it going? Hope the weather is better there – it's like 2007 all over again here. I'm sure Rihanna is planning on re-releasing 'Umbrella' soon. Seriously, it's that bad!!! Anyway – did you see the memorial? Any hot French dudes? xxxxx

Even in a text message, Kaitlynn still manages to spew out all the words from her head at once and for the first time since I arrived, I realise I miss her. I'm about to tell her about Olivier but stop myself. What exactly is there to tell? That I've met an attractive man who has been kind to me because I'm a bit of a Sad Sack. Instead, I keep it simple and stick to the facts.

Weather has been amazing. Not seen my great-grandfather's memorial yet but have seen others – very touching. So glad I came. xx

Back in Arras I almost collapse through the revolving door. I'm completely shattered but on the whole, I think my second attempt at touring alone went well. I trudge towards the lift, staring down at my feet, which are throbbing in my shoes. I contemplate treating myself to something comfier, when all of a sudden, I'm met with a hard impact, stopping me dead in my tracks.

My head snaps back up instinctively and I'm face to face with a woman with a blotchy face and puffy, red-rimmed eyes. Her hands clasp my arms and I'm able to make out her French mumbling of 'Excuse me', but instead of relaxing her hands as

I expect, her grip tightens uncomfortably and she looks me in the eye. Her nose is moist with watery mucus. She starts to speak in her native tongue so quickly, I don't recognise one word. The same sounds come out over and over, but I don't know what they mean. She starts to shake me. I realise I'm just staring at her pathetically, trying my best to understand. Eventually, she lets go and huffs before storming towards the exit. My hands are trembling and I look up to the receptionist with widened eyes.

'Did I do something wrong?' I ask.

He shakes his head. 'No, madame, you did not. The lady's son is missing and she was asking if you'd seen him. She is very worried for him as he is only six years old,' he says, sympathy etched into his features.

My stomach lurches. *Oh God.* I just stood there like a fool, completely helpless because I'm so uneducated I couldn't even recognise a frantic mother when I saw one. I feel terrible. 'Is someone helping her?' I ask, like that's going to fix everything.

Fortunately, he nods. 'Yes, the local police and some hotel staff are searching. He had let himself out of the room about an hour ago while the lady was taking a shower.'

I clasp my hand to my mouth. 'Oh no, that's awful.' I know exactly how that poor mother must feel. My mind casts back to the day I lost Kieran in a shopping centre. He was just four years old and I can remember the feeling of panic flooding my body as if it were yesterday. Eventually, once your cavities are filled with the terror, despair consumes your every nerve, brain cell and organ, diluting all rational thought. You can only think about what you did wrong, how you let it happen. It's truly awful. *The poor woman.* 'Is there anything I can do to help?'

'Thank you, madame, but the family speak no English, and not many of the local police here do. Although you mean well, your help could hamper their efforts.' Heat creeps across my face. 'It is kind of you to offer, though.' He smiles sympathetically, and it's clear he pities me for being so inadequate. Feeling the need to be alone, I turn to walk to the lifts.

'Cath?' Familiarity forces me to spin on my heel. Olivier is standing at the revolving doors in his red tour guide T-shirt, and I sink into myself. I can feel my face still clutching the tingling heat of my embarrassment and I've already rubbed my eyes, so there's a good chance they'll be ringed with smudged mascara. In the space of about sixty-five seconds, I'd presumably gone from presentable to Worzel Gummidge, and *this* is when he decides to walk in.

'Are you okay?' he asks, and I realise I haven't acknowledged him with anything more than a confused expression.

'Sorry, I …' I rub my face and start again. 'Did you know there is a woman outside who has lost her son?' The real reason for my flustered state is the missing boy and not the sight of Olivier before me. I shake my head a little, trying to rid it of that intrusive little thought.

'I know. Some of my passengers are assisting her. She'd been on my tour this morning and her son is such a sweet young boy. Inquisitive too. We think he's gone off to explore and that nothing sinister has happened, but there are some busy roads around so we do need to find him soon.' His tone is steady and calm but the V-shaped furrow on his brow might as well be branded on.

'If you want, I can help you search?' I say, before remembering my hindering linguistic skills. 'I mean, keep you company and be an extra pair of eyes. I know the boy doesn't understand English and I'd probably frighten him if I approached him alone and couldn't reassure him.'

The furrow momentarily disappears, before coming straight back. 'Yes, that would be useful. I just popped in to make a phone call to the office and my mobile phone has run out. Give me a moment.'

A few minutes later, we are heading towards Place des Héros as Olivier fills me in on the boy's description and what he was last seen wearing. His name is Nathan. I'm impressed by Olivier's calm, methodical approach, and I think some of it rubs off on me. 'The police are checking the train stations and toyshops, but today Nathan was quite obsessed with the old buildings and churches. I've asked the police to check the town hall but it's falling on deaf ears. The mother is so frantic she can barely communicate and hasn't been able to suggest any rational place he may have gone. She has some of the other tourists comforting her now. The town hall is a stunning Gothic building and the belfry is so high – it can be seen from many a street in Arras. I think he'll have gone there.'

'Well, it sounds as good a place as any to start looking,' I say, already picking up pace.

The square is quiet when we arrive. It's a midweek evening and there are just a few people dotted about at tables outside of the café bars. We walk through a cloud of cigarette smoke, past a couple of men enjoying a beer. They don't look up. It's easy to see how a young boy wandering the streets alone may have gone unnoticed. Thankfully, he should be easy to spot to those of us looking out for him thanks to his distinctive red jumper.

'Nathan's mother told police that the boy knows to go into a shop and ask for help if he's ever lost, but at this time, there aren't many shops open.' Olivier's words come out as a conscious stream, rather than him speaking to me directly.

'Poor mite. He must be petrified,' I say as we reach the town hall. 'Do you think he's gone inside?'

Olivier checks his watch and shakes his head. 'It is closed for the day now. Let's walk around it. Perhaps we can ask a few people nearby.' He doesn't wait for me to reply; instead, he charges ahead, on a mission. My chest flutters a little, breaking tension I hadn't even realised was there. Just like his knowledge of history, his proactive demeanour draws me to him, but I don't let that thought linger for long. Instead, I scold myself for thinking it at all when my head should be focused on finding the boy.

I have to run a little to catch up to Olivier's long, powerful strides and when I do, he's already speaking in French to a passer-by. I can tell by his facial expression and tone that they can't provide anything helpful. 'Let's keep looking,' I say and he nods.

We make our way around the building, and once we're out of the square, we see a couple of police officers. Olivier approaches them for an update while I wander up and down, checking doorways for tired little legs. I hear someone jogging towards me and turn around to see Olivier coming to a halt. 'They've finally come to check the town hall, but so far they have nothing.' My heart sinks to the pit of my stomach. I don't say anything, but the 'what if' questions are popping into my head as though a machine gun is firing them through my brain, and I almost choke on my own tonsils as I try to swallow.

All of a sudden, a spear of light penetrates the dark thoughts. It comes so quickly, I can't get the words out, so I tug at Olivier's sleeve until he slows down and I can form a sentence. 'The arches' is all that comes out. I'm out of breath but I don't know why. 'Kieran.' Olivier looks at me, confused. 'Kieran used to hide away when he was scared. I'd find him in his wardrobe, under his bed, in the shed. Anywhere but in the broad light of day. If you think the boy probably came here, we need to check the arches at the front. It's the only place to hide,' I say, already breaking into a jog.

Olivier doesn't speak but he's keeping pace. Once we've rounded the corner, we come to a halt and my body sags a bit with disappointment. The arches aren't as deep as I'd initially thought, and the posts much skinnier. I can practically see without walking under them that there's little room for hiding. 'You look,' I say, unable to face the disappointment of him not being there, nor could I reassure the little lamb if he was.

Olivier's Adam's apple bobs, and he nods before walking slowly under one of the arches. I look away, back across the square to where I was sitting eating with Olivier and the Americans on my first night in Arras, without a care in the world. What a contrast. Roused by Olivier's whispering voice, I turn around to see him slowly emerging from the corner post. I gasp, clutching my hands to my face as I acknowledge the blond boy in a red jumper, balancing on his hip. The boy is clinging to Olivier's neck and has his face buried in Olivier's sweater while Olivier continues to whisper to him in French, gently stroking his back. My chest cracks and all the air comes out. The sensation makes my eyes tingle and moisten.

'Oh God, you've found him!' I run over, stopping a metre or so before them so as not to startle the child. 'Is he okay?' I ask, scanning him over and resisting the urge to take him in my arms.

'He seems to be. Frightened, tired, and hungry but otherwise okay,' he says through a watery smile.

I open my mouth to reply, but as I do, the two policemen we saw a few minutes ago come bounding over, immediately entering into a conversation I don't understand a word of. One of the officers speaks into his radio, presumably informing everyone of the good news. Olivier hands over the boy to the other officer and there is some back-patting and handshaking before the officers leave with the boy and Olivier crumples in half.

'Are you okay?' I ask, placing an arm around his shoulders. It's a moment before he stands tall again, and I allow my arm to flop down as the gradient of his back increases.

'I'm so relieved. What his mother must have been going through, I don't know. I'm so glad he's been found in good health.' He rubs his face with his hands. 'I can't believe I didn't look there first – it was such an obvious place. I was convinced he'd want to be up in the tower or sitting admiring the building from afar.'

'You can practically see the entire space from here,' I say, gesturing towards the arches. 'He must have been tucked away in a tiny ball.'

'He was,' he says, staring at the building.

'He's safe now.' I sense pensiveness. Seeing how much he cares gives me a pang of something in my stomach. It's a mixture of affection and sadness, to know there are men in this world like that and yet Kieran's father, and my own come to think of it, never even gave us the time of day.

'Yes. Now I need a drink, will you join me?' His crinkled brow backs up his statement.

I nod.

'I want to speak to the mother again but will do it tomorrow. The police will be with her a while. There's a bar just off the square. It's quiet.'

'Okay.'

We take a seat in a corner inside and Olivier goes to the bar, returning with two large beers. He hands me mine before sitting down and taking three large glugs of his own and letting out a sigh.

'You'll be in the news tomorrow, hailed a local hero,' I say, trying to lighten the thick atmosphere.

He raises a smile but there is no jubilation behind it.

'What is it?' I ask in a more serious tone.

'I just can't help but think of how wrong today could have gone. That child could have been hit by a car, kidnapped ...' He trails off and sips his beer.

'I know that. But you found him, safe, and now he's back with his mother where he belongs. Imagine how she feels?'

'I know. You're right. It's just been a hell of a day.' He raises his glass. 'I couldn't have done it without you, though.'

I shake my head, unable to accept the praise. 'His mother approached me, just before you arrived at the hotel. She was frantic but I couldn't understand what she was saying so I just stood there staring at her like an incapable idiot.' It was my turn to take a long draw of my beer.

'That wasn't your fault.' His tone is comforting.

'I know, but if I could understand the language a little better,

I would have understood her problem. I could have offered to help or reassured her.' I sigh.

He rests his head on his hand and looks me directly in the eye, causing the hair follicles on the back of my neck to tickle. 'You're quite hung up on this whole language barrier thing, aren't you?'

I sigh. 'Yes, I suppose I am. I feel so stupid. But that isn't all. I love the sound of the French language, it sounds so …' I feel the heat in my cheeks again as I realise how foolish what I'm about to say will sound, but I've committed to the statement and swallow hard before choking out the word. 'Romantic.'

As I say the word, I have to look away, but I can tell he's smiling. Fortunately, he does his best to make me feel comfortable by shrugging. 'They say it is the language of love.'

'Exactly,' I reply, with more confidence than I feel.

'My offer still stands. I will teach you some French. In fact, I'd enjoy it.'

His face is hopeful: a half-smile, a slight rise of the eyebrows and his head cocked slightly to the side. 'Are you sure it wouldn't be an imposition?'

'I'd enjoy it,' he repeats, slowly and much louder to ensure I'd got the message.

I chuckle and notice his brows press together. 'Sorry, you just did the "speak slower and louder" thing that English people are renowned for.'

Fortunately, he laughs too. 'Well, that was your first lesson!'

'Thank you,' I mouth, loud and slowly.

He pats his stomach. 'Are you hungry? I didn't think I was before but it must have been the adrenaline. Now I'm famished. They do good food here if you want to eat?'

My stomach growls in response and I clutch it, hoping he hasn't heard. 'That would be lovely'.

'Great.' He claps his hands together. 'We can start our first lesson now.'

'Okay,' I say, glad to see his lifted spirits.

Olivier disappears to ask for some menus and returns with them and two glasses of wine a minute or so later.

'Okay, well in France, we like to enjoy a glass of wine.' He places the glasses on the table to make his point. 'One of the first things we teach our children to say after mamma and papa is: "*La vie est trop courte pour boire du mauvais vin*".' He speaks so quickly I can't so much as pick out a sound other than vin, which I know is wine. I frown. 'It means that life is too short to drink bad wine. It's a very important lesson, no?' His eyes dance mischievously. And I go along with his joke.

'English kids are tougher – they drink aged whisky.'

He laughs before lowering his eyes to the menu. 'So how about this? Do you see anything you recognise?'

He hands me the leather-bound copy and I scan the list. 'Omelette, hamburger, pizza. I think I'm better at French than I thought.'

He purses his lips, but I can see the humour glinting in his eyes. 'Okay, okay.' He waves a hand at the menu. 'Further down, madame.'

'*Poisson* is fish,' I say, reading the heading from one of the sections.

'And do you like all fish?' he asks, raising one eyebrow.

I pull a face to indicate I don't because I daren't tell the truth, which is that I only really eat chip shop fish or fish fingers – and of course the tuna in an occasional *salade niçoise*. I put the anchovies on the side.

'Then you must learn which fish is which.' He folds his arms smugly.

'*Sole á l'orange*. Sole with orange sauce?'

'Good, but again quite an easy one. Any others?'

'*Moules* are mussels. And that's it.' I stare blankly at the rest.

'You're better than you thought. We pronounce it "*moule*" though.'

'Why put an s on the end then?' I ask.

He shrugs. 'Why do women buy so many pairs of shoes when they can only wear one at a time?'

'*Touché.*' I smile. '*Moule.*'

'Perfect.' He smiles.

We talk through the rest of the menu and I'm quite surprised by how much I recognise. Some words I've seen on products at work, some I just know or are easy to work out. By the time the waiter comes to take our order, I feel confident enough to ask myself.

I decide to be adventurous and confidently say, '*Moules frites, s'il vous plaît,*' to the waiter, taking a satisfied breath when the waiter just nods as if it was normal.

'Eek!' I screech. 'He understood me.'

'Well done,' Olivier says once the order is complete and the waiter has gone. 'Using language is the key to mastering it.'

Olivier continues to teach me useful phrases while we eat our meal, and he asks me basic questions in French and I reply. He's a good teacher, patient, calm and thorough just like I thought he'd be, and the French lessons keep any potential awkward silences at bay. By the end of the evening, I've ordered wine and dessert for us both, requested the bill and thanked the waiter for a delicious meal. As we sit finishing our drinks, I'm feeling quite accomplished.

'Well, I think lesson one has been a success.' He holds up his glass and I chink mine against it.

From across the table, his eyes rest on mine, that lightning blue piercing me. Instinct urges me to look away, but I'm unable to; instead, I find myself running my fingers through my hair to straighten it out in case he's looking at what a tangled mess it is.

'I was wondering …' His smooth voice breaks through the silence. 'I'm off on Saturday and thought it may be nice to drive over to the coast. The weather forecast looks good and I'm ready for a day relaxing on the beach if you'd like to join me?'

My heart leaps and I have to reassure myself that he can't possibly see it punching through my chest like some cartoon depiction of love. Is it a date? I haven't been on a date for such a long time.

'I'd love to.' Somehow, I manage to sound casual.

'Fantastic. If you like, we can visit Étaples in the morning and have an afternoon off war history. We could even use it as an opportunity for another French lesson,' he says and my heart shrinks before I plaster on a smile.

'Wonderful.'

Chapter Eighteen

I've already changed twice. I don't know what to wear to the beach in France, or any beach for that matter. Last time I was on a beach I was much younger and much slimmer. *Should I even take swimwear?* My phone buzzes, breaking my mild state of panic.

Don't forget ton maillot de bain! O x

I Google the translation and smile because it's like he'd read my mind. Then a new wave of panic sets in: I'll have to wear a swimsuit, in front of Olivier. I pull out the two token costumes I'd chucked in the case 'just in case'. I'd not actually expected to need a costume on a WWI tour of rural France, but it's what you do when you go on holiday, isn't it? One is a hot pink bikini that has little bits of sand ingrained in the fabric from its one trip to Dorset many years ago, and the other, a plain black one-piece that I'd bought with the very best of water-aerobics-based intentions, is so old the stitching has started to fray, but I do seem to remember it was quite flattering thanks to a control panel that was great for hiding my 'mum-tum'. I shove it in my large canvas shopper, which, for today will be doubling as my beach bag.

I stand up to leave but sit back on the bed again just moments later. *I should try them on first.* I check the time and I have a few minutes. *What if I look hideous?* I take a breath and stuff the costume and my towel into the bag – I think being blissfully unaware of how I look will suffice.

The number of white gravestones at the military cemetery in Étaples is overwhelming. Neither of us speak as we pay silent respects to the fallen and somehow, Olivier's uncharacteristic silence says a lot. There are a few other visitors around but the place is quiet and still, granting earned, eternal peace for men. *I should live a better life.* I shouldn't fall back into my rut of work and cleaning. We each get one chance at life, and if this vast number of gravestones represents something it's how precious life is. I take out the letter that my great-grandfather wrote shortly after his arrival in 1915.

'I'll leave you to read it,' Olivier says.

Instinctively, I place my hand on his forearm and our eyes catch. 'You don't need to.'

My dearest Elizabeth,

We've begun our gruelling training. The conditions here are dreadful. There are men with the most horrific injuries who've come back from the front line to convalesce and men deemed well enough to be sent back who seem to have lost their souls. For they are without fear, pride and hope; instead, they're filled to the brim with resignation.

We have been told of what awaits us down the line, but until we're there, it's hard to imagine how one will cope. The men who do return home won't ever be the same again but this is the hand we must play for our great Nation.

All my love to you and Rose,
Will

Olivier swallows. 'The conditions were terrible. They only got worse too.'

'I remember reading how Wilfred Owen described it as "vast and dreadful".'

'You know more about the war than you give yourself credit for; you'll be after my job next.' His lips dance playfully, and I can't help but grin at the compliment.

***

'I hadn't expected this,' I say as I take in the white, sandy beach when we pull up in the pretty town of Le Touquet. Olivier turns down the radio that has been blasting the Foo Fighters all the way here. His singing was certainly interesting.

'It's beautiful, isn't it?'

We trudge through the sand and find a spot to lay out our towels. The sun is beating down but there's a strong breeze coming off the sea that keeps the temperature at a comfortable twenty-three degrees.

'This is the life,' Olivier says, sprawling out on his towel. I hadn't noticed him take off his T-shirt and the tanned, defined torso I'm greeted with surprises me a little. I'd not given much thought to what was beneath his red uniform before, but now I've seen it, it's all I can think about. I turn away before he catches me looking because that *would* be embarrassing.

The tide is out and the water glistens under the sunlight in the distance. Children squeal, running around after kites. Seagulls 'keow' overhead. I relax into my own towel and look up at the blue sky, shielding my eyes from the sun with my hands. I'm in paradise, and the grey skies of Berrybridge seem like forever ago.

I don't know how much time has passed but when Olivier sits

up and opens the cooler that he'd brought, I'm parched, and ready for whatever he has inside.

'Freshly squeezed orange juice for you, madame?' He hands me the bottle, which I press to my forehead, grateful for the coolness. It has one of those bottle stoppers that teenagers of the Eighties used to affix to their shoelaces.

'Did you make this?' I ask, noticing the lack of a label.

'I pressed the oranges myself this morning.' He grins but doesn't meet my eye. I want to tell him he never fails to surprise me, but instead I thank him and tell him how delicious it is once the first tangy sip hits the spot.

When he's drunk half of his juice, he turns on to his side and props his head upon a sandy hand. 'How come you're here alone, Cath?'

I splutter a little. 'I beg your pardon?' I realise straight away that I sound abrupt, but his question has taken me by surprise and I want to bide my time and fabricate a reason that isn't as pathetic as the real reason, which is simply that I didn't have anyone else to come here with.

'I suppose I'm wondering why you are single.' Using the fingers of the hand he's leaning on, he rubs his forehead. 'I'm sorry, it is none of my business. The warmth of the sun is probably making me feel too comfortable.' He bats at the words with his hand and I relax a little, unsure as to why I over-reacted.

'No. No, it's fine. I got pregnant young and had bigger fish to fry than dating men. My son's father left before Kieran was even born. He wasn't ready to be a father he said, then moved away and I haven't heard from him since.'

'I can never understand men like that.' He lets his words hang in the air for a moment but then shifts his tone. 'You haven't dated anyone?' he probes, keeping his eyes on mine.

'No, I've never considered it. Kieran's always been my priority.' I tug at a piece of cotton on my towel, unable to meet the strength of those bright blue lightsabres.

152

I'm expecting more questions or at least a 'why?' but instead, he shrugs and says, 'Fair enough.'

I let out a sigh. 'I've told you all about me, now it's your turn. What's your story?' I ask in a tit-for-tat exchange. His top lip tightens slightly before he breaks into a smile.

'I had a girlfriend back in school. We were together many years but as we got older, we drifted apart.' He dusts sand off his arm. 'The year we turned twenty-one, she left to go travelling the world and I never saw her again.' He raises his hand to suggest it was no big deal, but I sense some remorse. Perhaps she was the one who got away. I'm about to offer some sympathy when he opens his mouth to continue. 'Why are you not seeking a Mr Right?'

The question throws me a little, even though I was expecting it. I'd never really thought about it. I'd only asked him because it was unusual for a good-looking, kind man to have reached forty and remained single. Perhaps there was a small part of me that was curious too.

'For a long time, it's just been me and my son. I had a brilliant, hands-on mother and since she died my pet brother moved in.' Bemusement sweeps his face, but I don't want to have to explain my naff joke, so I continue. 'I'm never alone enough to think about it. In short, other than lust after the handsome lead in a romantic comedy or the dishy weatherman on the local news, I don't really think much about men.' He listens intently as I speak, which is a little unsettling because none of the men in my life pay any attention to me whatsoever. Normally, I don't talk about touchy-feely things like this because I don't know anyone interested enough in how I feel.

He smiles. 'You're an independent woman. I get it.'

'You could say that I suppose, but I don't always feel like one. I think a woman on a punctured life raft is more accurate.' I find the sand with my fingers and watch them sink into its softness.

'You speak from the heart and I love how honest you are but you shouldn't be so negative.'

I let my shoulders sag. 'I'm not. I suppose I use humour to deflect sometimes.'

'The tide is coming in. Shall we go for a swim?' And with that, the subject is deflected.

I look across the sand and children are splashing in the surf. The sun is only just hot enough to penetrate my skin so I seriously doubt it's hot enough to heat the English Channel to an acceptable temperature, but I don't want to come across as soft. 'Let's do it.'

Olivier is already on his feet, and I hadn't realised earlier but the navy shorts he has on are swimming shorts so he's sea-ready. I, on the other hand, need to change. Holding my towel around myself, I slither out of my shorts and vest self-consciously hoping none of my bits are flashing the poor unsuspecting people behind me. Quickly, I step into my costume, pulling it up and taking the time to adjust it in all the right places before daring to drop the towel. Olivier had the good grace to walk towards the water, ensuring my privacy (from him at least), so I jog a little to catch him up, willing him not to turn around and see everything jiggling about in a far-from-*Baywatch*-esque motion.

As expected, the water is freezing and dipping my feet in is almost too much to bear, but Olivier runs in until it's knee-deep and dives in head first before bobbing back up and beckoning me in.

'Come on. You have to get in quickly – once you're in, you'll love it,' he shouts above the crash of the surf.

I inch a little deeper, so the water laps my ankles and turns my feet into blocks of ice. I'm pretty sure I've lost the feeling in my toes. 'You're right. It's lovely but I think I'll just stay here.' I smile.

Olivier is now swimming at a leisurely pace. 'Come on, it's invigorating. You just need to get your head under.'

My head? I'm struggling with my ankles.

'Fine.' If there's one thing I've learned about the British since being here, it's that we're made of tough stuff and I'm not a wimp. I take a deep breath and run towards the breaking waves until I'm deep enough the water poses too much resistance to run any further, and then I flop forward into what I hope resembles a dive. The initial shock of the cold water takes my breath away but as I swim, my muscles warm up quickly and it does feel quite pleasant. *The old salt water.*

'See, invigorating isn't it?' Olivier swims over to join me. 'I much prefer this to sweltering on a hot beach down in Spain at the height of summer.'

'I think there's room in my life for both,' I say, laughing.

We run back to our towels, collapsing into them when we arrive. The breeze is like an Arctic blast now I'm wet, but he's right, it *was* invigorating, and I feel giddy and alive. I sit propped up on my arms. My legs are almost dry already with just the odd water droplet scattered around my goose bumps, but my costume is wet.

'Here, have my towel.' Olivier puts his towel around my shoulders and sand grains fall from it, sticking to my arms. He's already plonked his wet bottom in the sand before I have time to protest.

'Thank you.'

'Thank you for humouring me and coming for a swim. In fairness, I didn't think it would be quite that cold.' He shakes his head, sending water droplets everywhere. 'Not many women I know would have gone in. You're brave.'

'Or an utter dingbat. Those women probably have more sense than I do.' I chuckle. 'It's not a proper trip to the seaside if you don't go in though, is it? That's what I used to tell Kieran anyway.' Olivier looks at me for a moment and smiles warmly sending a new wave of shivers through me.

A ball lands by my feet, sending a puff of sand into the air, and I throw it back to the young boy bounding towards it.

'Once we dry off, I'll show you the town,' Olivier says. 'But first, how about our next French lesson?'

The town of Le Touquet is as perfectly whimsical as I've come to expect from my limited experience of French towns, with narrow streets lined with stunning French architecture. The summer crowds have descended and the bars and restaurants seemingly reap the rewards. Aromas of garlic, fish, and ale fill my nostrils as the rays beat down, making all the glass in the town sparkle.

'I could live here,' I say, as we amble through the crowds.

'You'd need a lot of money and besides that, if you lived here, you wouldn't appreciate it as much.' He's right, of course. I think of all the things I could see or do back in England that I never get around to. 'Arras gives me the best of everything: Paris, Lille, the coast and even the channel are all close by.'

'I suppose I have it pretty good too,' I muse. Not Olivier-good, but I have a roof over my head, a job and a wonderful son and that's a lot to be thankful for.

Olivier stops outside a traditional-looking bar-come-restaurant. 'Here we are.'

There are some wooden bistro-style tables and chairs outside and we manage to grab one of the few remaining.

The temperature has picked up so we both order the *salade de la mer*, after Olivier assures me that shrimp will be the only seafood I'll find in there and then he orders a bottle of wine I've never heard of: *Louis Jadot, Macon Village Chapelle aux Loups*. I make him teach me how to say it because it sounds so wonderful and I love how the shape of the words feel in my mouth.

Perhaps I'd soaked up too much of the place but I'm a little lightheaded. France is a drug running through my veins and, caught in the moment, I feel brave enough to put a few words together. '*Je suis chaud*,' I say confidently, adding what I believe to be a French accent and hoping I've pronounced it right. Sometimes it's difficult to know what you actually sound like.

Olivier's eyebrows shoot up pushing away any shred of hope I had of accuracy.

'Er, yes. I am hot. Now we're not getting the sea breeze.' I say with less confidence.

He smiles and his eyes fill with mirth. 'Ahh, I knew what you meant. It's probably not something you should go around telling everyone though.'

'Why ever not?'

He leans across the table, so his lips are close enough to brush my ear and whispers; 'You've just told me that you're horny.'

I gasp, hiding my face with my hands as my cheeks blaze. 'But, the words … Oh, dear God!'

Gently, he peels my hands away and I see he's been laughing. 'Listen, it's a common mistake.'

'Of course it is, the words mean I am hot.' He laughs again and I sigh. 'Well, I've definitely learned a valuable lesson today.'

My phone buzzes and I welcome the diversion. 'Sorry, it's probably my son.'

It is.

Mum, I'm thinking of getting a perm. Is your hairdresser's any good or shall I just get it done here in Leicester?

What the …? I do a double take.

'Is everything okay?' Olivier sits forward, concern creeping into his features.

I relax my forehead, 'Yes, at least I think so. Is there such thing as a quarter-life crisis?' *Kieran isn't even old enough for one of those yet.* Olivier lifts an eyebrow. 'Sorry, I need to just …' I wave my phone before tapping out a reply.

Are you being bullied? xxx

I pause, before adding the word 'online' because he's at university now and those online trolls target adults too.

It pings back straight away.

What? NO!!! It's fashion, Mum. Haven't you seen it?

Seconds later, another message pops in below.

Mum – er – MEET ME AT MCDONALD'S??

My heart aches for him and it just goes to show that you can need your mum at any age. I look up at Olivier, conscious of my rudeness. 'I'm sorry, this son of mine is behaving rather oddly. Just one moment.'

Kieran, love. You know I'm in France, I can't meet you at McDonald's, but when I'm home we'll spend some quality time together. Love you xxx

I press send and put my hand to my chest. 'I think my son misses me.'

'Of course he does. Moving away to university is a big step, especially if it has always been just you and him.'

'He wants me to take him to McDonald's. It's like he's reverted back to being a little boy again, and now he's talking of getting a perm.' As I shake my head, another message comes in. I look apologetically at Olivier. 'Last one, I promise.'

God, Mum, no! The haircut is CALLED the meet me at McDonald's!

My heart sinks. In a case of good timing, the waiter brings our wine. I take it straight from his hand and have a big glug of it.

'Something else?' Olivier looks quite puzzled and I dread to think what my face might be doing.

'I'm sorry. I know I've not been much company since we got here. Kieran isn't missing me after all and he doesn't want to meet me at McDonald's; that's just the name of some hair trend or something.'

He reaches across the table and puts his hand on my arm, causing frissons beneath it. 'I'm sorry. I'm guessing you were hoping for him to be missing you? Right now, he's a young man having fun. Once that wears off, he will miss you. Trust me.' Something about the way he says *trust me* makes me believe it will happen.

I nod, afraid my voice will come out all wobbly if I try to admit it.

'This is just what teenagers are like.'

'I know,' I say sombrely.

Olivier's lips form a hard line as he raises his glass. '*C'est la vie.*'

'*La vie,*' I reply, lifting my glass and taking another sip of wine. Olivier bursts into a fit of laughter and I glare at him in confusion.

He places his right hand on his heart. 'I'm sorry, I shouldn't laugh, again; it was a knee-jerk reaction.'

'What did I do this time? You told me to *say* "la vie" so I did. How could it go so wrong from there?' I fold my arms, convinced he's just nit-picking this time. And then he explains.

'Well, I feel like a prized idiot. Perhaps languages just aren't my forte.'

'Don't be silly. I shouldn't have laughed – it was, how do you say it … cute.'

It's like flying ant day in my stomach. *Olivier just said I was cute.* I think I'm acting nonchalant as I smile and take a sip of wine but my cheeks are burning. I press my cold glass to them in an effort to subdue the undoubted redness and then I fan myself. 'It's hot, isn't it?'

'I, er …' He struggles for a polite way to say: *not really, it's actually just pleasantly warm.* 'We can sit inside if it would be more comfortable?'

My heart squeezes. Somehow, aside from laughing at my faux pas just moments earlier, he always manages to say and do things that put me at ease. I can feel my heart rate dropping and the tingling subsides in my stomach. 'It's such a beautiful day – outside is fine. I think I just drank my wine too quickly.'

Over dinner, we practise some of the French phrases I've already learned, and I inform Olivier that I'm moving out of the hotel and into an Airbnb room tomorrow.

'Oh no, you should have said. There are some gîtes for rent in my village and I know the owner well. He's not been lucky with rentals this summer and I know he'd give you a good deal if I arranged it.'

He's too kind but I really can't fathom why he's taken me under his wing.

'Thank you but I'm sorted. It's a bedsit thing above a shop in Arras. It will do and it's still close to the train station, which will be useful. I'll miss the hotel because I feel comfortable there but I'm going to be living alone when I get back to England. It shouldn't be any different here.'

He seems to accept that. We talk about other things – my favourite places so far, what else is on my itinerary and so on – and before we know it, two hours have passed.

'I think I'll have to bring you back here. There's so much we haven't done: the pools, crazy golf, dinner …' His eyes meet mine on the word 'dinner', zapping me. I can't help but wonder if he meant to do that to me, or if it's all in my head.

Chapter Nineteen

I've found a job. Complete load of bollocks it is, but it will get me out of your hair. Am I OK to stay in your grand palace for two more weeks until I can sort a flat out? Gaz

I read the message in Gary's voice complete with the sarcastic tone I know he intended and slump on the bed in relief. At least I'd be able to get the empty-nest syndrome business dealt with and start walking the path laid out for me. It would be impossible while caring for that man-child.

Congratulations. That's great news about the job – I knew you could do it. Yes, of course you can stay for two weeks.

I pause before hitting send. Something occurs to me, something I should have done a while ago, and that is to stop being such a blooming pushover. I add a few more words to the message before hitting send. I don't even put my phone down because I know he'll reply straight away, and he does. His messages come through short and snappy, and I smile because I know it's his stream-of-consciousness style.

Fix the bathroom mirror?
It's not really in my skill set as an engineer.
I don't have the right tools.

I'm about to reply but it's time for some tough love. He can't keep relying on me to help him out of difficult situations. It's quite bizarre that he's coming to me for help with a tricky situation that I've purposely put him in to make him more independent. I laugh at the irony and put my phone down. *Gary can figure this one out on his own.*

The phone buzzes endlessly as I pack the last few bits in my suitcase. Only once I've finished do I check it.

Do you have any tools?

Don't worry yourself, I've found your little toolkit.

All done! Happy now, slave driver?

You don't have any plasters, do you?

I giggle at the last one and send a short reply now his lesson is over.

Thank you – plasters in the cupboard above the fridge.

I settle the bill at the hotel and set off on the five-minute walk to my new room, suitcase in tow. Olivier had offered to help me move but he was heading off on an overnight trip to London this morning and could only help at some ungodly hour that Kieran would probably consider 'time to leave the club and get a kebab'. Having him make all that effort to help me pull one wheelie suitcase was unnecessary, but he was persistent. He only agreed to let me do it alone when I told him in no uncertain terms that no way was I getting up at silly o'clock in the morning.

It's a damp, soggy day and the temperature seems to have dropped a few degrees. As I reach the apartment's proximity, I double-check the address and map on my phone. It should be right ahead. I take a few steps forward trying to spot it when I see a man leaning in the doorway smoking a cigarette.

'Er, *excuse moi? J'ma—*'

'You are here for the apartment?' he says, sparing me the excruciating exchange.

'Yes.' I nod eagerly.

'Come this way.' He enters the building without stubbing out his cigarette.

I follow him inside, taking a quick look around to see if there would be any witnesses, should I never re-emerge, but the folk of Arras don't seem keen on the rain and there isn't a soul in sight. Apprehensively, I climb the steps.

The ingress to the apartment is a cracked and peeling, off-white door, which creaks as the man, who I realise hasn't yet introduced himself, wiggles the key and shoulder-barges it open.

'Excuse me,' I say politely. 'Would someone be able to fix that? I'm just not sure if I'd be able to manage it.'

He looks up at me with brown, unsympathetic eyes before taking a drag of his cigarette and swinging the door open. 'You have paid in full through the website, but any damages must be paid for.'

A musty smell hits me as I cross the threshold and take in the dingy room. There's an unmade bed, kitchenette and old TV, and I realise that the photographs on the website were perhaps overly sympathetic. The bathroom has been built out of louvred doors and takes up a small corner of the room by the bed. My chest tightens. A jingling sound prompts me to look right, to where the man is holding up the keys. I take them and he disappears down the stairs.

It takes two hands and all my body weight to get the door to close. When it's shut, I slump against it, letting out a sigh. It wasn't as though the hotel was luxurious, but it was comfortable, clean and welcoming. Here, there's a brown patch on the ceiling that I actually hope is damp and not something even worse. The pile of linen folded on the bed is crisp and white. It smells clean, which is something, but not enough to stop the creepy-crawly feeling up my arms.

The romantic image I'd had of living independently abroad for a while like some young and trendy gap-year student is shattered. Even after I make the bed and the stained mattress is covered I can't settle, and for the first time since I've arrived, I start to miss home. I miss Kieran and to some extent Gary, but only because I'm so used to having him around. My eyelids start to feel hot and moist. Within seconds, a tear blobs onto my cheek and my nose starts to run. Without a better option, I wipe it on my sleeve.

'Pull yourself together, woman,' I say aloud. It's not exactly the worst hurdle I've had to overcome in my time, but it's probably the worst place I've ever slept. I stand up and rub my eyes, before forcing myself to go to the shop for cleaning supplies.

Three hours later, every surface has been disinfected. I'm thankful for the hard vinyl flooring but I wouldn't have ruled out scrubbing a carpet with disinfectant had I needed to. Either I've become accustomed to the foul smell or it has gone and the place is slightly more habitable.

I've worked up quite a thirst, but the thought of going and sitting in one of the nearby bars alone is daunting. After the day I've had, I want somewhere comfortable and familiar.

The clean air-freshened smell of the hotel feels like home when I walk in. I take a deep breath of it through my nose before walking over to the bar area, where barman Kevin is kneeling down stocking the fridge.

'Hi, Kevin,' I say, sliding onto a stool.

'Cath, you're back already.'

'I missed the ambience of the lobby.' My tone isn't convincing, nor would anyone describe the lobby as ambient. It's plain, slightly dated and very green.

'Are you struggling to settle into your new place?' Kevin's English is quite broken and heavily accented but still much better than my French.

I shrug. 'It's not what I expected but it will do.' Boring Kevin the barman with my problems seems a bit sitcom-esque, and in real life, I can't imagine he cares a great deal about my bedsit. I order a white coffee in French and Kevin looks at me with a raised eyebrow.

'You've been learning some of the language?' he says.

I'm about to reply and tell him about Olivier's lessons when all of a sudden, a loudly groaned 'Kevin' comes from behind me. I turn around and see the pretty female tour operator from the other day. She slumps onto the stool next to me and starts speaking to Kevin in French. I try not to listen, not that I'd understand much anyway. I don't feel isolated this time. Instead, the noise of chatter and simply being around people is comforting. Much more so than the flat. I screw up my eyes, wishing I could just go upstairs to bed and not back to that hellhole bedsit, when the woman's phone rings. The first word she says catches my attention.

'Olivier?'

My chest thumps and I listen as carefully as I possibly can while pretending to sip my wine. I don't understand much of her hurried speech, so I listen to her tone. It's light and she laughs. She doesn't sit still – one minute she's leaning forward and the next running her fingers through her hair. Suddenly her tone gets angrier before she simmers down again. The next few words from her mouth I recognise and they are a vice around my stomach.

'*Je t'aime*,' followed by another word I don't pick up.

My mouth goes dry.

Chapter Twenty

The brown spot on the ceiling is definitely just damp. I consider myself a bit of an expert now, because I've been staring at it for about an hour, putting off getting up and dressed because I quite frankly can't think of anything to do with my day. I can't shake the feeling that Olivier was giving off 'signals', and it's consuming me, but why would he be if he was in love with a gorgeous blonde?

I need to pull myself together and remember why I came here. Taking my phone off the side, I use the voice-activated dial. 'Call Kieran.'

It rings for a while and goes straight to voicemail. I try Kaitlynn. She answers after a few rings.

'Cath, hi.' Her voice is thick with sleep.

'Sorry did I wake you?' I check the time and it's just gone nine here so it's only just after eight back home.

'Yes but it's fine, I need to get up anyway. Is everything okay?'

I stumble over my words. 'Yes, I just … I'm checking in, just seeing if those tills are running smoothly, that's all.' My voice cracks a little at the end.

'Er, yes. Everything is fine. Are you really okay, Cath?'

I sigh; I've never felt more alone. This bedsit, being in a foreign country all alone, and Olivier stringing me along playing me for a fool is all starting to feel too much. 'I think I'm a bit homesick, that's all.'

'Well, believe me, there is nothing to miss here. It's still raining, work is the same, your son is still at uni and Gary is still vegetating on your couch. In brighter news, my manicure has lasted.'

'That's good, about your manicure. I know all the other stuff, I just … I don't know. I think I even miss Gary.'

Kaitlynn scoffs.

'Okay, that was a little bit dramatic. I wish I could just pop home for the day and come back, but I haven't budgeted for that.'

'Stop being ridiculous!' she barks. 'Holidays are a bit like dog years: what feels like seven days to you when you're away, is really just one day here. Honestly, to me it's like you've only just gone.'

She has a point. It has only been two weeks. 'I think it's because I've left the hotel.'

'Haven't you made any friends?' She sounds distracted, and I can hear her filing her nails in the background.

'It's not that easy when you don't speak the language, and it's even harder now I'm in a bedsit.' I draw a breath. 'One of the tour guides has been helping me learn French and we've been out for food and drinks a few times.'

'Well, there you go then. If you're feeling down why not give her a call and arrange to do something today?'

'She's actually a *he*. Not that it matters.' I just wanted to correct her because it felt odd she referred to Olivier as 'her' but as soon as the words come out I regret them and brace myself for Kaitlynn's reaction.

'Oh, is *he* now?' *Here we go.* 'Well, well, well.'

'It isn't like that,' I say before she goes getting any ideas. Now I know what I know about him, it *really* isn't like that, but I don't want that conversation right now.

'So, this tour guide is just teaching you French for fun, is he?' Her tone is teasing but I can tell she wants the gossip.

'It isn't like that. I actually think he feels … *felt* sorry for me.'

'What does he look like?'

'What does that matter?'

'It matters to me.'

I sigh. 'He's handsome I suppose, dark messy hair that seems to flop one way or the other depending on his mood, tanned skin.' *That looks like caramel.* 'And the bluest eyes you've ever seen.' As the words leave my mouth, I realise how foolish it was to think that someone like him could possibly be interested in a plain Jane like me.

'Oh my God! You love him!' she shrieks.

'Shhh,' I say, as though he could hear her if she spoke any louder. 'No, I do not! He's *with* someone.'

I can feel her disappointment through the phone. 'Well, just as it was about to get juicy! You could have started with that little nugget.'

'It's irrelevant. The point I was trying to make was that I've not been completely alone and I've been learning French. You turned it into something else. Too much *Love Island* perhaps?'

'Er, until you've watched *Love Island*, you can't knock it with your condescending tone, and actually your "the bluest eyes I've ever seen" comment was the giveaway.' She uses a mock 'Southern Belle' accent to mimic me.

'Okay, so he's attractive and kind but his partner is very attractive and younger than me and I'm sure they're very happy.'

'Partner? So he's gay?' She lets out a dramatic groan.

'No, he's not gay.' She's exasperating sometimes.

'Why did you say "partner" then?' I can hear more nail filing.

For goodness' sake. I need some older friends. 'Because I don't know if the woman is his girlfriend or wife.'

'Well, find out!'

'What does it matter?'

'Because if he's as old as you and he's not married to her, then it can't be serious.' Her tone is nonchalant, and I think she thinks she's being wise. Her youthful insight, while way off the mark, is endearing nonetheless.

'Well anyway, I didn't come here for a holiday romance. I'm not interested in men in England and I'm not interested in them in France.' I know the words are true as they spill out of my mouth, but they don't feel right. I'm twitchy and niggled and I know it's to do with Olivier, but I can't honestly say why. So what if I find him attractive? Plenty of men are attractive.

'Are you a lesbian?' she asks, breaking my thoughts.

'Not since you last asked me.'

'I don't get you.'

'There's nothing to get. I'm content, and the whole idea of meeting someone and falling in love makes me feel quite queasy.' She giggles down the phone but I'm not joking; the thought of giving my heart to someone and feeling so vulnerable and exposed is nauseating. Almost allowing myself to believe Olivier was one of the good guys and convincing myself we had a connection was enough. He lied to me and I can only assume he felt sorry for me. At least if I only count on myself, I will never be let down.

'You're so odd, Cath!' I practically hear her headshake. 'Well, I have a date next Saturday. I'm hoping this manicure lasts one more week otherwise I'll have to get another.' She draws out the word another, and I'm glad to be on a new subject or subheading at least.

After the phone call, I'm able to refocus myself properly. I'm here in France for three reasons:

One – to fulfil my great-grandfather's dreams on behalf of my grandma.

Two – to soak up some culture other than that of Gregg's sausage rolls, braap-ing teens and Brexit discussions.

Three – to have some me time, spoil myself and not have to constantly worry about my giganta-kids.

None of these goals include Olivier, but I'm tempted to add a fourth:

Give Olivier a piece of my mind for lying about being single. I shudder. Whatever his intentions were, they were not good.

I don't quite feel ready to complete my great-grandfather's journey. I'm too wound up and going to his final resting place is too special to have my head wrapped up in a man. It needs my full attention. Instead, I decide to visit the Wellington Tunnels after picking up a leaflet about them from the hotel and becoming intrigued as to how some medieval tunnels helped save the city of Arras during the Great War.

A large group are hovering by the entrance, so I take a seat on a grass verge outside. A message has come into the 'chitchat' group from Cynthia asking how I am. Martha has thankfully found the full stop on her 'eyepad' but those capitals are still going strong. She wants to know if Olivier is looking after me. I can't bring myself to reply so I tap out a quick 'hello, how are you both?' and fill them in on some of the places I've been to.

After five minutes or so, the crowds have dispersed, and I pay myself in and make my way down to the tunnels with my headset on. Soon, I'm engrossed in the history of how the tunnels were expanded by the tunnellers of the New Zealand division and practically turned into an underground city, when that familiar red coat catches my eye.

It's *her*. She's all shiny and polished, like a beacon, leading the large group of tourists to the balcony where I'm standing. As they pour on, I'm shunted to the side. 'Sorry,' I say, before wondering why I'm apologising.

'No, we are sorry. I have a full coach today,' Olivier's partner says, before doing a double take. 'Have I seen you before? At the hotel?'

I can't believe she recognises me. The notion makes me shrink inside myself and regret having accepted my hair as being 'rinsed' this morning when I knew that trickle of a shower hadn't got all the conditioner out. I swear I'd have had more success riding a camel around the Sahara and waiting for it to rain. My heavy, greasy strands cling to my scalp.

'Yes,' I croak. 'I've actually been on a few of your tours, with the other guide, Olivier.'

Her face breaks into a smile, a big warm one, like the kind of smile people in romcoms have when they're newly in love. Think Julia Roberts in *Notting Hill*. 'Ahh, he's probably told you all about me?' I wince. Poor girl. He's deliberately kept her quiet. I can't lie and say yes, because he hasn't, and I can't tell the truth either – that he's had the chance to tell me about her and didn't – so I just smile in what I hope is a warm and friendly way. 'He's always the favourite of us both, but since he's not here, I'm giving a guided tour in English if you want to tag along? You're a customer, after all.'

She's far too nice for him to be treating her this way, and I daren't tell her I'm not a *paying* customer in case she makes assumptions. Nor do I want to tag along, but she's so bouncy and happy that I really can't say no. 'That would be wonderful, thank you.'

'Great. I'm Elena, if you need anything, otherwise, enjoy!' Her English is impeccable. Even better than Olivier's.

She's a very enthusiastic tour guide, patient and knowledgeable, just like Olivier. I can see why they're well suited. My chest feels heavy as I think back to how interested in me he became when I spouted out a few facts about the war. He obviously has a *type*. Albeit a very odd one.

'Where are you from, love?' a plump lady with plum-coloured hair and a Northern accent asks me.

'Berrybridge,' I reply quietly, not wanting to be rude by talking over Elena.

'Are you here alone?' she asks, and I try to keep the irritation from showing when I reply.

'Yes.'

'Me too,' she whispers.

Suddenly, my frustrations dissolve into relief. 'Really?'

'Yes, I come every year, usually with my family but my sons are all grown up now and my husband was too busy with work. It's the anniversary of my great-great-grandfather's death tomorrow. He was killed in the war.'

'I'm sorry,' I whisper. 'Mine too. I'm here retracing his footsteps and to visit the memorial where my great-grandfather is commemorated. He was killed in Ypres.'

She looks me over. 'You mean great-great-grandfather?'

I shake my head. 'No, my grandmother had my mother when she was around forty. Rare in those days, I know.'

'If you're staying in Arras, we should meet up for a drink. I'm sure we'd have lots to talk about,' she whispers.

'Yes, that would be lovely,' I say, hoping I don't sound as desperate for a friend as I am.

She smiles in response, and we listen to Elena's tour.

After arranging to meet the plum-haired lady, whose name escapes me, in the bar later, I decide to head off back to my studio for a rest. As I'm leaving the museum, Elena jogs up behind me, catching me up. 'Did you like the tour?' she asks.

'Yes, very informative,' I say politely.

'I don't know if you're booked on any more with Olivier but be sure to tell him you did.' She grins. 'I love him, but he thinks he's better than me at everything.' For the first time, I notice her name badge – Elena Durand – and I remember Olivier introducing himself as Olivier Durand on the trip to Ypres. 'Anyway, it was nice to meet you ...' She pauses in anticipation of my name.

'Cath.' A flicker of what looks like recognition passes her face, but I might be imagining it.

'Cath,' she repeats, holding out her hand to shake. I spot a beautiful diamond ring on her finger. It's either platinum or white gold, I never can tell.

'Nice to meet you too.' I walk away, sombre. They are just two incredibly nice people. I bet she'd offer to give me French lessons too. I replay all the times I've been with Olivier and how I misread the signals so badly and almost laugh. I'm a rusty old fool is what I am.

Except I didn't misread the fact he *said* he was single. Or did he? Thinking back to our chat on the beach, he actually just brushed over the question by talking about the past. Very clever. I start putting all the pieces together. Olivier and Elena do separate tours and both work erratic hours. It's perfectly feasible that Olivier could seduce unsuspecting tourists and she'd never find out. It's probably a twisted little game he plays, preying on lonely single women, making them feel special just so he can put a notch on his bedpost. God only knows what he could be up to in London right now. Bubbles of rage rise in my chest, and I turn back to the museum before spinning back again. I should tell Elena, but not now, not here. I will wait until Olivier comes back and confront him first.

Before I head down to the hotel bar, I pull out my phone. There's a message from Martha asking how things are and repeating Cynthia's question about Olivier so I tap out a quick response telling her what I've been up to and asking about her leg. Before I hit send, I add: 'Olivier is married!'

When I arrive at the hotel bar, Kevin is handing my new plum-haired pal a G&T. 'Oh, hi.' She scrunches her shoulders up and smiles as she spots me walking over and pats the seat next to her. I stifle my amusement when I think about how I've obviously been doing 'making friends' all wrong when purple hair seems to have it down to a T.

'Hello,' I say, settling into the chair. 'Sorry, I didn't catch your name earlier.'

'It's Jackie. Now tell the man what you're drinking.' She bangs a hand on the bar.

'Large white wine, Cath?' Kevin asks before I open my mouth.

'You know me too well.' I smile at him.

Jackie is already giving me the lowdown on her entire life, and by the time Kevin plonks my wine in front of me, I reckon I could probably get at least a level seven in the 'Jackie GCSE'. Still, she's very nice, and it's good to have some company. I learn that her great-great-grandfather is buried in the cemetery in Arras and she's heading there tomorrow for the anniversary of his death.

'I'm sorry, my husband tells me I talk too much but I can't help it. Tell me more about you. Do you have family?' She takes the front of her hair and tucks it behind her ears.

'I have a grown-up son too. He's just gone away to university in Leicester.' She's looking at me with a slight raise to her eyebrows and a narrow smile. She's waiting for more. 'And my brother Gary is living with me at the moment.' I know the burning question is coming, so I supply the answer. 'I'm not married or with anyone.'

'Gosh, a pretty woman like you, single.' She lets out a dramatic breath.

I look down at my wine and slosh it about in the glass to avoid having to say anything.

'Have you met the other tour guide? The man?' she says suddenly, eyes twinkling.

'Yes.' I sip my wine.

'He's a dreamboat, he is.' She cackles to herself and sips her drink.

'He certainly catches a few eyes,' I say dryly.

'He's spoken for, though,' she says with a sigh. 'That lovely woman, Elena, was gushing about how she and her new husband work together – could you imagine working with your husband? I'm sure the enthusiasm will wear off and she'll reach the "can't wait to go away without you" phase of love soon enough.' She winks and I force a smile in response. I'm pretty sure Olivier has already reached that point.

'Well, good luck to them.' I sip more wine, allowing the heat of it to fill my body.

'They both did a tour introduction thing the other day and they did seem pretty cosy together. Lots of banter and that kind of thing. Both lovely, though.'

Jackie keeps ordering drinks and while I become chattier and more carefree, her demeanour doesn't alter in the slightest. By the time Kevin announces that the bar is closing, the world is slightly filtered and looks a bit like one of Kaitlynn's Instagram pictures, all hazy and in soft focus. I wobble when I try to stand up straight.

'Will you be all right getting home?' Kevin asks.

'Of course.' As I speak, the hand I'm resting my body weight on slips off the stool I was using to steady myself. It happens in seconds, sending me crashing to the floor, causing a vague pain in the side of my bottom.

'Oops. At least there's plenty of padding there,' I struggle to say.

'I'm walking you home,' Kevin says sternly.

'Ooh, I like a man who takes charge,' Jackie says. 'I'll see you in the morning, Cath.' She winks before glaring at Kevin. 'And you make sure she gets home safely.' I know I should feel embarrassed, but my inhibitions have been neutralised.

Kevin links his arm through mine to steady me, and I allow his sturdy frame to carry most of my weight. The heat from his body feels nice. The pavement sways like I'm on a ship, and I can only just get my feet to land one in front of the other. It makes me giggle and I look up at Kevin expecting to see him giggling too but his jaw is hard set and his eyes are intent on the road ahead. He looks like a man on a mission, and that makes me giggle more because he reminds me of an action hero.

Inside I'm giddy. *I like wine.* It's been a long time since a knight in shining armour has escorted me home and Kevin is a fine knight. His tight black T-shirt grips his tanned biceps like any red-blooded woman would, given half the chance. *He's barely older than Kieran*, I have to keep reminding myself.

I'm about to step down a ridiculously high kerbstone when all of a sudden, Kevin yanks me tight to his chest and I fall into him as a flash of red whizzes past.

His eyes are just inches from mine. 'For a moment there I thought you were making a move.' I chuckle nervously, but a little niggle in the back of my head tells me I'll regret saying that in the morning. It was just a little joke, I reason.

'Cath, you could have been killed by that bus just then.' He shakes his head and I'm sensing a lack of amusement.

'You're very serious, Mister.' I squish his cheeks.

'You're very drunk. I should have been a more responsible bartender.'

'Jackie wasn't even drunk. Do you think she Rohypnol-ed me?' I widen my eyes humorously.

'No, I just think you, being half of her size, should have drunk half the alcohol,' he says dryly.

***

Grogginess consumes me when I wake up the following morning, and sunlight streams through my window because I neglected to close the blinds before I went to bed. For a moment, I lie silently, staring at the ceiling, but memories of last night start pelting me like hailstones and I groan, pulling the duvet over my head. I hate being so drunk and losing control. I'll have to apologise to Kevin and probably Jackie.

'Shoot.' I sit up and snatch my phone off the bedside table to check the time, relaxing when I realise I haven't slept in. I can just about remember arranging to go to the cemetery with Jackie this morning. The sudden movement makes the room spin and my stomach lurches. I dart into the bathroom, thankful for its proximity to the bed, and retch into the toilet, heaving up nothing but bile. Champion limbo dancers haven't even seen such lows.

Jackie is sipping orange juice in the bar when I arrive. After a can of full-fat Coke and a shower, I'm feeling more like a human. Jackie, on the other hand, looks like she's had twelve hours' sleep and a facial.

'Well, good morning,' she chirps, lifting her large sunglasses to get a better look.

I wave my hand in the direction of the sunglasses. 'Put them back on – you don't want to see this,' I say, with considerably less enthusiasm.

'I take it the head isn't great this morning?' Her body shakes as she giggles.

The head? I wish it was just the head. 'I'm not much of a drinker,' I say.

'You don't say.' She slides a glass of orange juice towards me and it's gone in three gulps.

I hear footsteps behind me, and whoever it is catches Jackie's attention.

'Kevin!' she screeches, while my internal organs plummet. 'Make this woman a strong coffee will you, love?'

I turn around, forcing myself to look him in the eye. 'Kevin, I …'

He places a hand on my shoulder. 'There's no need to apologise. I shouldn't have served you so much alcohol.'

'It wasn't your fault. It happened so quickly – I was merry and fine and then I wasn't. I'm sorry.' The movement of the revolving door catches my eye and my heart rate picks up when I see Olivier walk in. Instinctively, I want to dash over to him and confront him about lying to me and tell him what he's doing is wrong, but I don't have the stomach for it just yet. Maybe after I've eaten. His eyes catch mine but his usual bright smile doesn't appear. Instead, he gives the slightest nod of acknowledgement and goes straight to chat to the man on reception.

There's a release of pressure as Kevin removes his hand from my shoulder and walks to the bar, but I barely notice. My mind is on Olivier and his sudden change in demeanour. What has *he* got to be cross with *me* about? I rerun our last conversation in my head. He offered to help me move and I'd declined, then he said he'd catch me when he returned from London, which is now. Maybe it's because he didn't get what he wanted from me when we got back from the beach. I didn't invite him in, not that he asked, but perhaps he thought I would. Whatever it is, he didn't win the little game he was playing so now I'm just an annoying tourist he can't wait to see the back of. He's probably already onto his next victim. Or perhaps Elena has mentioned that she's met me. Maybe I've taken his game too close to home.

'Are you ready?' Jackie has gathered her faculties and is getting to her feet.

'Yes, let's go,' I say enthusiastically. For once, I can't wait to get out of the hotel.

'I just want to buy a poppy.' She points to the British Legion charity box on the bar and I twitch because it means walking over to pay at reception. If I stay here, I'll look like I'm avoiding Olivier, which I am, but I want to look casual so I follow her.

'Did you have a good trip to London?' I ask Olivier, who is leaning on the reception desk.

He lets out a long breath and rubs his chin. 'It was okay. There is always a lot to cram into two days but the tourists enjoyed it.' His tone is flat and he barely makes eye contact with me.

My stomach feels twisty and I don't know why. I want to know what I've done to upset him. I can't exactly give him a piece of my mind if he won't even look at me. 'Have I—'

'Let's make tracks.' Jackie interrupts me and it's probably for the best. I need to forget about this man and rid myself of all the unusual stirrings he seems to conjure up inside me, both pleasant and otherwise.

'Yes, of course,' I reply, before turning to Olivier. 'I'm glad you had a good trip.' He gives another slight nod as I walk off.

As unusual a place as it is to go to forget a man, the cemetery seems to be working wonders. Jackie – with her endless supply of conversation – gives me the chance to drift in and out of thought. She's actually got a fascinating story about her great-great-grandfather, and that part does catch my attention, especially since I don't have too much information on my own great-grandfather. She has newspaper cuttings about his death and he was some heroic sergeant who died in Arras, shielding two men from sniper fire. Those two men went on to survive the war, and one even wrote a book, which he dedicated to the man who'd saved his life. Jackie says she'll write the name down for me so I can buy a copy.

We find the pristine, white stone bearing his name and she places the poppy on the flourishing flower bed before it, and then she closes her eyes in silent prayer. I look away to allow her some privacy and watch a bird, hopping from headstone to headstone.

'Right. I always have a drink after doing this. Are you with me?' She pops her face around me to get my attention.

'Sounds good, but it will be non-alcoholic for me. I'm still ashamed after getting so drunk last night.' And after all the warnings I'd given Kieran about binge-drinking too.

'Oh, you only live once,' she says. I don't know what my liver has done to her, but she certainly wants to punish it.

'Exactly! And I don't want to spend the rest of it feeling rotten,' I say laughing.

We head to a bar with a pretty outdoor terrace near the hotel, and by the time we've sat down, Jackie has convinced me to join her in having *one* glass of wine. It's unlike me but I feel a little bit odd, like I just want to throw caution to the wind and I can't put my finger on why. There's a cheese grater working overtime on my insides, and I just don't really care about what people think or who I'm supposed to be right now.

Without thinking, I order a bottle of *Louis Jadot, Macon Village Chapelle aux Loups*, in French without hesitation. It just rolls off my tongue, but the feeling of smugness I'd expect for sounding natural and un-panicky doesn't come.

'Well that's impressive, you dark horse.' Jackie gives a little squeeze of her shoulders like a grandmother might when their precious grandchild says thank you for the twenty pence she's just given them. I've noticed she does that a lot.

Once the cosy wine fuzz embraces me, confiding in Jackie seems like a good idea. I don't know her that well, but if I call Kaitlynn, who I *do* know well, with an update on my Olivier encounter, I can predict her advice will cover all bases from: 'screw him and find a new man' to 'get on Tinder'. A second opinion is probably quite wise.

I stroke the stem of my wine glass and can't make eye contact. 'You know that tour guide, Olivier?'

Jackie chuckles. 'My eyes turn into emoji hearts whenever I see him. Of course I know who he is.'

'He's been teaching me French. That's how I could order the wine.'

'Oh, he's so lovely like that, you know. One of those *do anything for anyone* types. Great with the old folks.' She takes a sip of her wine and I study her face. I'm looking for a sign that she thinks there must be something in it, but I see nothing. 'There was a lady on our tour who was really interested in the local agriculture for some unknown reason and he sat with her for an hour on the coach going through the different tractors or whatever it is those types talk about. In fact, I think he was leaving her some books at the reception this morning.'

His moves are strange, but they work – I'll give him that much.

My insides feel like they're being sucked down a vacuum. Jackie excuses herself to go to the bathroom and I guzzle half of my next glass of wine, and then I laugh because everything makes so much sense.

Maybe Olivier is just a nice guy.

Olivier is also *paid* to be a nice guy.

Olivier has a beautiful new wife.

Maybe he wasn't pretending to be single; maybe he just didn't mention his wife because it's none of my business. It's not like anything happened between us and it could have. I'd misinterpreted his kindness for attraction, for the simple reason that I'm not used to men being kind to me or interested in me. I'd *wanted* it to mean more. Maybe he isn't a cheating so-and-so after all. Elena must have been working and he clearly only invited me to Étaples and the beach because he felt sorry for me. When I think about it, he hasn't flirted or made a move. He's done nothing but be a *nice guy*.

God, I'm a foolish bint. I laugh again.

'What's so funny?' Jackie asks, sitting back down.

'Ahh, I'm just happy. In fact, I think we should get some food, stay out late, and have some fun.'

'Well, I'm game,' she says, clinking her glass against mine.

Chapter Twenty-One

I am not a drinker. I feel worse than I did yesterday morning and I regret each and every drink I had yesterday, even the first. The room is spinning and I sit up to try and steady myself but the movement makes it worse. I know if I stand up, I'll vomit. I check my phone and there's a reply from Martha:

MARRIED

I CANT BELIEVE THAT

MY SATELLITE MUST BE WONKY OR SOMETHING BECAUSE I DID NOT PICK THAT UP

Oh no. I can't deal with this right now.

I fall back to sleep.

When I awake the next time, I feel a little bit more human, but I'm famished. Another message has come in on my phone, from Cynthia this time.

I wouldn't have guessed it either.

I glance outside and it's pretty grey, so I throw on some blue jeans, a white T-shirt and grab my grey hoodie. The few cafés nearby still have their chairs upturned on the tables and I've no idea if they serve breakfast, so I decide to head to the hotel and eat there.

It's fairly quiet, which I'm thankful for as it means I shouldn't have to talk to anyone. I press the lift button because the stairs would probably defeat me in my fragile state, and as the doors slide open, a pair of sharp lightning-blue eyes strike me.

I swallow hard. 'Olivier?' All the words I'd wanted to say escape me.

'Good morning, Cath,' he says flatly. The fact he is mad with me when I'm mad with him throws me, and I find myself asking how London was. Again.

'Grey, drizzly and busy.' His tone is definitely clipped and he turns to walk away, but I don't want him to go. The change in him has got underneath my skin. I've caused the change somehow, and I need to know why. I need to confront him about lying too. Perhaps then we can put all this behind us and be friends again, especially now any silly ideas I may have had about a little holiday kiss have been firmly imprisoned somewhere in the back of my head.

Instinctively I put my arm out to stop him, but I haven't thought of the words to accompany the action and just blurt out the first thing that pops into my head. 'It's nice to see you back.'

His jaw tenses and relaxes again in a flash. 'Yes, there's no place like home.' With that, he nods curtly and walks towards reception.

'I know you haven't been honest with me!' I shout after him and he turns, setting his eyes on mine. There's a hollowness to them and his mouth turns down ever so slightly. If I didn't know better, I'd misinterpret his guilt for sadness. He shakes his head and walks off, leaving me too gobsmacked to go after him.

I grab a coffee and a croissant and sit in the back corner where, hopefully, I'll be left to my own devices. What was the head shaking about? Did he just not care about lying? And what was that comment *there's no place like home* about? What does that mean? Was it a hint? Does he want me to go home? Maybe he was just homesick? Or has he been watching *The Wizard of Oz* on the coach?

I'm angry with myself for not confronting him. I should have asked why he lied to me, and the fact I didn't is going to keep bugging me. So is the fact he's annoyed with me. What right does he have? What reason? I think that's bugging me the most, so I have to figure this out. When he left he was fine; when he came back, he wasn't. The only thing that happened between those two points in time was my conversation with Elena.

I tap my fingers on the table while I rack my brain trying to remember everything I'd said to her. I'd mentioned Olivier but had I mentioned the free trips? That could be a reason for him to be mad but I didn't think so. Perhaps I'd told her about the French lessons? I don't think I did but I couldn't rule it out. I rest my head in my hands.

'Cath?' I recognise the caramel tone before I even look.

'Elena, how nice to see you,' I say, plastering on a huge smile.

'Can I join you?' It's the last thing I need, but I can't say no, so I gesture to the adjacent chair. I suppose now is as good a time as any to set the record straight.

'Olivier is upstairs if you want him,' I say in a fine demonstration of how un-bothered I am about the two of them being together. I suspect the only beneficiary is myself.

She waves her hand. 'I see enough of him.'

I take a deep breath. 'Elena, I hope I didn't cause any problems between you and Olivier the other day?'

She frowns as she tips a sachet of brown sugar into her coffee. 'In what way?'

'I don't know, I just think I may have upset Olivier. He's been a bit off with me since he got back and I wondered if it was something I'd said to you?'

She shrugs it off. 'He can be a drama queen – I wouldn't worry.'

'But did I get him into trouble or anything … with you I mean?'

Her eyes lift to meet mine. 'Olivier does not answer to me.'

'I know … I mean … of course not.' God, why can't I get anything right? 'There hasn't been—' Her phone rings and the rest of my words come out as air.

'My husband,' she says apologetically.

I sit on pins as she chats away happily. From her tone, there's no animosity between him and her, so why is he angry with me if she isn't mad with him?

'Sorry about that,' she says, stuffing her phone into her pocket. 'What were you about to say?'

'Oh, it's nothing. Olivier seemed a little out of sorts since he returned from the UK, but I'm guessing he just missed you?'

She throws her head back with laughter. '*Moi?* Not a chance. I'm the slave driver in this business and he'll have been glad to escape my bossy demands. Honestly, the men in this business can be quite useless.'

I smile. 'So, are you one of the bosses?' I ask, genuinely interested.

'Yes, three of us own the company: myself, Olivier and my husband, Julien.'

Wait? What? My heart spasms. 'Olivier isn't your husband?' *And he owns the company!*

She laughs heartily. 'What? Ew. No! He's my *brother*.'

Like the iron bolts on *The Crystal Maze*, everything starts clicking into place.

'But if you're married, why do you have the same name?'

'I never changed it. All my business contacts know me as Durand.'

'If you aren't cross with him for giving me free trips and private French lessons—'

'He gave you *free* trips?' She gasps.

I gulp.

Then she winks. 'He's such a Casanova when he wants to be, which is never.'

I let out a sigh of relief. 'So if I haven't jeopardised your relationship, why is Olivier mad with me?'

She shrugs. 'You'll have to ask him that.'

Chapter Twenty-Two

Nobody at reception seems to have any idea about today's trip – where it was to, when they'll be back – and Elena had left before I thought to ask. I wanted to wait for Olivier, so I'd got myself comfortable in the bar area a few hours ago and I've been here ever since but he could have gone on a quick trip to the cemetery in Arras or back to London for two days for all I know.

At midday, Kevin arrives for his shift. 'I hear you were out partying again last night?' he says as he slings his backpack behind the bar.

'I wouldn't call it partying *exactly* but we had fun.' By about eight-thirty, we'd discovered that sleepy little Arras wasn't quite the place for partying. 'I was in bed for ten … We call it an all-dayer back home.'

He shakes his head. 'Why are you here and not out seeing the sights?'

I sigh. 'I'm waiting for Olivier to get back from wherever he's gone today. He seems off. I think I've upset him.'

'You know, I saw him last night and thought the same, so perhaps something has happened in his personal life. Anyway, the trip today is just a coach drop-off in Paris. He doesn't usually go but maybe Julien was busy. He normally comes back here afterwards to meet guests and sign people up for excursions.'

A short while later, the bus pulls up. Sure enough, the doors open and Olivier hops down the steps and walks in.

My heart starts to thump in my ribcage and any vague plan of action becomes a distant memory. He's looking straight ahead and doesn't see me so I jump up. 'Olivier?'

When he turns around to face me his shoulders slump a little with recognition, zapping my confidence. 'Can we talk?' I ask.

He checks his watch and sighs. 'If you wish.' His eyes flick to Kevin at the bar. 'Shall we get some fresh air?' He doesn't wait for me to reply; instead, he turns back towards the door.

I follow him out through the revolving door he freed me from on my first day here and he heads for the train station, where he sits on a bench just outside. 'Okay, what would you like to talk about?'

I decide to be upfront. 'You're mad with me.'

His lips part to speak but instead, he lets out a breath.

'Just tell me what I've done to upset you. We were getting on so well and I thought we were ...' I decide not to say what I really thought we were because it seems so imaginary, so ridiculous now. 'Well, friends.'

'We *are* friends. Nothing has changed.' He folds his arms.

'Why are you being so ... different?'

'I'm not.' His words come out like a bark. Or maybe a bite, since they catch me so sharply.

'Okay.' I decide to play along with his charade. 'Well, can I take you to lunch one day this week in exchange for another French lesson?'

For the first time since we sat down, he turns to look at me, and I notice his eyes look heavy and moist. 'Cath, I don't think it's a good idea. Perhaps Kevin can give you lessons. Anyway, I got you these from England.' He pulls out two large Galaxy chocolate bars and thrusts them into my hand.

'Wait. What? Why Kevin?' I say, ignoring my chocolatey commiseration prize, though I am touched he remembered I missed them.

'I saw you both. Embracing in the darkness of the streets when I was on the coach coming back to the hotel from London.'

Cogs whiz and spin in my head but I can't remember *embracing* Kevin. I think I'd remember a clinch since the last time I'd *embraced* anyone was probably about the same time I got pregnant with Kieran. An *embrace* would stand out. I would remember.

'I don't know what you're talking about.'

'You looked as though you were about to cross the road just there and then Kevin took you in his arms.' He points to one of the roads coming off the square roundabout and snippets of memory start coming back to me. 'You know, it doesn't matter. You're free to do whatever you like.'

'That? That wasn't an *embrace* – that was a drunken idiot being helped home by a guilt-ridden bartender.'

His forehead crevices. 'So nothing happened between you and Kevin?'

'No! I'd stumbled, and he caught me. He's lovely and all, but he's barely any older than my son.'

He sinks back into the bench and looks across towards the hotel. 'Oh.'

'I blame Jackie.'

He looks puzzled.

'You'll know her when you see her. Anyway, long story short, she can drink and I can't, but that little fact didn't stop me from trying to keep up.'

The conversation doesn't put me at ease like I thought it would. I'd hoped that once the air was cleared, things would go back to normal, but something else is hanging in the air, bugging me.

'How come thinking I was cuddling Kevin changed your attitude towards me?' My voice comes out as barely a whisper, and at first, I can't be sure if I've even spoken at all.

He glances at me before dropping his head in his hands. It's now or never; if there *is* something between us, then this is his chance to admit it.

'Honestly? I don't know.' His whole body sags before silence envelopes us.

'Oh,' I say. 'I should go.' I need to get away. This whole situation is everything I don't want. The mixed signals, the confusion, the uncertainty. At least back home I know who I am, what I mean to people, and while to some I may not mean much, I know who I can give my best self to. Here, I don't know anything, and it scares me.

'I'll see you around,' I say. I start walking back towards the hotel, and the words sit uncomfortably in my ears.

'Cath. Wait.' I hear footsteps running towards me. I turn to see Olivier standing there, shoulders sagging as he catches his breath, features crumpled. 'Can I take you out to lunch tomorrow?'

'Lunch?' I say, once again confused. 'Another French lesson?'

He shakes his head and something like hope fills my chest. 'To apologise for being such a grump.'

My heart sinks. 'Okay,' I say, the rest of my vocabulary blocked by something.

A wide smile breaks across his face and his body relaxes. 'Good. Great. I'll pick you up around ten.'

Okay.' I force a smile.

He turns to leave and then spins back, almost colliding with me. 'Would it be okay if we called it a date?' *A date?* My heart flips and I try to smile but my mouth twitches nervously and I don't think it quite happens.

All I can manage is a nod.

'Great. I'll see you tomorrow.' He smiles. 'I should go and apologise to Kevin. I've been a bit rude to him. Perhaps tomorrow at lunch we can work on some French vocabulary. The word for *idiot* perhaps? Spoiler alert: it's *idiot*.' I smile, glad to see him back to his usual, cheerier self.

'I'll see you tomorrow,' I say, managing to keep my cool as my insides do a Cirque du Soleil practice.

Once he's gone, I deflate until I'm just a blob of skin and innards that's subsided on the bench. I can feel the onset of another argument with my subconscious. *You got as much as you could have hoped for*, she says. I assume my subconscious is a she because she's me. I haven't really thought about it before. '*What if I got too much?*' I argue back.

I spot a familiar plume of purple hair emerging from the hotel. If anyone's going to take my maudlin mind away from my Olivier musing, it's her. 'Jackie!' I yell across the square. She peers over her large sunglasses and waves when she spots me.

She's a bright vision in her geometric print dress, skipping across the grey square, and I wish I had my own sunglasses on just so I could look at her without risking my eyesight. 'Good morning, Cath love. How are you feeling?' she asks, plonking herself down on the bench beside me.

'I'm not going to lie, I've felt better.'

'I don't think Arras was ready for us.' She chuckles. 'What are you up to today? I can't remember whether we made plans or not?'

I laugh. 'I can't remember either. I'm not quite sure. My priority was getting some breakfast and I've managed that. I suppose I'm at a bit of a loose end.'

'Me too. I was just going to browse the shops. I was thinking of going to Lille but I really can't be bothered. There are some nice little shops in Arras if you fancy joining me?'

I check my watch. 'Yes, that sounds perfect.'

Jackie doesn't have the same sense of urgency while shopping as the American women, so we meander at a steady pace, looking in all the clothes shops. I even treat myself to a new top. It's all floaty chiffon and flowers and makes me feel like I can pull off boho chic. *I think I'll wear it to lunch tomorrow.*

'So, who are you meeting tomorrow?' Jackie asks as she squeezes her feet into some soft leather sandals. I'd happened to mention I was going for lunch when I was browsing for a top.

'Er ... well ...' My stumbling causes her to look up. If I say his name I'm going to have to tell her the whole story. So I do.

Her eyes widen when I say 'Olivier', and the anticipated questions come rolling in, so I fill her in completely.

'Blimey,' she says after. The shop assistant is looking at us impatiently as Jackie has been sitting wearing the sandals for so long he probably thinks she's itching to do a runner. She hasn't even looked in the mirror yet.

'Sorry,' Jackie says to the assistant eventually. 'I'll take them.' She removes the shoes and hands them over to a visibly relieved assistant. 'It all sounds so romantic, especially him taking you to Mametz Wood and swimming in the sea at Le Touquet.'

'Well, that's the part I'm having trouble with. We've built up a good friendship up to now, and I was going to ask him if he wanted to keep in touch when I left and then he asks me on a date, which I found myself getting excited about, but I'll be going home soon and a holiday romance will just get messy and complicated and a friendship is much more manageable.'

'Breathe,' Jackie says, but it barely registers. If only I hadn't got drunk that night, Kevin wouldn't have caught me, Olivier wouldn't have gone all weird and we could have both carried on as we were.

She regards me with pursed lips and folded arms.

'You need to pay.' I nod towards the counter.

Chapter Twenty-Three

My floaty new top goes beautifully with my blue jeans and tan sandals. I feel like I've made an unobvious effort, which is a balance I never quite manage to achieve at home. The bit of colour I've got from the sun sets the top off well and my hair has a shine to it that I haven't noticed before. I feel more comfortable in my own skin than I have in a long time.

The unfamiliar sound of the buzzer makes me jump as I'm doing my mascara; it smudges, and I realise it's the first time I've heard it since living in the studio. It makes me wonder how often I'll hear the doorbell when I'm home, now Kieran's friends will no longer be calling for him. I wipe underneath my eye, grab my bag and keys, and head downstairs to meet Olivier.

When I open the door, I gasp. He isn't wearing his usual red T-shirt, as I've come to expect, but a crisp white shirt that clings to his arms in all the right places, and some cornflower blue chinos and tan loafers. The difference the outfit makes is quite staggering and I'm so glad I've worn my new top.

'*Bonjour, madame,*' he says.

Nerves wash over me, inhibiting my facial muscles. '*Bonjour,*' I manage.

'Shall we?' He holds an elbow out for me and I take it. We walk the short distance to his car and he unhooks his arm and holds the car door open for me. I look at him with a frown.

'Where are we going?' I ask, assuming we'd be walking to somewhere local.

'I thought we'd try somewhere a little bit different.'

He's grinning, so I don't ask where because I sense he's enjoying the mystery. Instead, I take in the beautiful rolling hills and farmland as we zip along the country roads. I don't know how much time passes, but I start to see signs for Reims and the intrigue becomes too much.

'Okay, I have to ask – where are we going?'

'We're going to a vineyard.' He glances at me momentarily, before fixing his eyes back on the road.

'A vineyard?'

'Yes, the Calais region is not renowned for its wine, so we're heading towards the Champagne region.'

I think back to my fifteen-pound glass of champers on the ferry and get little twinges of excitement as I snuggle down into the car seat. I really am living the life of luxury. I feel my phone vibrate and a text comes in from Kaitlynn.

How are things? Are you still alive? K x

I smile; I'm sure it's only been a day or two since I last texted her.

All is good. I've been shopping and to the beach. It really is beautiful here and the weather has been fantastic. Heading to the champagne region today. Living the high life, I am! I don't know how I'll ever return to my normal existence again ;) x

She replies straight away.

Who with? x

I tuck my phone away because I feel foolish talking about Olivier behind his back while he's sitting right next to me, even though he doesn't seem to be paying attention.

We turn up a long, golden-pebbled driveway and head towards

a beautiful white chateau at the top of the hill. Fields of grapevines stretch as far as the eyes can see on either side of us.

'This place is stunning,' I say.

'It belongs to an old friend of mine. It's a small family business – they don't mass-produce their champagne so you probably won't have seen it in the UK, but what they do make is exceptional.'

His friend? That comment makes me realise how little I actually know about Olivier. 'What an amazing place to live and work. I've never seen anything like it.' My voice is all breathy with excitement and awe.

'You ain't seen nothing yet.' He winks.

He parks up and we walk across the crunchy gravel to the house. Before we reach the door, it swings open and a lady dressed in a black and white housekeeping uniform beckons us in with a smile. She speaks in French, but I'm impressed with myself when I'm able to pick up on a few words.

'Michael is in the private garden,' I say quietly to Olivier, ninety per cent certain that's what the woman said.

'*Très bien.*' He smiles at me.

'So, how do you and Michael know one another?' I ask Olivier as we follow the housekeeper down the hallway and past a sign that says '*privé*'.

'He and I went to school together. We remained friends, but with our work, we don't get to see one another as often as we we'd like.'

'Olivier!' A tall, slim man with thinning black hair stands to greet us as we step outside some French doors (or are they just *doors* here?).

'Michael, it has been too long,' Olivier says in English, before grabbing Michael and pulling him in for a hug.

'It's so good to see you.' Michael's face is bright and happy as he regards his old friend. 'And you must introduce us.' He looks at me, stooping to shake my hand.

'Michael, this is Cath, from England. I had to make friends with her when she expressed an interest in the Great War.' His eyes dance with humour and I laugh nervously.

'Ahh yes, you history types are a rare breed.' Michael's English is impeccable, but I suppose he has plenty of English guests here. 'Let me get you both a drink.' He doesn't ask us what we'd like; instead, he pops into the house and returns a moment later empty-handed.

'Please, take a seat.' He gestures to the cast-iron patio set and Olivier pulls out a chair for me before sitting between me and Michael. The private garden is very pretty, with a small manicured lawn area and plenty of flowers and shrubs growing around the borders. A wooden love seat sits proudly at the top end and the patio furniture is positioned closer to the house. The sun falls directly on the patch of grass, but a gentle breeze blows in from the vineyards beyond.

The housekeeper comes out not long after we're seated. She's carrying a tray of champagne flutes and a metal ice bucket containing a bottle of champagne, with condensation running down its sides. It's one of those free-standing ice buckets that you see in fancy restaurants, the kind on a tall stand that sits beside the table.

'Madame,' she says, placing the glass down in front of me.

'Is this champagne that you've produced here?' I ask Michael, once the bubbles have been poured.

'Of course! You don't think I drink that mass-produced rubbish, do you?' He winks then smiles, making me laugh a little. He has an air of boyish mischief about him and I already like him.

I take a sip of the rich, creamy bubbles, which fizz gently on my tongue. 'This is very good,' I say, setting my flute down gently.

'Thank you. My family have been perfecting our methods for generations,' Michael replies.

Olivier raises his glass in his hand to point at Michael. 'Michael has been working at the vineyard since he was in kindergarten, back when his grandparents used to run it. That's when we first met. I liked to play with toy trains and Michael liked to collect grapes.' He laughs easily. 'When we were a little bit older, I'd come over for the weekend sometimes and we'd earn pocket money grape-picking.'

'But mostly it would end in a grape-fight,' Michael adds wistfully.

Olivier laughs. 'Yes, until your grandmother caught us and then she'd shout at us and dock our pay. In fact, didn't we have to pay her once because we'd wasted so many?' They both burst out laughing.

I smile, enjoying the little snippet of Olivier's history, picturing the two of them.

'Damn right we did. I'd do much worse nowadays. These grapes are more precious than my own children.' We all tinkle with gentle laughter.

The housekeeper comes back and puts a dish of green olives out before returning inside the house.

'Now *these* you have to try.' Michael holds the bowl out towards me and Olivier, and we both jab a cocktail stick in and take one dutifully.

'Mmm. These are delicious,' I say after cramming one into my mouth. I'd only ever tried the ones from work before, and to be honest they didn't do much for me, all tough and salty. These, on the other hand, are to die for – they just melt in your mouth, bursting with flavour.

'My wife is always after the perfect accompaniment for our champagne. This is her number one nibble,' Michael says, jabbing a cocktail stick into one for himself.

'Is your wife here today?' I ask. I'd love to meet her. I find the whole idea of a family producing champagne fascinating. It isn't the kind of career path our school advisers would ever have put us on back home.

197

'Yes, you'll meet her later on. She's gone to the market.'

When we finish our wine, Michael takes us to the front of the house, where a golf buggy awaits. 'It's time to see the vineyard,' he says, jumping into the driver's seat. I sit in the back, leaving Olivier to choose who to sit next to. He slides in next to me. We drive down the bumpy path while Michael explains about the vineyard, how it's expanded over the years, what the different types of grapes are used for and how they absorb different flavours from the earth, depending upon what is growing nearby. Olivier doesn't say much, but I'm guessing he's seen and heard it all before, or, like me, he just enjoys listening. It is such a wonderful place to bring me to. It's not somewhere I'd have ever thought to visit if it wasn't for Olivier, but all my senses are suddenly alive with the peaceful sound of the birds, the bright leafy-green vines following the curve of the land and stretching into the distance, and the sight of the juicy, almost ripe fruit hanging from them in their abundance.

After a while, Michael pulls the buggy to a stop. 'Lunch is served,' he says, gesturing to a red and white gingham tablecloth spread out in one of the fields. A wicker picnic basket has been set out next to it and there are plates and glasses there too.

'Oh my goodness. This is wonderful.' I clasp my hands to my mouth.

'I'm glad you approve,' Michael says.

Olivier has already jumped out and has walked around to my side to help me out. I take his warm hand and climb out but Michael doesn't move.

'Aren't you joining us?' My smile wavers – the thought of just Olivier and I together in this beautiful setting suddenly sends tremors through me. I suppose that is what a *date* entails.

'I'm afraid not. I have châteaux guests arriving at 3 p.m. and have an orientation to set up. You kids have fun.' He drives off, waving a hand in the air as he does. I leave it as long as I can get away with before turning around to face Olivier.

All I can crank out is a 'Well.' Which he echoes.

'Come and sit down.' He takes my hand and leads me over to the spread, and I sit down, crossing my legs. Olivier starts to unpack the picnic and shortly after, hands me another glass of champagne, which I'm incredibly grateful for.

'Cheers,' he says, clinking his glass against mine.

'Cheers,' I say quietly.

There are cured meats, cheeses and more olives in the hamper, plus fresh bread, and strawberry tarts for after. The rich tastes explode in my mouth and while I'm in food heaven, I can ignore the tension of being in this romantic spot with such a handsome man.

We chat through lunch, and I'm thrilled to be able to get part of the way through our conversation in French, with the odd minor correction or suggestion from Olivier. I can't believe how quickly I'm able to pick it up with him on hand.

As I'm finishing off my strawberry tart, I'm acutely aware of Olivier's eyes on me. I dust off my lips just in case any escaped crumbs are lingering there, though the thing was so delicious, I'd be disappointed in myself if I'd missed them. Once I've swallowed my last bite, I dare myself to look at him.

His eyes are there, like I'd felt they would be.

I swallow hard.

'Cath, yesterday you asked me a question and I didn't give you my full answer,' he says.

My mind goes blank. I don't remember a question – not one he didn't answer anyway.

'You asked why I cared so much when I saw you and Kevin together.'

I gulp as hope fills my chest cavity.

'The truth is, I shouldn't have really,' he says, and the hope starts to leak out. 'But, I've started to really enjoy your company and the thought of no longer being able to spend time with you disappointed me a little.' Well, that was hardly an expansion on what he'd already said; in fact, it was less hopeful. 'That's why I asked you to lunch today.' It still isn't what I'm hoping for. His eyes bore into mine, as though he's trying to say so much more, but I don't speak *eyes* or *glances* – I need words.

'Well, you don't need to worry about that. I haven't been with a man for a long time and I'm not about to start looking for one now, so I'm all yours, available for sightseeing, teaching French and taking on picturesque picnics.' I give a tight smile. Something flickers across Olivier's face – a shadow, a momentary relaxation of his muscles, which quickly reform.

'Of course. Perfect,' he says with a pinched smile. We both sip our champagne and I can tell by the thickness of the atmosphere that we both need it. The sound of birds tweeting breaks the tension a little, and I gaze up to see them soar overhead.

'Sorry, I'm not really making much sense here and I talk for a living! The truth is …' His words startle me a little and I lower my head to look at him. 'The truth is: I do like you, Cath. A lot. You're different, in a good way, and you don't take life too seriously. You're fun and always make me smile and I've enjoyed touring the battlefields with you so much. I love how you're as passionate as I am about the history here and how easy it is to just talk to you. I love how you're so easy to be around and how your face lights up when you smile. But most of all, I just like being with you, in a museum, or a vineyard or on a bench in Arras.' He takes an uncertain breath, 'So, I suppose, when I saw you with Kevin, I was perhaps a little jealous.'

My heart flips. Bright, colourful thoughts are racing through my head at one hundred miles per hour and I can't pluck one out to focus on, and instead, my head is like the murky brown you'd get in primary school when you mixed the entire tray of paints together for 'experimental' purposes. It renders me speechless.

'You don't have to say anything. I know this is one-sided and you've made your position very clear; I just wanted you to know the truth.' This is the strangest, most ridiculously crazy thing that's ever happened to me and I'm afraid if I speak, it will be an outlandish stream of gushy thanks. I lean over and kiss him on the cheek. It's a knee-jerk reaction because I can't find the words, and as soon as I pull away, I feel the heat rush to my cheeks . As I go to sit back down, he takes my face into his hands. My eyes are just inches away from his piercing blue ones. I can feel the warmth of his champagne-tinged breath on my face. He doesn't speak or look away, but somehow his eyes have conjured up fireflies that are darting about inside me. Then he leans forward.

His hot lips press against mine gently. Slowly, he pulls away an inch, pressing his forehead to mine. I run my fingers through his soft hair and he lifts my chin so our mouths meet again. This time we fall into a rhythm. A slow tempo that gradually increases. His hands are entwined in my hair and I run mine down the back of his shirt. He pulls me in closer like he can't get enough. Below the bellybutton, things stir that haven't stirred in a long time.

Eventually, the tempo slows even more and he pulls away, resting his head against mine. 'Oh, Cath,' he says breathlessly. 'I don't know what came over me. I just couldn't h—'

'Shh,' I say, pressing my finger to his lips. 'Don't say anything. It was … perfect.'

He lies back on the blanket and tugs my arm so I fall down beside him. Side-by-side, we look into to depths of the blue sky embellished with the odd fluffy white cloud that almost looks too perfect to be true. I feel his fingers find mine and entwine themselves, and we lie like that until Michael comes back to collect us.

Chapter Twenty-Four

I wake with a start. The emptiness in my stomach is probably the cause. I'd fallen asleep last night practically floating above the bed after goodness knows how long spent in an Olivier-infused daydream. We hadn't kissed again yesterday, but I can still taste Olivier's sweet champagne lips. Now, in the stark light of day, I'm horrified. *How could I have let that happen?* Saying goodbye to Olivier isn't something I've been looking forward to, but now we've kissed it feels impossible.

I replay that one kiss over and over in my head, searching for a sign that it was a mistake. Something to clutch on to and say 'ah well' about, but all I remember is the deliciousness, and the way in which we were so synchronised, as if we fit together, and the way Olivier kept glancing at me afterwards. When Michael introduced us to his wife and showed us the oak barrels he ferments his vintage champagne in, Olivier never took his eyes off me. My skin still tingles now as if he's left a part of himself on me.

Once I'm showered and dressed, I can focus more on the day. I almost cancel, because seeing Olivier is probably not a good idea, but I promised to help him out today, and I owe him that after all he's done for me. I make my way across to the hotel where I'm meeting him. He has a group of year seven school-children from the UK – thirty of them – to transport from a hostel on the outskirts of Arras to the 'P'tit Train de la Haute Somme' and has asked me to join him.

Because it is a coachload of children, Elena is coming too, which I'm apprehensive about because having his sister there adds a whole new dimension to things with Olivier. I'm glad the two of them are already sitting together when I board the coach – it means I can sink into a corner. I say hello to Elena and smile self-consciously at Olivier who jumps up and insists on sitting with me.

The children are lined up nicely outside the hostel when we pull up. Olivier, Elena and I get off the coach to help them all on board while the driver stays seated, reading the newspaper. The children are all aged between eleven and twelve and should hopefully be quite manageable. There are three schoolteachers accompanying them: two men and a woman, so between us, we should have some semblance of control.

Olivier gets on board while Elena stands by the door, high-fiving children before cautioning them to be careful when climbing the high step. The children file on board in a flurry of excitement, interspaced by the odd frazzled-looking teacher, and I begin to doubt my earlier belief about them being well behaved. I follow the last teacher on board and see the female staff member has taken the seat at the front, next to Olivier, who gives me an apologetic look, but I'm quite glad to put off any awkward conversations that may crop up. I sit behind the driver, who is still reading his paper, and Elena sits next to me just before the door closes.

'So, you and Olivier, hey?' She dives right in just as the engine starts to rumble.

My cheeks tingle. 'He told you?' *So much for avoiding awkward conversations.*

'He didn't need to. I know where he took you yesterday and I saw his beaming smile after. He really likes you,' she says.

203

I glance around, hoping her voice is quiet enough and the engine noise loud enough that the conversation *is* just between the two of us. 'We had a really nice day. The vineyard is beautiful,' I say, politely.

'It really is. I'm glad Olivier took you there.' She glances around, obviously also hoping that nobody can hear us. 'Many years ago he used to go all the time with his girlfriend.' I feel a pang of something.

'He told me about her. Didn't she go travelling?' I say, letting Elena know he's already told me about his ex.

'She did. He was a mess when she left and since then, he hasn't been up to the vineyard,' she whispers.

There's a heaviness in my chest. He hadn't really let on how much it affected him when his girlfriend left, but it's not really any of my business anyway. It's just strange that she left so long ago and he still hasn't been able to face going back to the vineyard.

Elena leans in close. 'It was all my fault too.'

'What do you mean?'

'He didn't tell you?' Her eyebrows are gathered in and I shake my head, confused.

'Olivier and I lost our parents the year he turned twenty. I was just sixteen and he became my guardian. He and his girlfriend always planned to travel the world together, but after that, he refused to go. I could have stayed with my grandparents, but he refused to leave me. His girlfriend still wanted to go because she felt it was a now-or-never decision, something she needed to do before she settled down.' She falls into a thoughtful silence whilst I sit back in shock. I had no idea how much Olivier and I had in common. Perhaps the fact he too had so much responsibility at a young age is why I'm so drawn to him.

'I'm sorry about your parents,' I say after a moment.

'It's okay, it was so long ago now, and time is a great healer. They were wonderful people, though, and that's how I remember them. The tour company was theirs originally, so naturally, Olivier and I took over after their death – well, mostly Olivier at first as I was still at school. Julien joined the business about five years ago as it grew and that's how I met him.'

'Olivier never mentioned that he owned the business.' So the free excursions really were due to his own generosity.

'Olivier is quite modest, and besides, "come and see my coach" doesn't have the same pulling power as "come and see my Lamborghini" does.' She throws her head back and laughs.

'So how come Olivier hadn't been back to the vineyard, if so much time has passed?' I have to know.

Elena twists her mouth. I knew there was more to it. 'The last time he went there was to propose to his girlfriend. He thought if he showed her how serious he was about building a life together, she'd change her mind and stay.'

'But she didn't.' My words come out in a whisper, and Elena shakes her head morosely.

'He still saw Michael, but they always met up somewhere else after that. I think you've broken his spell.' Elena grins.

I want to dispute it and say that he's probably just moved on and it's all a big coincidence, but I remember the kiss, and the way his eyes were all over me and I wonder if perhaps I have broken his spell. It's a bittersweet thought.

Laughter erupts, breaking my thoughts. It's the female teacher. I can't see her properly, but I can see that she's sitting side on, facing Olivier. She laughs again, tossing her hair back, and I imagine Olivier telling one of his terrible jokes and I smile because he'll be thrilled that someone appreciates them.

We turn into a car park outside the museum and the female teacher stands up and yells at the children to be quiet and listen (in French). Then, once the children are calm, one of the male teachers instructs them to file off calmly. Elena jumps off and runs into the museum, presumably to sort out the tickets, but I remain seated until everyone is off. One of the male teachers is shouting at the children to line up as I walk over to the museum. He only looks like he's in his mid-twenties. Once the children are lined up, he turns to me. 'Hi, I'm Mr Buchannan. Mike. I'm a history teacher.' He holds out a hand, which I shake. 'That's Mr Mitchell, another history teacher, and Ms Clarke is the French teacher.' He gestures to the other two staff members.

'I'm Cath,' I say, 'I'm just helping out.'

My eyes wander over to Ms Clarke, who hasn't left Olivier's side since they got off the coach. I can hear her chatting to him in French and convince myself she's just brushing up on her skills, but there's a lump of ice in my stomach that makes me feel quite unusual. I turn away and find myself facing the schoolchildren, who are all chattering in little groups, looking more like a chubby caterpillar than the neat line they were asked to form.

'Check Ms Clarke out with that guy,' I hear one boy say. 'She's all over him.'

I try to ignore the comments, but as we enter the museum, they start to gnaw away at me and I don't know why. Olivier is just being his typical friendly self but Ms Clarke is being, well, keen.

We each take a group of six children to explore the museum before we go on a train ride. I end up with six mini versions of Kieran, so at least I know what I'm doing. Surprisingly, they're quite interested in all the different engines that were used in the Great War, taking a particularly keen interest in a small, rusty engine that had been used to transport artillery to the front line. There were even a few 'oh my Gods' when they saw how some trains were powered by bicycle.

Every now and then, I glance over at Olivier, who is often stooping down to the height of the children and pointing something out or explaining something animatedly. They are all engrossed and I wonder how he is so good with children, not having any of his own. He's a natural, I guess.

Ms Clarke is barking orders to 'get down' at one member of

her group who has boarded one of the trains. As I turn to walk down the aisle between two train tracks, I tense as I see Olivier walking towards me. 'Hello, you,' I say quietly, with a sizeable dollop of fake confidence in my tone. The children are distracted by a small medical train, used to transport injured soldiers from the front line, and are oblivious to our lingering eye contact. We haven't spoken about our kiss yesterday, and I can feel something – *tension?* – hanging in the air.

A girl comes over and hovers nearby. 'This is a great place, isn't it?' Olivier says, noticing our company. I smile in response, but I'm desperate to talk to him. I want to make sure he knows that yesterday was wonderful, but that I don't expect anything from him. I can't. Not with me going home soon. It's a holiday romance or fling. Actually, it's neither of those things. It's a holiday friendship sealed with a kiss. God, I'm driving myself crazy. It's like Kaitlynn has crawled into my head. I'd give anything to go back to worrying about whoops deals and electricity cards.

'It's time to head to the platform,' Olivier says and I round up my group, glad of the distraction. The railway is a narrow-gauge kind, and so the trains are much smaller than regular ones. There is a choice of open or closed carriages and we opt for the latter for safety purposes. The last thing any of us wants is to have to scrape a splattered pre-teen off the inside of a tunnel. The carriages are big enough that three whole groups of seven can fit into one, which are broken into open sections of three.

I bundle my children in and take a seat on the wooden bench. Ms Clarke hovers close to Olivier, and I think she was hoping to share a carriage with him. I catch a glimpse of disappointment when he climbs in with his group and closes the door, unaware she was trying to peer in, seemingly after a seat.

He sits directly behind me and his back touches mine above the wooden seatback of the bench. The hair follicles on the back of my neck tingle with electricity.

Soon, we're on our way. My boys are fairly calm and one, in particular, reminds me more of Kieran at that age than the others. That funny age where they start to feel much older and more capable at life than they really are. Most people dread the pre-teen and teenage years, but I used to think it was cute when Kieran was that age. As the train trundles by the Somme canal, I sit back and take in the stunning views. The boys do too but there is the odd mumbling of how boring it is. I smile to myself because twelve-year-old Kieran would have said the same if his friends were by his side but would have loved it otherwise.

'Miss, how come you're in France if you're English?' a cherub-like blond boy asks.

'I live in England. I'm here for the same reason you are – to learn about the First World War,' I say.

'How come you're on our trip then?' another boy asks.

'I'm in France for a while, and my friend, Olivier—' he turns around and waves in acknowledgement '—has been taking me on some of the trips, so today I'm helping him out to say thanks.'

That seems to be it for the questions and we all return to silence. Soon after, the train goes through a narrow tunnel, taking us into the pitch black. I feel an arm come over my shoulder and a hand finds mine. Its warm familiarity sends my stomach into Cirque Du Soleil mode. As we approach the sunny daylight, his fingers slip away and our focus returns to the children, but there is a niggling question in the back of my head. *What are we doing?*

The train journey is quite long and doesn't stop anywhere. After we've seen the beautiful poppy fields, we turn around and head the same way back to the station. 'We've got to do all of that. Again?' whines one of the boys.

I nod. Even the precarious zigzag back down the hill doesn't excite them and soon they're jabbing each other in the ribs and playing a good old-fashioned game of *slapsies*.

'So where else have you been?' I ask, trying to generate some interest in the trip.

The blond boy shrugs. 'A museum. Some trenches.' He doesn't seem too interested.

'My great-grandfather was killed in the First World War.'

'Really?' He looks me over. 'You don't look *that* old. My great-grandad is still alive and the war was a hundred years ago,' he says and I laugh.

'My grandmother had my mother at an older age and my mum didn't have me until she was in her thirties.' I can see the cogs turning in his head, but I don't think he fully computes.

'So he was a war hero?' he asks eventually.

'I suppose he was,' I say.

'Cool.' He looks back out of the window.

'I have an idea,' Olivier says, shuffling sideward on his bench so he can see into both mine and his sections. 'Let's play I spy, in French.' A few children groan but decide to join in anyway, and I'm pleasantly surprised at one girl who starts the game off with unbroken fluency. Her chosen letter is 'A' and I'm stumped.

'*Arbre*,' one boy says.

'*Très bien*,' she says with a smile. I'm a bit lost but glad the fighting has stopped. I mouth 'thank you' to Olivier, who gives me a gorgeous lopsided smile.

It's a short-lived respite and soon the slapsies recommence to a greater extent. There's a wail as one boy ends up in floods of tears after another caught his eye with a fingernail. Others laugh whilst a few continue to complain of boredom. The carriage is starting to descend into chaos.

'Let me see,' I say, beckoning the injured boy to come over. I inspect his eye. It's red but he'll live. 'It's quite funny that you're injured on this track,' I say. He doesn't look amused. 'Because it was used to transport injured soldiers to safety.' The fighting escalates, and the injured boy thumps the inflicting boy whilst my head is turned. They both stand up and in the confined carriage it looks quite menacing.

I stand up and put my hands on my hips. 'Quiet, now. Every one of you.' I speak from the back of my throat in my loudest, sternest voice. Everyone across all three sections of the carriage turns to look at me. I'm quite relieved because if they didn't, it would have been embarrassing. 'That is quite enough. You are here to learn about the war, not prat around fighting. Now sit down!' All eyes are still on me. I take out one of the plastic wallets from my leather folder. I'd brought them in case anyone was interested. 'My great-grandfather was killed in the First World War and this is a letter her wrote to his family in England.' It's the one from Étaples and I read it out. Everyone remains silent. 'Do you see what men had to go through? Some of those men were only six years older than you. In fact, some lied about their age and came to fight when they were only a few years older than you are now. They fought for their country and their friends, not among themselves.' I think I've made my point now and the carriage is much quieter so I go to put the letter away.

'Miss, can I see?' Eye-gouger asks. I look up to read his face, and he looks genuinely interested.

'Okay,' I say, handing it over slowly. 'Be very careful with it.' He nods and a few others shuffle closer to his side to get a better look. Soon, the children are passing it around carefully and asking questions all about him and where I've been.

When we pull back into the station, the kids are more subdued, and the teachers take them outside to sit on the grass to enjoy a picnic. Elena, Olivier, and I grab coffees in the café and sit outside on a terrace overlooking the station.

'You were fantastic on the train; even I was scared of you. I thought we'd lost the crowd at one point,' Olivier says, stirring milk into his coffee.

'It's just kids for you. If I had a pound for every time Kieran and his mates fought, I'd still be staying in the nice hotel.' I grin.

'Well, thank you, I was starting to panic when the game of I spy didn't work. You're a *naturel*.'

'I'm just glad we didn't have a full-on re-enactment of hand-to-hand combat.' I sip my coffee. 'It's hard to imagine how such a beautiful little train ride was built for the horrors of war,' I say, sipping my coffee. It burns my mouth and I wince.

'It was also used to rebuild the area after the war, so in some ways it's a symbol of hope,' Olivier says. 'It was then used for transporting sugar beet. Which I don't think is a symbol of anything.' He grins.

'You're off duty now.' Elena nudges him.

'It's okay,' I say. 'I like listening to Olivier's war trivia.'

'Hey, if you like hearing Olivier's tales, you should come for dinner tomorrow night. I'll cook. He can talk.'

I'm about to say yes but Olivier groans and knocks the wind out of my sails so instead I fumble for words and an 'Oh no, I couldn't possibly' comes out.

'You must!' Elena insists and I'm cringing inside. It's obvious Olivier doesn't want me to go.

I bat my hand in an attempt at flippancy. 'Olivier probably just wants to rest. He's been working so hard.'

'It's not that, Cath. Elena is a terrible cook. The worst,' he says, grinning mischievously.

I giggle, probably too hard, but it's what comes out with the relief I feel. 'Well, I'm sure you're not, Elena. Besides, it's not as though I'm used to fine dining or anything. In fact, between you and me, I'm actually a fan of cut-price tinned meats.' They both look at me, confused.

'Well, you have been warned.' Olivier is mock serious. 'Honestly, she is the only French person I know who can't cook.'

'Brother, you are very cruel,' she says, but there is a sparkle to her eyes that suggests she's taken it all in good humour.

'So I take it you *can* cook?' I ask Olivier.

Elena throws her head down onto the table and groans

dramatically. 'Oh please, is there anything this man can't do?'

I giggle. Obviously, I don't know him as well as she does but I had got that impression.

He puts on an overly modest expression. 'I've been known to dabble a little in the kitchen.'

'He's like Raymond *bludee* Blanc.' Elena's pronunciation of bloody packs a lovely punch, but I have no idea who Raymond Blanc is. I'm assuming he's a chef of some sort.

Olivier laughs. 'I cook simple, homely French food. That's all. I've tried teaching this one but she has no patience. Like you can make a *quick* casserole.' He shakes his head.

'Speaking of patience, I'm going to round up those children. It's almost time to leave.' Elena disappears before either one of us replies.

'So, you're a dark horse,' I say, teasingly.

Olivier's brow crevices. 'You have some strange expressions.'

'I mean you're a man of many hidden talents.' I'm smiling but I allow it to fade. 'Elena told me about how you cared for her after your parents passed away. I guess you had to be good at a lot of things.'

He draws a deep breath. 'Elena talks too much.'

'I'm sorry. I didn't mean to pry. I—'

'It's okay. Elena has this habit of telling everyone everything.' He sips his coffee. 'I should be flattered because she always sings my praises, but sometimes I think she has this rose-tinted image of me, still through her naïve sixteen-year-old eyes.'

'Surely you're being harsh on yourself there. And unfair to Elena.'

'She remembers me as this hero. I shielded her from a lot of the details about my parents' deaths at the time and I always made sure she was well looked after. She was my number one priority. But in the background, when I was alone, I struggled. I missed my parents, and I had a lot of responsibility.'

'Of course you did. I'm a single parent – I know how it is.

212

When my friends were out clubbing, I was at home feeding a baby and changing nappies all alone. It's hard. Going straight into parenting a teenager at such a young age must have been a lot to handle.' I place my reassuring hand on his.

He swipes at some crumbs on the table. 'I started taking pills to help me sleep. I'd wake up, cook, clean and make sure Elena was okay and had everything she needed, then once she went to bed, I'd take a pill. Then I started taking different pills during the day, for anxiety, just to take the edge off, and when the doctor wouldn't prescribe them anymore, I bought them illegally.'

I let his words sink in for a moment. 'After what you went through, nobody could blame you for that,' I say, thinking back to the days where Kieran was a baby and would cry for hours on end and I'd feel like a complete failure because I didn't know how to fix him, so I'd cry too. I know what that kind of isolation feels like, and if there was a pill I'd known about that would remove that helplessness, I'd have taken it too.

'It's hardly the perfect image that Elena portrays. I was basically a drug addict. I feel so guilty when she coos about what a great brother I am, but she doesn't know my secret.'

'Olivier, everyone has secrets, and the very fact that Elena thinks you did a great job is evidence that you did. I've never told Kieran about my struggles because he doesn't need that weight on his shoulders, so it's understandable that you kept it from her. I know what it's like to be so young and have such great responsibility, and it's hard, but here we are, on the other side, enjoying life.' I raise my cup to him and he smiles.

'I also wish I could have told you everything on my own terms. Elena latches on to people and tells them her life story.'

'Well, I'm glad she did because I've finally uncovered an imperfection. You're not perfect through nature or choice, you're perfect because you had to be.' I hold his gaze for a moment. 'It's intimidating being around someone who is too perfect, you know.' I smile so he knows that I'm joking.

213

'Well, if you don't like perfection, you should come to Elena's dinner tomorrow. I'm sure she just wants to get to know you better. Either that or it's her way of getting you and me together. Who knows what goes on in her head.' He laughs.

'I would love to come to dinner.'

Maybe then we will finally talk about yesterday.

Chapter Twenty-Five

I'm jiggling with nerves. Olivier is picking me up soon and he's going to drive me to Elena and Julien's house. A family gathering is uncharted territory and I'm going to be out of my comfort zone. Jackie and I had been to Lille to go shopping earlier, and she seemed to think I was making a big fuss over nothing, but she has no idea about my background. I'm a single parent and I work in a supermarket and here I am in the middle of some French romance with a handsome, intelligent man who is way out of my league. Things like this don't happen to me. *But it isn't a romance*, I remind myself. *It can't be.*

A familiar little red car pulls up and Olivier honks the horn. I take a breath and climb in. 'You look beautiful. I love your dress,' he says as his eyes pass over me, making my skin tingle. Goose bumps pop up on my legs.

'Oh, this old thing?' I joke, but I'm too nervous to be convincing. It's a red, flowery sundress that I bought today, and I must admit, I did think I looked good as I passed the mirror on my way down; but if I'm not careful, Jackie will have me bankrupt.

We pull up to a well-kept property out in the countryside. It's a pretty peach bungalow with a dark oak front door, gravel driveway, and lots of garden space. There are potted red flowers by the door, which swings open as we approach it. 'You're here!' Elena bounces down the driveway, hugging us in turn.

'You have a beautiful home,' I say.

'Thank you. You should see Olivier's.' She winks at him.

We walk inside and cooking aromas travel through the hallway. 'It smells good,' I whisper to Olivier, who purses his lips. The house is fairly minimalistic and simple inside. Pale cream tiled floor, pale cream walls, and light oak furniture. We're greeted by Julien as we enter the kitchen. He's a handsome blond man who looks like he goes to the gym. His face is friendly.

'Hello,' he says. His accent is much thicker than both Elena and Olivier's. 'I've set up outside.'

We all take our seats and Julien pours out some red wine. 'I feel terrible that you're all having to speak English just for my benefit,' I say, sipping mine. An explosion of dark, rich red fruits hit my taste buds.

'Oh, don't be silly. It's second nature to Olivier and me, and this one—' she jabs Julien '—needs the practice.'

I'm glad Olivier doesn't say anything about my French lessons because I'm not ready to showcase my talents (or lack of) just yet.

'Would you like bread?' Julien hands the basket of fresh crusty bread rolls around the table.

Olivier leans over to me. 'I'd seriously recommend eating the bread.'

Julien gives a look of mock-sympathy. 'I agree. I tried to salvage this meal by turning the heat down, but I don't know.' He shrugs.

'I can hear you,' Elena's voice echoes from the kitchen. 'I think this time I've done okay. I've gone for *French-edible* cuisine.' The men laugh quietly and Olivier murmurs that it would be a triumph if she's succeeded.

She brings out a cast-iron crockpot and places it in the centre of the table before removing the lid. Steam gushes out. '*Voilà.*'

'It smells delicious.' I glare pointedly at the men.

Elena beams with pride. 'It's *boeuf bourguignon*. As our guest, you can try it first.' She dollops a ladleful on my plate and the rich aromas of onion, beef and wine fill my nostrils. I can't wait to tuck in because despite my apprehensions, it smells delicious, but I wait politely until everyone has been served.

'*Bon appé*tit,' Elena says, raising her glass. The men exchange glances of caution and I shake my head at their rudeness. Everyone else breaks off hunks of bread and scoops up the stew so I follow suit.

The flavour is quite unusual, not at all how I remember the dish, though whenever I've made it, I've used one of those sachets that you just add water and raw ingredients to. I don't have a crockpot either so it goes in my Pyrex dish in the oven.

'This isn't your worst. It actually has flavour this time,' Olivier says chewing a piece of bread. 'Though your beef would make a sturdy pair of boots.'

'I'll take that as a compliment because at least you're eating it this time. I used all the herbs I have. Parsley, basil, rosemary, sage. You name it,' Elena says.

That's why it tastes so odd. The beef is very chewy but no worse than how mine sometimes comes out. After a few mouthfuls, the odd taste starts to become sickly, so I adapt my bread-to-stew ratio accordingly.

Julien pushes his plate away when he's about half-done. 'I'm sorry, my love. I can't finish.' He stands up and walks over to a disappointed-looking Elena and wraps his arms around her. 'You have many talents, my dear, but cooking isn't one of them. I know you tried your best.' He kisses her on the neck and she feigns hurt and then giggles.

'I tried.' She sighs. 'Sorry, Cath.'

I feel terrible for her, but she's taking it in her stride.

'I was always more interested in boys than cooking.' She looks to Julien and grins, and I'm glad she gets that little sliver of a dig

217

in. 'Anyway. I thought this might happen.' She walks into the kitchen and returns with a brown paper bag. 'So I got these.' She pulls out some ham, cheese, and tomato baguettes and the men cheer. Elena shrugs. 'One day, I will cook a meal that leaves you begging for more.'

The informality of the baguettes changes the dynamic of the meal and soon we're sitting back in our chairs, chatting and laughing. Julien tops up the wine glasses but Olivier covers his glass with his hand, refusing another drink. 'I'm driving Cath home.'

I feel guilty he can't just relax and have a drink so I offer to get a cab. The horrified look on his face suggests that it won't be an option.

'Why doesn't Cath just stay at your house?' Elena suggests, sending my thoughts into a crazy spiral of morning breath and clean pants all over again, never mind the tension it might create now things have progressed. We still haven't talked about our kiss.

'I couldn't intrude,' I say.

'It's fine, Olivier has the space and you guys can walk from here. Come on, Olivier, then you can have some fun with us.'

He looks a little unsure and I watch him nervously. I've already protested so the ball is now in his court.

'Of course. You're more than welcome to stay,' he says eventually.

'Okay then. That's settled,' Elena says, sloshing wine into Olivier's glass.

The evening continues to be one of warmth, love, and laughter. There are points where I feel like an outsider, looking in. Especially as Julien slips into his mother tongue as the alcohol takes effect. But being an outsider isn't a bad thing. It's been a long time since I've shared a family meal. Gary grunting across the breakfast bar about corned beef hash and being skint doesn't really cut the mustard.

218

At midnight, we decide to call it a night.

'It has been lovely having you over, Cath,' Elena says.

'Perhaps she'll come again if you promise not to cook,' Olivier says in jest but a pang of sadness hits me because I know there probably won't be a next time.

'Ha-ha, brother. I think I've found the one thing you suck at.' She smirks as Olivier frowns.

'Comedy!' We all laugh.

'Goodnight, sister.' He leans in and kisses her on the cheek. 'Night, Julien.'

'Thank you both for a wonderful evening.' I hug them both.

Outside, there are no street lamps. It's pitch black bar the light coming from the downstairs window of Elena's home and the moon above. We walk side-by-side in silence, listening to the chirping of crickets. The red wine dances through my system, making me feel giddy and excitable.

Olivier slows to a standstill and puts his hand on my shoulder. 'Look up.'

'Oh my.' I gasp at the number of bright stars filling the inky black sky.

'There's no light pollution here – it's great for stargazing.' We stand still for a moment, looking at the sky. I don't know about Olivier but my head is full of wonder. Wonder for what's actually out there, what space is, and the mind-boggling concept of it going on for infinity.

'Space is the biggest mystery known to man.' Olivier speaks quietly as if reading my mind.

A breeze comes from nowhere sending a chill over me. 'Here, take my jacket.' Olivier has already taken it off and is draping it over my shoulders.

'Thank you.'

'That bright star there is Jupiter.'

I squint. 'Where?'

He leans in close, so his cheek is pressed against mine, and he points to one of the brighter stars. The feel of his skin on mine is like little jolts of electricity.

We continue to walk down the quiet road until a large country farmhouse-style building comes into view. 'Home sweet home.' He waves an arm towards the property.

'It's beautiful,' I say, taking in the giant version of Elena's house. It's a rustic, two-storey, double-fronted property with a long driveway in front.

Inside, it's homelier than Elena's. Family photographs adorn the walls and evidence of Olivier's parents is everywhere, from the Welsh cabinet filled with china, to the numerous floral oil paintings; so it comes as no surprise when he tells me it was their house.

'Elena wanted me to have the house to show her gratitude to me. We inherited it jointly but she wouldn't hear of keeping it in her name. I have tried to pay her half but she won't accept it.'

'She really looks up to you,' I say.

'I know. But she doesn't know what a mess I was.'

'Why didn't you tell her then? It might have made you feel better.' She doesn't seem unable to cope with the truth to me.

He sighs. 'At the time, I had to look like I was keeping it together. I was all she had, and if she knew I was hooked on pills, she might have worried unnecessarily. By the time I'd got myself off them, too much time had passed, and I think she would have been upset that I'd kept it from her for so long.'

'That makes sense. It's in the past.'

'The problem is, she blames herself for the fact I didn't travel the world or meet someone else after my ex had left. But the truth is, I didn't meet anyone because I was in a fog. My eyes were open but I couldn't see what was going on around me.'

My stomach clenches. He's right. Elena *does* carry that guilt. I've known her all of two minutes and I know that. 'You should just come clean. She'll understand.'

He nods. 'Would you like a coffee or anything before bed?'

The conversation is closed, and it definitely isn't the time to bring up whatever our thing is.

'A coffee would be great.'

While he's in the kitchen, I sit on the sofa and take in the well-lived-in room. There's a photo on the oak TV cabinet of Olivier, Elena, and two other people who I assume to be their parents. Elena has certainly got her mother's elegant beauty, and Olivier has his father's boyish good looks and mischievous glint in his eyes.

'Here you go.' Olivier hands me a steaming mug of coffee and sits on the chair to my right.

'I enjoyed tonight,' I say, between blowing into my coffee and taking cautious sips; the roof of my mouth is still rough from yesterday's hot coffee incident.

He smiles. 'Me too.'

We sip our coffees until Olivier breaks the silence.

'So, just one more place to visit until you complete the journey of your great-grandfather. Are you ready for it?'

'I think so.' I swallow. 'Would you be able to come with me?' I look at him hopefully.

'I wouldn't let you go without me.' Olivier glances down at his cup, shakes it and drinks the last of his coffee before rinsing the cup and putting it to drain by the sink.

'Did your son get his perm?'

The mention of Kieran hits me like a club to the stomach. I haven't thought about him in days, never mind checked in on his latest hair fads. It's so unlike me and the feeling of guilt penetrates my wine-infused merriment.

'I don't actually know,' I say honestly. 'I feel like a terrible parent – I don't even know what hairstyle my son has! I'll have to call him tomorrow.'

'Home feels so far away when you're on holiday.' Olivier's comment is flippant and he's right, but I must keep up to date with my home life. I'll be heading back there, after all, and soon,

Olivier will be a distant memory. There's that club to the stomach again.

'Are you okay?' he asks, picking up on the sadness, no doubt etched in my worry lines.

'I was just thinking about how sad I'll be when I do have to leave here.'

Olivier's face doesn't move, but I notice his jaw tense and relax, and then he smiles. 'We'll have to make sure you make the most of your time here then, won't we?'

'I don't really know what else there is to see until I go to Paris, other than Ypres of course,' I say. 'I've done what I came here to do.'

'There's lots to see. There are plenty more World War I sites to visit, you could move on to the Second World War or visit more vineyards or the coast or—'

I giggle. 'I get it. I just wish I'd planned my time better. I have a week left and don't want to waste it. I could do with a rest day, though. Jackie wore me out shopping today.'

He laughs. Well, I've got to go into the office in the morning for a few hours, but I'm not running an excursion so I'll come back and we can spend the day relaxing here if you like? Who knows, a rest day might be what you need to really plan out your last few days.'

'That sounds like a plan.' And hanging around here would certainly beat hanging around in my bedsit.

After chatting for a while, Olivier shows me to the guest room. It's a cosy double room with an en suite and it feels like a penthouse suite after staying in my grubby little studio.

'Here's a T-shirt to sleep in, and there are clean towels in the bathroom and spare toothbrushes and things, but if you need anything else, just let me know.'

'Thank you,' I say, holding his gaze for too long.

'Goodnight, Cath,' he whispers.

'Goodnight,' I whisper back, but he doesn't budge, and instead, we continue to look into one another's eyes with our faces just a foot apart.

He runs his finger up my arm slowly, tracing my collarbone when he gets to the top. My body is frozen, aside from the parts directly beneath his touch, which fizz with warmth.

He rests his forehead on mine as he takes a step in, close enough that our bodies touch from the knees up. Using his head, he gently pushes mine back and our lips meet. I pull his shirt, wanting to feel him as close as possible, and he pushes me back up against the wall and jams his knee between my legs, pinning me against the solid surface. The kissing gets faster and I weave my fingers through his hair, clutching handfuls of it for dear life. *This is not addressing the problem, Cath!* My subconscious is screaming but I ignore her. *I'm having this moment and keeping it in my memory forever.*

He breaks away. We're both panting. I haven't been kissed like that ever, I don't think. 'I've wanted to do that all night,' he whispers in my ear. His hot breath sends tingles down my spine. 'Goodnight, madame. I'll see you for breakfast,' he says, before leaving.

He leaves me slumped against the wall.

Wanting more.

Chapter Twenty-Six

When I wake up, I've no clue of the time. The wine has left me groggy but so has the lack of sleep. It took me ages to drop off after that kiss, and I'm beginning to think Olivier should come with his own personal warning label: *Caution! May Cause Insomnia.*

I trundle downstairs, encouraged by the delicious smell of sweet pastry. 'Good morning,' Olivier shouts cheerfully from the kitchen.

'Morning,' I say slowly, wondering what on earth is going on. 'Are you baking? It smells gorgeous.'

'I woke up early so I made a *tarte au citron*, which is my speciality. Then I made fresh croissants for breakfast.' He looks pleased with himself and I can't blame him – they look tons better than the fresh bakery ones at work.

'I'm impressed,' I say as he places a warm croissant in front of me. I sit on the barstool and tug at the bottom of the T-shirt, which now feels incredibly revealing.

'I couldn't sleep. Baking relaxes me so I thought I'd start off the pastry and head back to bed, but I just got into the groove.' He looks up from buttering his croissant and flashes me a half-smile.

The warm, buttery taste of the croissant is to die for, and I feel no shame in asking for a second. The food is almost enough to mask the huge elephant in the room, but I feel silly bringing it up. I don't really know the protocol for hot, steamy kisses and whether or not they require a debrief. I just know that *I* do.

'I need to head into work for a few hours. You can make yourself at home. It's a nice day so you could enjoy the garden.' He walks over to the patio doors and swings open the curtains. To my surprise, there's a small outdoor swimming pool set into the crazy-paved patio, with two wooden sun loungers by the side.

My insides squeeze with glee. 'Ooh, you have a pool,' I blurt. 'It looks like my idea of heaven.'

'We don't always get a long swimming season here in northern France, but the weather for the past few weeks has been great so I've finally had some use. Feel free to relax out there. Elena is going to pop round soon with some things you might need.'

My chest fizzes with excitement. This house, the pool, Olivier. It's like a dream, or a Disney bubble or something. It's a far cry from my terraced house back home, so I don't take much persuading.

Olivier has been gone about twenty minutes when the doorbell rings. I can see through the glass panel to the right of the door that it's Elena. I swing the door open. 'Hi.'

'Good morning. Did you sleep well?' she asks and her words are layered with additional meaning.

'I did. It was a much comfier bed than the one at my studio.' There's no point going into how I still couldn't get to sleep for other reasons.

'Good.' She pauses as though contemplating another question, and a part of me wants her to ask what's on the tip of her tongue, but instead she holds out a shopping bag. 'Anyway, I have to get to work, but I brought you some essentials. There's a swimsuit in there, which should fit you. I haven't worn it because I bought it then changed my mind and forgot to return it. Don't tell that to Olivier, though – he hates that I'm so careless with money.' She winks.

'Thank you, this is great. It's a shame you can't join me.' And I really mean that. Some girlie company is just what I need.

'Sorry. Another time maybe.' She hugs me and skips down the driveway to her car. 'Bye!' she shouts and then she leaves. Everything is silent: the house, the fields outside, me. I take the bag inside and empty it onto the kitchen counter. I'm relieved to see the swimming costume is plain black. Being a sweetheart, Elena has also thrown in sunglasses, sun cream and a few French magazines. Soon, I'm lounging by the pool like a movie star, wishing every day could be like this one.

Remembering my plans to ring Kieran, I take out my phone. There is a good chance he won't be up yet, but I decide to ring anyway. As I suspected, it goes to voicemail after a few rings so I leave a message in the hope he'll get back to me.

'Hi, it's me: Mum. Just wanted to see how you are. Call me back. I think it's free now to call abroad but if not I'll p—' *Beep.* I sigh. They never give you long enough to speak.

While I have my phone out, I decide to ring Kaitlynn.

'You stayed over!' she shrieks down the phone when I fill her in. I imagine a flock of birds leaving her vicinity immediately.

'Only out of convenience, don't get all excited,' I say. 'His house is amazing. It's a rustic pile in the countryside. I'm currently lounging by his outside *pool*.' I allow some uncharacteristically girlie excitement to tinge my tone.

She gasps. 'No way?'

'Yes way. But pools and houses aside, I do really like Olivier. He's just so …' I can't describe him without coming over all gushy and I don't want her to think I've fallen for him or anything so I go for an anecdote. 'He baked a lemon tart this morning because he couldn't sleep. I haven't tasted it yet, but it looks and smells amazing.'

'Are you sure he isn't a figment of your imagination? Who the hell wakes up and rustles up a bloody lemon tart?'

I'm smiling. 'I don't know. He's just different from the men back home, or at least the ones in Berrybridge.'

'I'm lucky if I can get a guy to pop to Gregg's for me, never mind whip up a bloomin' pastry. So has anything happened between the two of you?'

I pause. On one hand, if I tell her, it will make it a *thing*, and I'm trying for it not to be one, but on the other hand, I really need to tell someone and I don't know when I'll next see Jackie. I can't talk to Elena about her brother, and I think I'll go mad if I don't let someone know. 'We've kissed. Twice.'

She gasps. 'Oh my God. Is it a full-on holiday romance?'

'No, I don't think so. We've been spending time sightseeing together but really, that's just his job so there's nothing to read into there. Last night, his sister had invited me round for dinner; he was there. We were tipsy and got caught up in the moment. We slept alone, though, before you ask.'

'Hang on, you said you kissed twice. What happened with the other kiss?'

'He took me to his friend's vineyard and set up this beautiful picnic for us. He kissed me there but again, it was just being in the moment.'

'Are you blind or incredibly dim?'

'Excuse me?' I'm quite taken aback.

'How do you get caught up in the moment twice? The man has taken you off on a picnic, which I'm guessing had nothing to do with his tour company? You've met his family for dinner and now you're lounging by his pool. Do you really think that nothing is going on?' She sounds frustrated.

'I know how it seems, but we're just having fun. I'm coming home soon so what would be the point in anything happening between us?'

'I think it's too late for questions like that,' she says solemnly. 'Be careful, Cath.'

I laugh nervously. 'I will. I am.'

'Well okay then, but you at least need to admit to yourself that this is more than a holiday fling.'

'Maybe if I was your age I would.'

She sighs. 'Well, keep me posted and I'm here for you, okay?'

'Of course.'

We say our goodbyes, and when I put my phone away, I start thinking about her words. If she thinks this thing between Olivier and me is a big deal, am I just deluding myself? I push myself to think about going home. I've always known it was coming, but I hadn't actually thought about how it would be going home to my empty house.

I close my eyes and imagine it. Saying goodbye to everyone here, boarding the train and arriving home to my empty nest before heading back to the supermarket job I know and love.

I can do that. It's what I've done for years.

I force myself to think deeper, to think about actually saying goodbye to just Olivier, and my chest clenches so hard it's painful. Maybe Kaitlynn is right. I think about calling her back to see if she has any answers, but I already know what she'll say. She'll tell me to step back because I'll get hurt. She'll tell me to focus on why I came here. There's only one old romantic I know who could possibly offer any advice. It just won't be quick.

I open Facebook Messenger on my phone and go to the message Martha sent me. I smile at the familiar partially punctuated, caps lock text but feel bad for not replying sooner.

HI CATH HES MARRIED. I WOULD NOT HAVE GUESSED THAT. ARE YOU SURE M XX

Still smiling, I tap out my reply.

Hi Martha,

I'm sorry it's taken me so long to reply. I've moved out of the hotel and don't have Wi-Fi in my new studio. Anyway, I'm glad you arrived home safely and I can certainly say that France isn't the same without you ladies here. Anyway, your instinct

was right. Olivier is single. Basically, I'd put two and two together and won a loaf of bread.

I actually wanted to ask your advice on something. Olivier and I have grown quite close (Calm down – I know you're squealing!). We've even kissed. The problem is, I'm leaving in six days and wonder if I've let things go too far and if I should cut all ties with him now before it gets messy.

Give Harry a hug from me.

Cath x

I stare at the text with my finger hovering over the delete button, but instead, I hit send. What the heck do I have to lose?

To distract myself, I pick up one of the magazines Elena brought. They look just like the glossy, celeb-filled mags I see every day by the tobacco counter at work, except I don't recognise the cover girl. I flick through but my basic French skills don't afford me any word recognition, so I settle for looking at the pictures and imagining what the words say. I've fabricated a very interesting story about an obvious plastic surgery addict when my phone buzzes. It's a message. My heart skips. It's from Martha.

SO GREAT TO HEAR FROM YOU HONEY. FOUND THE FULL STOP BUTTON NOW. DARN EYEPAD. STILL CANT TURN OFF CAPS. ANYWAY BACK TO YOUR PROBLEM. YOU HAVE TO FOLLOW YOUR HEART HONEY BECAUSE IN LIFE THERE IS LITTLE ALL ELSE. IF YOU WANT TO SPEND TIME WITH THAT MAN THEN YOU SHOULD. WHAT IS THE POINT IN STOPPING NOW. HAVING YOUR HEART BROKEN A FEW DAYS EARLIER WONT MAKE ONE HELL OF A DIFFERENCE. YOULL JUST SPOIL THE LAST FEW DAYS OF YOUR HOLIDAY AND EITHER WAY YOURE GOING HOME SAD. BUT YOU NEVER KNOW. LOVE IS POWERFUL AND IF YOU TWO ARE SUPPOSED TO BE TOGETHER THEN YOU SHALL BE. KEEP ME POSTED. M XX

I rub my eyes. The capitals and lack of punctuation make the message a bit hard to read but her message is clear. She's right – what's the point in moping around for the next six days? I will still be sad to leave either way so I might as well enjoy my time here.

Then something occurs to me. Olivier. Shouldn't I talk to him about this? He might be having the exact same mental dilemma. I suddenly feel all hot and clammy so I jump in the pool, hoping the cold shock will clear my head, but it's a lovely temperature.

I spend an hour drying off in the sun and pop into the house in search of juice. I glance at the bookshelf in the lounge on my way past and see the book Olivier was reading when I met him in the café that day: *All The Light We Cannot See.* He's finished it I notice, as I run my finger down the spine, unsure if that bears any significance. *He's committed.*

I find the orange juice and glasses and pour myself a drink. I can't help but want to look around the house. There must be some undesirable qualities that this man has. The laundry room is clean and tidy. Just a pile of neatly folded bedding sits atop the washer waiting to be put away. The kitchen has been cleaned post-bake-off and the *tarte* sits on a wire cooling rack. There is an immaculate open-plan dining area with a vase of freshly cut flowers on a sideboard behind the table amidst ornaments of various shapes and sizes. The door by the front entrance opens into a downstairs loo, which has scented candles on the window-sill. He's like Gary's polar opposite, I think with a smile.

I shouldn't be snooping, I tell myself, but I can't stop; it's like a compulsion. I'm already climbing the wooden stairs to the first floor. The room I stayed in is off to the right, and I can see the house bathroom and two more doors off the landing. I open the first. It's a small study with a pine desk, a computer and hundreds of travel guides and information books mostly centring on the war. *Nothing unusual here.*

The other door must lead into his room. Opening it feels like a real invasion of privacy, but my hand is already twisting the knob. As the door creaks open, I'm greeted by the sight of a perfectly made bed. I let out a small laugh and slump against the door. There isn't so much as a pair of jeans strewn over the chair in the corner. *This man is immaculate.* I walk over to the window, just curious about the view he sees each morning, and I'm not disappointed. Fields of green and yellow stretch as far as the eye can see. There are hills in the distance, and below the sill is the grey patio and pool, framed by a neatly cut green lawn.

A feeling of sadness hits me on Olivier's behalf. He has this wonderful life and nobody to share it with. He obviously would like to find someone. I can tell by the way he is around me, and because he kissed me. But I'm just not the right someone for him. I'm the warm-up act getting him ready for the real talent. Martha overlooked one vital detail in her message: Olivier's feelings.

As I turn to leave, I notice a small pill bottle on the bedside table. I'm on autopilot as I cross the room and pick it up with a trembling hand. It's a prescription bottle but the name and date have worn off. I've seriously invaded his privacy now. I place the bottle back down, fussing with the position to make sure it's exactly as I found it. Then I slip out, close the door and go back to the pool area.

Once I'm sat down, all kinds of things whizz through my head. Is he taking the pills again? Was he trying to talk to me about it? Is it my fault? I grab my phone seeking a distraction and I'm surprised to see a missed call from Kieran. I call him back straight away, hoping to catch him. Normal life is the perfect distraction.

'Hello, love,' I say before he has a chance to speak.

'Hi, Mum.' The sound of his voice shocks me. The familiarity of it brings back so much feeling and emotion. My eyes start to sting with moisture.

'Oh, Kieran. I've missed you.'

'Give over, Mum.' There's humour in his tone and I know it's because he's missed me too but he's too macho to say.

'I feel like I haven't seen you in ages.'

'It's not been *that* long. Are you still in France?'

'Yes, I've six days left here in Arras and then I'm going to Paris for a few days before coming home. It would be great if you could come home that weekend?'

He pauses to run some mental calculations. 'Yeah, probably.'

'Did you get your perm?' I ask keenly.

'I did. Shall I send you a pic?'

'Please, love.' I haven't made my mind up as to whether I'll laugh or cry when I see it but I'm definitely intrigued.

From the corner of my eye, I see Olivier step out on to the patio. Instinctively, I shout 'Hi.' And he shouts it back.

'Who is that?' Kieran asks.

'Oh, it's a … er … friend.' I glance at Olivier and mouth 'my son'. He smiles and sits on the lounger next to me.

'A *male* friend?' Kieran's tone is teasing.

'It isn't like that.' My hand becomes clammy around the phone. It's a strange conversation to have with Kieran, especially since Olivier is sat next to me. I come over all squeamish.

'Well if it is, it's okay, you know?' he says. There are so many things I want to say, that mostly centre around denial, but that was a very mature thing for Kieran to come out with and so I simply thank him. University must be doing him good.

'Anyway, I'm playing five-a-side soon so I have to go. Love you, Mum.'

My heart swells with love. I can't remember the last time he said that. 'Love you too, son.'

'How was work?' I ask Olivier when I've put my phone and all thoughts of pill bottles away.

'It was dull. I'm not a fan of office work. It's more Julien's thing but I have to do the accounts as he needs training so he's swanning off to London today … but, I get to spend the afternoon here with you.' He takes my hand and kisses it. My stomach somersaults and immediately after, knots.

232

'Olivier. I think we need to talk,' I say, sliding my hand from his.

A crease forms between his eyebrows; then he relaxes and looks down to the arm of the lounger. 'I know. But first, you have to try my *tarte au citron*.'

I put my head on the side and give him the kind of look I used to give to Kieran when he tried to put off tidying his room.

'Honestly, you won't want to feel all maudlin when you eat it. It's a fresh, happy flavour and should be enjoyed while fresh and happy.'

'It's a good job I've had a swim then,' I say dryly.

He saunters off into the kitchen and soon re-emerges with the tarte, whilst balancing some forks on two small plates in his other hand.

'Here you go.' He hands me a piece. It's even topped with icing sugar, and the lemon curd sits neatly in the pastry – none oozing over the side like it would be if I'd made it. I jab a piece with my fork and pop it in my mouth. The buttery pastry is the perfect base for the deliciously sweet and tangy lemon curd.

'Mmm. This is heavenly. Seriously.' I close my eyes to savour the taste even more. 'I want you to come home and live with me.' The last sentence pops out as a joke but straight away I realise the awkwardness of it, especially when Olivier doesn't laugh.

'I'm glad you like it.' He's already eaten half of his piece.

My phone buzzes and it's the photo of Kieran. He has his tongue out and he's pulling a 'rock on' gesture with his free hand – the other, I assume, is taking the picture. His perm looks okay, very similar to the hairstyles many boys have these days. I'd just assumed their curls were natural, not permed. I show Olivier.

'The perm,' I say.

'He's a handsome young man,' he says, shovelling the last forkful of tart into his mouth.

Now is as good a time as any to say my piece. 'Okay, the talk. Shall I start?' I want him to say no and take the lead because I might just be over-reacting in his eyes, but he doesn't. Instead, he gestures for me to go ahead. I take a deep breath and decide to keep it light. 'I've had so much fun with you. I've really enjoyed your company—'

'Me too,' he interrupts.

'But I only have six more days left and then I'll leave and this will be all over.'

He's peeling a piece of dried-out wood off the armrest of the lounger. He doesn't look up. 'I've been thinking about this too. I wondered if I should keep my distance, but I can't.'

'Don't you think the more time we spend together, the harder it will be to say goodbye?'

'Can't you stay longer?' His tone suggests he knows I can't.

'I have a son, a job, and a home. I can't afford to lose any of those things, just like you can't lose your home and business here. And besides, staying longer would just make things worse.'

'What is your suggestion?'

'I've thought long and hard about it. We can either stop seeing each other now and draw a line in the sand, or we can enjoy the next six days together. Either way, we can stay friends when I leave.'

He sits back in the chair, looking into the distance. 'I can't stop seeing you, Cath, not while you're here.'

My chest fizzes with excitement at the thought of the next six days together. It's the right decision, definitely. A wonderful six days, then back to the life I know and love. What could possibly go wrong?

Chapter Twenty-Seven

The next few days are heavenly bliss. I join a couple of Great War tours. There have been plenty of knowing glances and stolen kisses and the world has felt a much brighter place. It's now day four, which is our planned visit Ypres but first, Olivier wanted to show me the museum at Passchendaele.

From the car park, we walk past what looks like a building site. It isn't until we're right next to it that I realise what I'm looking at. 'Is this …?'

'A small piece of battlefield? Yes.'

The pulped ground is punctuated by the gnarly remains of trees and barbed-wire posts. Wooden planks lay across the mud to enable easier passage.

We continue walking to the museum, which is housed in a quaint, Flemish chateau.

'Do you want "tour guide" Olivier or just the regular charming and handsome version?' I glance his way, grinning.

'I'll take a bit of both.'

The gas masks, the weaponry, the lives and fears of everyday people are all completely unimaginable. I try to imagine my great-grandfather wearing these clothes, carrying these weapons whilst crossing the wooden boards I saw outside. Bullets flying and explosions deafening him as he went. He thought he might die here. I know that because of his final letter. He was resigned to it and fought anyway. His only hope was a prayer for survival.

I become aware of my heart racing. As we watch a short film about a raid on a village and the horrific bayonetting of a local man, I snuggle into the nook of Olivier's arm. It's hard to imagine why someone who had more than this, who had real love and a family, would want to volunteer for war. Chances are, he'd have been conscripted in time for the Somme offensive anyway but he didn't know that back in 1914.

We make our way through the replica underground bunkers, which take us out into realistic-looking trenches. 'It's hard to imagine trying to stay alive down here, isn't it?' I say as the reality sinks in. I try to imagine the bombs and bullets whizzing overhead, not knowing what direction they're flying in or where they would land.

'They think about three hundred and twenty-five thousand Allied men died here alone, and as you know, Miss Poetry, the conditions were much worse than what you see here. Men and horses died because of the mud, not just the fighting,' he replies. I think back to the replica battlefield we'd passed when walking from the car park.

'Then there were diseases and trench foot on top of the smell and the rats. Ten per cent of soldiers fighting this war were killed,' Olivier continues. I can only see the side of his face, but there's moisture glazing his eyes and it makes tears prick at my own. 'Here.' His tone changes to one that's more upbeat, 'Do you see this?' He jumps up on the bench and points out a metal panel. 'It's a loophole for snipers to look out across no man's land. Some snipers could make a shot right through the enemy loopholes and kill their targets.' It's hard to imagine they had the equipment back then. I stand on my tiptoes to peer through the hole and Olivier puts his hands on my hips and lifts me slightly so I can see better. The poor souls wouldn't have stood a chance.

'I just can't understand why my great-grandfather enlisted,' I say. 'I can't imagine why anyone would do that. Not when they have a wife and child at home.'

'There was a strong sense of national pride and the propaganda was heavy.' He reaches in his pocket and pulls out his phone before showing me the screen. 'Here are some of the posters.'

I scan them. 'Women in Britain say go. Your king and country need you.' I read the headlines of two of the colourful posters aloud and take in the equally compelling images. The rest are just as powerful. Coupled with the media outlets back then it was easy to see how people wanted to fight for their country.

'Thanks,' I say and Olivier shrugs, stuffing the phone back into his pocket. 'I suppose things were different then. These days people vape or do the ice bucket challenge under peer pressure; back then, it was saving your country.' I sigh at the trivialisation and the phrase 'you don't know you're born' springs to mind.

Outside the museum is a beautiful, serene lake, and families make the most of the warm summer sun by eating picnics by the stunning vista. Children play happily in the playground nearby. It takes me a moment to adjust to the contrasting scene.

'I'm glad we came here,' I say as we take a seat looking out at the view. 'It's helped to complete the picture of my great-grand-father's war journey. I feel like I've seen the beauty he wanted to share with my grandmother and I feel like I truly understand his bravery and the horrors he faced.'

Olivier puts his arm around my back and squeezes me close, kissing my head as I lean in to him and for a moment we glance across the lake.

'I think I'm ready to walk the final footstep.'

We arrive in the pretty town of Ypres a short while later and once again, I'm surprised at how small it is. It's not Neuve-Chapelle small, but because of the casualties suffered, I just expected it would be a bigger place. We park near the Menin Gate, but I don't want to look at it yet, not properly, though its dominance of the town hasn't gone unnoticed.

I want to visit the 'In Flanders Field' museum and learn all I can about the third battle of Ypres. The museum itself is a beautiful building dominating a square in the heart of the town. I take particular interest in the third battle of Ypres, in 1917. My great-grandfather was killed on the 27th of August after an advancement during a heavy storm. The men had been neck-deep in mud and had walked overnight through wind and rain. By the time zero hour came, they were numbed by the cold and barely able to move. They were sitting ducks for the German machine gunners. I close my eyes and put myself there, imagining the sounds from the museum at Albert for background noise.

Little shocks of emotion flare my nostrils and flood my eyes. I break down, heaving out the sadness that's built up over the past three-and-a-bit weeks. After all the battles my great-grandfather took part in, all the wretched conditions he lived in, the training, everything, he was killed just stuck in the mud, waiting to be shot. Killed like he was nothing. I don't know why his body was never found, perhaps it lies in the beautiful fields he was so fond of. I take a tissue out of my bag and clutch it to my face. Olivier wraps me in his arms and strokes my hair.

'I'm sorry.' I sniff. 'It's just so profoundly sad. What a senseless waste of life.'

'I know,' he whispers into my hair still clutching me tight.

'Surely there could have been a better way.'

'Maybe.' Olivier holds me and for a few moments we stay like that.

'I'm ready to find his name,' I say.

When we exit the museum, I decide to buy a wooden cross topped with a red poppy. We call in one of the gift shops stocking British Legion merchandise and sit on a bench.

'Here.' Olivier hands me a Sharpie pen. 'I always have this with me when we visit war graves as most people decide to leave a message of remembrance.'

I take the pen and fiddle with it.

238

'Do you want to be alone?' he asks.

I shake my head. 'No, it's okay, I just don't know what to write. I'm not very good at this kind of thing. I never have the right words.'

'You're a caring, compassionate woman,' he says, catching my eyes with his. The back of my neck tingles. 'Most people want to thank the men for their sacrifice and tell them they'll never be forgotten.'

'Of course. That's what I'll put.' I pop the lid off the pen and write clearly:

> *William Edward Ainsley*
> *Lost but not forgotten*
> *27/8/1917*
> *Thank you for your sacrifice.*
> *From your great-granddaughter,*
> *Cathy*
> *xxx*

'That is perfect,' Olivier says as I place the lid back on the pen. 'Would you like me to walk with you while you lay it?'

I look at him with moist eyes and nod. A lump has formed in my throat. The fact that I'm here, the only person in the whole world who has ever made the effort to see the tribute to my great-grandfather, is almost a raindrop of relief in a lake of crushing sadness. 'Thank you,' I say eventually, but it comes out in a whisper. Sensing my emotion, Olivier places a comforting hand on mine, and enjoying the warmth and tingle beneath, I let it rest a moment. *He's good at this.* It must come from years of experience.

'Whenever you're ready,' he says, leaving his hand on mine.

Before I came I'd printed off the grid reference so I know where to find his name. We take the steps under the archway to the panel; poppy wreaths and crosses line the way.

'There he is. *Ainsley W.E.*' I point to his name.

'Honoured a hero for all time,' Olivier says quietly.

'Agreed.' I kiss the cross before gently placing it down on the immaculate stone floor beneath the inscribed fascia and stop to look at it. A simple name, a beautiful tribute, the end of a journey. I dry my eyes and turn to Olivier.

'Thank you for being here with me today. I'm so glad I've completed this journey for more reasons than I can even describe.' He kisses my head and I take out the last letter.

25th August 1917

My dearest Elizabeth,

If you get this letter, it probably means the worst for I've left it with a friend to post if I don't make it back from the battlefield. There have been so many killed that I can't be sure I will ever return home and I want you to know that you and Rose have been in my heart and thoughts since the day I arrived.

In many ways, I will die a lucky man. So many men out here haven't had the chance to love. I meant what I said in my letters to Rose. Peace will come, and when it does, you must visit this beautiful country by whatever means. See the world and open your horizons, otherwise what is this all for?

Live well, live full and live happy.

All my love, forever and always,

Will

'Let's take a walk,' Olivier says once the words have sunk in. He takes my hand gently and leads me through a grassy area on top of the memorial. It turns into a memorial pathway down by the river. It's a beautiful conclusion to the day. To the whole trip in fact.

'When you took me on that first trip to Thiepval, I realised what a truly good person you are. The fact you were so kind to your passengers, your sympathy for the war heroes, your passion to share their stories, and your knowledge is such a unique combination,' I say, looking at the vast countryside ahead while a gentle breeze blows my hair behind me.

'And here's me thinking you just liked me for my looks.' He laughs easily.

'Don't get me wrong, I admire those too.' It surprises me just how easy those words were to say.

'It was your innocence that attracted me to you,' he says.

'Innocence?' I nudge him in the ribs. 'You called me an independent woman during one of our first proper conversations.'

'You are. I mean here. You seemed vulnerable and lost, but at the same time, I admired how you came alone anyway because you had a goal to fulfil. Your great-grandfather would be proud of you.'

'I smile. Well, at twenty-four, I doubt he'd given much thought to great-grandchildren,' I say, laughing after.

'You know what I mean.'

'I know.'

We walk back to the memorial, Olivier's warm hand wrapped around mine, and we arrive at the stone my great-grandfather's name is inscribed on. Olivier pulls me into a hug and kisses my forehead. My nose starts to tingle and my eyes sting.

'I'll probably never come back here again,' I say through a sob. 'It's bizarre. He was killed long before I came along and I don't even know what he looked like but the connection I feel with him is there.'

Olivier squeezes me hard. 'You've brought his memory to life.' He steps back, holding me at arm's length and looks me straight in the eyes. 'Just by being here, by living, you've made sure he didn't die in vain.'

I wipe the moisture from my eyes. 'Thank you.'

We take in the view across the memorial park one last time before heading back down for the Last Post.

People have already lined the pavements underneath the gate and the road has been closed off. We weave our way through the crowd hand in hand to find a spot where we can see.

Everyone is waiting quietly, all seemingly lost in independent thoughts. I assume they are paying silent respects and follow suit. A short while after, five buglers in greatcoats march by, commanding our attention as they step onto the road and make their way down to stand in a line beneath the memory arch, marked with the names of over fifty-four thousand men who gave their lives for freedom.

It is such a moving experience, and I can already feel myself welling up before the bugle call to attention. The rough, forced sound begins and I allow warm tears to flow. It's such a sad sound, but strangely, it seems such a fitting tribute for the strong men, living in rough conditions, largely forced into war. After the Last Post is played, and the bugles are lowered, there's a minute's silence. A lump forms in my throat, making it difficult to swallow, as I give silent consideration to all the men who, just like my great-grandfather, were killed in the Great War.

***

We go for a drink back at the hotel, and just after Kevin has placed two glasses of apple juice in front of us, I hear Jackie's familiar voice bellow my name.

'Jackie.' I hug her as she walks over and she grins and tips her head towards Olivier in a 'what's going on here then?' sort of way.

'Olivier, it's nice to see you again.' She doesn't hug him; she just pats him on the hand he's resting on the bar.

'Hello,' he says with a vague look of recognition in his eyes.

'I'm just having a tipple before my coach arrives. I'm going home.' She sticks out her bottom lip in mock sadness.

'Of course. It's today!' I get a pang of guilt, realising I've missed her last day.

'It will be nice to get back to normality.' She smiles and then orders a drink from Kevin. *Normality.* The word pings around my head like a squash ball. A few days ago, I'd been okay with getting back to normality, but since Olivier and I decided to enjoy the last few days together, my feelings have escalated. We've been in each other's pockets and there have been a few more of those kisses that kept me awake before, except now they send me into a soft, dreamy sleep. I'm not sure normality is on my radar anymore. In fact, I may need the Hubble telescope to ever find it again.

Olivier excuses himself to go to the bathroom, breaking my thoughts. 'So, anything more happened between the two of you?' Jackie asks, with a twinkle in her eye.

I tell her everything.

'Oh, Cath. You'll come crashing down like a lead balloon when you have to leave, but I can't say I'd be able to resist him either.'

I force an unenthusiastic smile. The lead balloon might as well land on top of me.

'I just thought that we may as well enjoy our last few days together, but I didn't expect to enjoy them so much, if you know what I mean.'

'I got ya.' She winks.

'Oh, no. Not like that, more on an emotional level. We've really connected. I don't believe in soul mates, not after Kieran's father

244

ran off at least, but I do believe if there were such a thing, he could be it.'

'Oh, love. These holiday romance type things always feel more intense. I fell head-over-heels in love with a Turkish waiter when I was seventeen and I'd only known him a week. As it turned out, he had a besotted teenager for every night of the week.' She rubs my arm in sympathy. 'Not that Olivier is like that. I'm sure you two do have a real connection.'

'It's hard to tell. He's such a lovely man. I don't know if it's the fact he's so different to any man I've met before that is drawing me in. Either way, I'll miss him incredibly.'

Olivier is walking back towards us and Jackie starts rambling on about her plans for next week when she's home – they're almost all food-related. A man in a tour guide uniform walks in and shouts for anyone waiting for the 5 p.m. bus.

'That's me,' Jackie says, sliding out the handle of her cerise wheelie case.

'It's been lovely to have met you. I hope you'll stay in touch,' I say, hugging her.

'Definitely. You have my number.'

I let out a huge sigh as she follows the rep out of the revolving doors. 'All these goodbyes,' I say, imagining how hard the next one will be.

'Cath, I've been meaning to ask you something,' Olivier says.

'Okay.' I draw out the word. Something about the way he said it makes me think it's going to be a big ask.

'I wondered if you'd let me come with you to Paris?'

I pause. Shocked. I've been psyching myself up to say goodbye in three days and now he wants to *extend* this purgatory? No, it isn't a good idea. I bite my lip while I mull it over.

He must sense my discomfort. 'I'm sorry, I shouldn't have asked. Ignore me, I've just been caught up in the whirlwind of the past few days.'

The thought of going to Paris alone *is* quite daunting and

having Olivier there would mean I don't have to worry as much. Plus he'd know the best things to see and do and help me avoid tourist traps and it would mean I wouldn't be all alone, which I'll soon be experiencing a lifetime of anyway so I might as well say …

'Yes.'

His eyes widen. 'You mean it?'

'Yes. Of course,' I say, smiling.

'You won't regret it – I'm something of an expert.'

I laugh. 'I can believe it.'

Chapter Twenty-Eight

He's already waiting for me at the train station when I arrive. I'd almost bottled it and told him not to come. I can't shake the image of those pills by his bed. What if he's taking them again? Could saying goodbye in Paris make things worse for him? Especially since we've practically become a temporary couple, like those paper knickers you wear when you get a spray tan. What we have has offered momentary comfort and security but it isn't meant to last. Actually, that's a terrible analogy as those knickers are far from comfy or secure. If he feels the same as I do, saying goodbye will surely push him back to taking them – if he isn't already.

In the end, after all my reasoning, I decided to let him come, because being away somewhere new might be the best place to talk about them, if they come up. I can hardly tell him I'd been snooping in his room, can I? I'm hoping he brings them and they fall out of his bag or something. Somehow, I'm going to have to make sure it comes up because I can't go back to England knowing he could have a problem.

When I spot him, my stomach flips like a teenage girl's at a Harry Styles concert. He's wearing beige chinos and a white shirt that is tucked in beneath a brown leather belt. His hair has been cut but still flops effortlessly to the side, and he has a neat glossy-black weekend case on wheels beside him. My stomach is fluttery with excitement and nerves and when I say 'hello', it comes out all child-like and small.

He kisses me on the cheek and we go to buy tickets. Once on the train, I relax a little while Olivier pulls out his guidebook. He points out various things to see and do, and I find myself needing to snuggle in to him to be able to see properly. He smells delicious – like mint and lime – and I just want to bury my face in his chest. It feels like the most natural thing in the world, and that makes me feel a whole melting pot of emotions ranging from joy and desire to sadness and fear. In a way, it's nice to feel this way again. The start of a relationship is the exciting part after all, but saying goodbye is going to be as hard as saying goodbye to Kieran when he left for university. Perhaps even harder since saying goodbye to Olivier will be for good.

'Are you okay?' Olivier asks, as if reading my mind.

'I'm fine. I'm just happy,' I say honestly and force a smile. He kisses me on the top of my head and carries on talking me through the pages of the guidebook.

When we arrive at the Pullman Hotel, I'm in awe. There's a partial view of the Eiffel Tower from the doorstep. I'm giddy. Partly because I've never seen the Eiffel Tower before, but mostly because I never splash out on myself, and this is one of the first proper luxuries I've treated myself to in forever, if you discount the fifteen-euro glass of champers that seems like forever ago. I even have the extra bonus of Olivier by my side.

We go to reception to check in and while the receptionist taps away on her computer, Olivier pulls me into a hug and kisses me on the cheek, relieving the tension in my cheeks from all the grinning.

'Are you celebrating anything this weekend?' the receptionist asks. *Only living a dream.*

'No,' I say politely.

'We are, darling. Don't play down your special birthday,' Olivier says, sliding his arm around my waist and squeezing me gently. I wonder if he thinks I'm passing for thirty or forty.

'I am just seeing a notification on the screen that you have been allocated a room upgrade,' the receptionist says with her front-of-house smile. 'An Eiffel Tower view.'

'You sneak!' I say as we fall into the lift, giggling.

'She wanted an excuse to upgrade us, I could tell.' He shrugs.

The room itself is plain but ultra-modern and an improvement on the studio in Arras by gigantic proportions. The sight of the king-sized bed chokes me a little when my eyes land on it. I'd been so hell-bent on convincing myself I was going to be okay when I left that I hadn't really thought about the sleeping arrangements. 'We can top and tail or build a pillow fortress, or if you're still uncomfortable, I will sleep on the floor,' Olivier says, sensing my discomfiture. I don't reply because I don't really know what to feel, but the last person I had in bed with me was a tonsillitis-ridden nine-year-old Kieran who stole the covers and kicked them to the floor before finally dozing off with his knees in the small of my back.

When we step out onto the balcony, the view of the tower takes my breath away. 'Just wait until you see it all lit up at night,' Olivier says, sensing my awe.

'Can we go and see it now?' I ask, almost jumping up and down.

'We can …' I sense a 'but' and look up at him with impatience. 'But—' *there it is* '—I think you should *experience* Paris first. You should connect with the city on a deeper level and really *feel* it first. You'll appreciate the Eiffel Tower so much more after that.'

'Okay.' I'm not really buying it but I'll play along. 'What do you have in mind?'

Soon, we're wandering the narrow, winding streets of the Latin Quarter, and I can feel myself absorbing the diverse café culture. Perhaps Olivier had a point. 'This is the authentic Parisian experience. Much better than just dashing to take a selfie by the tower, don't you think?'

'You're such a know-it-all.' I bump him playfully.

'Hey! I was just about to share with you an interesting fact.'

'I'm so sorry.' I pull a mock-serious expression. 'Sorry again. I really do want to hear it.'

He narrows his eyes. 'Okay. The Sorbonne, or the University of Paris, was founded in the twelfth century in this neighbourhood, and back then, the language spoken at universities was Latin so the students walking around here all spoke Latin, hence the name the Latin Quarter.'

'Huh,' I say. *So it's just one big student village.* I giggle.

Olivier looks puzzled. 'What's so funny?'

'I'm just thinking about all the warnings I gave my son Kieran when he left to go to university, about student nights and girls, and here I am, romping around a student village with a strange man.'

Olivier puts a dramatic hand on his chest. 'I'm not that strange, I hope.'

I shoot him a playful sideways glance.

'How about we do something more grown-up?'

I raise my eyebrows, more than a little concerned.

He laughs and a piece of hair falls over his left eye. 'I was thinking more a walk in the Luxembourg Gardens, but we can do the thing you have in mind if you like?'

I hit him playfully and ignore his last comment. 'The gardens sound wonderful.'

The gardens themselves are serene and beautiful and contrast hugely to the packed streets of the Latin Quarter. We stroll the gravel paths, taking in the statues, and amble by the octagonal lake, watching children and their parents sailing model boats.

'How do you always get it so right?' I ask Olivier, as we stop to watch, hand in hand.

'It is my job.' He flashes a grin.

'I don't just mean that.' I tilt my head to the side. 'You seem to always say and do the right things.'

'I don't think I do.'

'You're hard on yourself.' He doesn't reply. 'That's my opinion of you, anyway.'

'From my point of view I've got things quite wrong.'

I consider his words. I suppose rattling around in that big farmhouse all alone probably feels like something went wrong somewhere, and honestly, I don't know how he ended up alone. There's no shortage of interest: the teacher on the train trip, the waitress in Arras, me.

'It's you, Cath. You listen to what I have to say and you're interested in the same things as me.' He picks up a pebble and skims it across the water. 'Not many people would want to listen to my history lessons, not these days anyway. Not even Elena, and it is her job too.'

'You're different to the men I know.' He twists his mouth and I laugh. '*Good* different,' I clarify. He leads me over to a bench where we take a seat.

'I'm going to miss you when you leave, Cath.' My chest aches in response to his words. I don't even want to think about it. 'I hope we will stay in touch.'

'Of course.' I touch his leg without thinking and immediately feel awkward and look out across the water to avoid meeting his eye.

He places a gentle hand on my chin, turning my head to face him. The breeze blows a ribbon of hair across my eye and he brushes it away gently before kissing me softly on the lips, sending a jolt of fizz through me.

'What was that for?' Not that I'm complaining.

'It's just a perfect moment. The lake, the sun beating down and you, here by my side. I wanted to … put a cherry on top.'

And what a delicious cherry it was too. 'Saying goodbye to you is going to be hard,' I admit.

'How about we don't talk about it or think about it until we absolutely have to?' he says.

'Okay,' I reply as he pulls me into a hug, but it's easier said than done.

We sit there for a while, just people-watching, silently, while enjoying the warm comfort of each other's bodies.

***

After announcing I was starving, which I really was (and still am) we end up back in the pretty seventeenth-century streets of the Latin Quarter. Olivier is leading me by the hand through one of the bustling, café-lined streets to his favourite Parisian restaurant. We've passed several decent-looking places and the delicious wafts of white wine sauces and butter and garlic almost turn me savage enough to be an extra on *The Walking Dead*.

'We're here,' he announces, finally. It's a pretty brasserie, with dark wooden bistro furniture on the pavement and floral hanging baskets swinging from the burgundy canopy. 'It will be worth the wait, I promise. The Latin Quarter is a bit of a tourist trap – you can pay a lot of good money for bad food.'

A smartly dressed waiter hands us two leather-bound menus and pours us each a glass of water.

'If you like chicken, the coq au vin here is the best in Paris.'

'Well, that's me sold. Although I'd have been sold by "a lot of good money for bad food". I'm famished,' I tease.

A little while later, our food arrives in earthenware pots. Fresh bread is placed in the centre of the table. The chicken is a tender infusion of burgundy, lardons and onion.

Olivier is sitting back in his chair with one arm resting flat across the table. The sunlight creeps beneath the canopy, striking his eyes and illuminating them. If he catches me looking, I'll have to look away. They're hard to look at directly when they're like that.

When I've had my fill, I follow his line of sight. He's people-watching, and the lively crowd is quite a sight at that. The eclectic mix of style and individuality could keep you entertained for hours.

'I feel so relaxed in your company,' he says eventually, and I smile. Sitting in silent company is normally something that would have me scrambling for words so as not to appear boring, even if it was just Kieran I was with. It's different with Olivier; there's an unspoken, mutual understanding that we both need time to think, that we're so used to time in our own heads we can't go cold turkey.

Back in our small hotel room, I'm suddenly aware of our proximity. Holding hands in the bustling city is one thing but standing on opposite sides of a king-size bed is another. Olivier undoes the top button of his shirt and walks towards me, taking my hands in his, intertwining his fingers with mine. 'I meant what I said – I will sleep on the floor or we can sleep at opposite ends. I don't expect any more than you're willing to give, Cath.'

I sigh with relief. 'Thank you.'

'I just want to see Paris and spend time with you before you go.'

'Okay,' I say.

'It's a warm night, let's sit on the balcony,' he says. We have drinks that we've brought up from the bar and we sit on the balcony in the balmy evening air. It's dark now, and the Eiffel Tower is lit up. It's the epitome of Paris to me – the Parisian symbol from every movie ever set here – but Olivier was right. Paris is so much more than the Eiffel Tower; it's just the icing on the cake.

Chapter Twenty-Nine

The following day I wake from a wonderfully deep sleep. The pillows are still wedged between us and I peer over to see the tanned skin of Olivier's chest rising and falling. He's still asleep. The temptation to run my fingers through the sprinkling of dark hairs on his chest is so compelling that I get up and go to the bathroom just to stop myself. By the time I've taken care of my ablutions and re-emerged, he's awake, and concentrating on something on his phone.

'Morning,' I say, patting the ends of my hair with a towel. He looks delicious lying there in the pristine white sheets, like a caramel swirl in vanilla ice cream. The shower did nothing for the compelling urge, and it takes all of my strength not to dive back in the bed.

'Good morning. I was just checking on some things for today and I've got plenty of ideas if you want to hear about them over breakfast?'

'That sounds perfect.'

'But ...' He looks me over and grins. I tug the towel a little tighter around myself, hoping I haven't revealed anything.

'But what?'

'Nothing.' He smirks.

Over coffee and croissants, Olivier talks me through the plans for the day, but I find myself drifting off into my own head. I haven't had a man in my bed in forever. That was a big deal for me. I know I'm a grown woman and that nothing even happened – we built a pillow dam, for goodness' sake, and it had the tenacity of the Hoover Dam – but still.

When I replay the night over, I'd actually slept like a baby despite the newness of the situation. I thought I'd be sleeping on eggshells, scared I'd break wind or snore or wake up with disgusting morning breath or something equally horrendous but nothing like that happened.

'Cath?' The sound of my name brings me back to the moment.

'Sorry, I was miles away.'

He grins. 'Somewhere good I hope?'

'You could say that.' I smile shyly.

'Anyway, I was wondering if you thought the plans for today sounded okay?'

I haven't listened to a word he's said since we sat down but I trust him implicitly. 'They sound perfect.'

'Great.' He tucks into his breakfast and I follow suit.

We take a champagne riverboat ride on the Seine, visit Notre Dame and walk a large chunk of the glamorous Champs-Élysées, where I spot bored husbands lugging shopping bags. I think about the comment Harry had made to Roland calling it the 'Chumps-Élysées', which makes me laugh. We carry on to the busy junction housing the Arc de Triomphe. It's a tourist's paradise and even I, a practical stranger to social media, am compelled to post a picture on Facebook.

We stop for a coffee in a café with a view of the Arc de Triomphe. 'And I thought you were here to stop me falling into tourist traps,' I say teasingly as we take a seat in the wicker chairs outside and I spy the extortionate price of a cuppa.

'Sometimes you just have to go with it.' He shrugs.

Our coffees arrive quickly, the staff seemingly eager to keep the in-out cycle of custom going.

Olivier is over-stirring his coffee. His lips are pursed, and when he draws a deep breath, I know he's about to talk about something I'd rather ignore. 'Is there any way we can see each other after you've gone?'

I've already thought about it and don't see a way. Saying goodbye is going to be tough – I don't want to have to do it again another time. 'I don't see how.'

'You could move to France, you could join the business. You were great with the kids last week – you're a natural.'

If things were different, I'd jump at the chance to spend my days with this gorgeous man, in a beautiful place, and have the fairy-tale happy ever after but that isn't real life and I have responsibilities. People don't just up and leave. 'I'm all Kieran has. Even though he's not around, he needs a home to come back to, and I'm not just talking about the house. *I'm* his home too. I'm all he has.' I get another stab of guilt for being away from him for so long.

Olivier glances down at the table. 'I had to ask.'

My chest feels heavy and I can't say the thought hadn't crossed my mind. 'I know.'

We sip our coffee, listening to the cars beeping at the busy junction. 'You could come to England,' I say.

'Spending more time with you is what I want so much, but I can't desert the business. I have to ensure its success so that Elena is taken care of. After she refused the money from our parents' house, I vowed she would always earn well through the business, but if I leave, I would fear for its survival. Both Julien and Elena lack strong business acumen. They're great with customers and have fantastic rapport and knowledge, but growth … I don't think they could make that happen.'

'I guess in this life, at least, we're just not meant to be,' I say sombrely. Olivier doesn't reply but he sort of twists his mouth

256

in sad agreement. 'A few months down the line we'd probably hate each other's guts, and surely having this bank of perfect memories is better than that. It's why the romcoms always end when the couple get together because the after part just isn't as good.' *I will actually never know.*

After our coffees, we head back towards the Eiffel Tower and I start to feel quite giddy. 'Are you finally taking me up?'

'Yes, but first we'll go back to the hotel and change.'

I shoot him a confused look. 'Why? I've waited for two days to see this tower. Please, can we just go up now,' I mock-plead with my hands.

'Then half an hour more won't matter.' He lets out a resigned breath. 'I've booked a table for dinner.'

I sigh. 'So I have to wait until after dinner?'

'No.' He draws the word out. 'We are going to walk the esplanade, take the lift to the third floor of the tower, explore the shops on the second and *have dinner* on the first.'

I get a sudden stab of guilt over not listening to the plans this morning and attempt to cover my tracks. 'Of course, I remember you saying at breakfast.'

'It was a surprise. I didn't tell you at breakfast – I knew you were away with the fairies.' He grins, shaking his head.

'I wasn't, I …'

'You're blushing.' He's still smiling, relishing in my embarrassment.

'If you must know, I was thinking about this attractive man I found in my bed this morning.' *I might as well make him blush too.* But he doesn't – he just smiles and walks on.

We stop on the bridge across the river and watch a glass-roof boat pass below. He turns to face me.

'What about this man in your bed? I hope he was a gentleman.' He raises an eyebrow.

'Oh, he was, but perhaps tonight, he won't be.' I wink and turn on my heel, heading towards the tower. He doesn't follow me straight away and I hear him jogging behind to catch me up a few seconds later.

We pass the tower and go straight to the hotel to get changed. In the room, the air feels charged and I feel lightheaded knowing it's my fault. As I run the straighteners through my hair, my mind wanders to the places I'd like his hands to visit. My lower abdomen flutters in a way that's no longer peculiar. 'I think I need some air,' I shout to Olivier, who is shaving in the bathroom.

I step out onto the balcony, pulling the door to behind me. As I look out at the tower, twinkling in the pinky dusk, I wonder if it would be the worst thing on earth to face the final frontier with Olivier. The thought both excites and terrifies me. But you only live once.

Chapter Thirty

The esplanade is busy with tourists. Armed police patrol the area, discreetly blending into the crowds, and tacky souvenir stalls have popped up nearby to capitalise on the evening flurry. My hand is wrapped comfortably in Olivier's, but there's still a tension between us. It's lingered since I made that comment earlier about not being a gentleman, and I'm not sure if I've broken what we had. I'm hoping we'll both relax a little when we sit down and have a drink.

We're ushered through the airport-style security and to the lift. There are quite a lot of people bundling in so Olivier and I shuffle backwards until he's pressed up against the side and I'm pressed up against him. I'd been facing him, to avoid having to face a complete stranger, but now it seems strangely intimate with my soft curves pressed perfectly into his firm indentations. The lift sets off on its diagonal, upward path, and Olivier looks into my eyes and brushes my windswept hair away from my face. We may as well be the only two people in the lift because everyone else has turned into colourful confetti and blown away.

The lift stops and my body deflates as we move apart to get out on the first floor. 'We need to get the next lift,' he says, pulling me by the hand. Soon we're in the glass lift heading to the top and taking in the whole of Paris. People say they feel Christmassy;

but right now I feel well and truly *Parissy*, and yes, that's a made-up word because no word in the English language can truly describe this feeling.

Unexpectedly, the champagne bar is more of a kiosk, but then why would you want to be inside drinking when you can be outside looking at *this*? The buildings below look like a Legoland construction, and between them, illuminated boats sail down the inky black river as the skyscrapers of La Défense glitter in the distance. It's fairly crowded, but we're able to find a vantage point offering perfect views. Olivier stands beside me, curling his fingers around my hand, sending a current of electricity up my arm and right through my chest. I'm desperate for him to kiss me. He doesn't. Instead, he does the next best thing and offers me a drink.

I hold our spot while he goes to get them. My body is still tingling with desire in his absence, so I take the time to relish the feeling. Other than watching romantic movies, *this* is my only experience of romance. I've always been somewhat overlooked in the past, like the dull bag of butterscotch beside the bright and funky Skittles packet. Not that I'm complaining. A drunken one-night stand brought me Kieran and I wouldn't swap him for being swept off my feet by a man, but I think any girl could be forgiven for getting excited while standing at the top of the Eiffel Tower accompanied by a wonderful, handsome man and a glass of champers.

But just like any dream, it will only last the night.

'For you, madame.' Olivier's hand pushes between two tourists whom I hadn't noticed had invaded my personal space and stolen Olivier's spot. He squeezes his shoulder through the minute gap and the rest of his body follows until he's back by my side.

'Did you know the base pillars of the tower are aligned with the four points of a compass?' he says.

'Did you know you don't have to try and impress me anymore?' I reply teasingly.

He pulls a mock-sad face. 'I thought you liked my trivia.'

'I do. I'm sorry. Tell me more,' I say, stroking his arm in a way that could be construed as flirtatious, but the merry dance of the bubbles has given me the confidence to go for it anyway.

'The Eiffel Tower was a radiotelegraph station and during the Great War, it intercepted enemy radio communications. It was almost scrapped in 1909 too.'

I tug at his ear and peer behind it animatedly, prompting a look of confusion in response. 'Just looking for your off-button.'

'Fine. What do you want to talk about?' He folds his arms, pretending to be offended, but the corner of his mouth twitches like he's stifling a grin.

Okay, I asked for this. 'Erm … Tell me where your favourite place in the world is?'

His arm slides around my waist and pulls me in close. The heat from his body radiates. 'Well, this is hard to beat.' He gestures with his plastic champagne flute, to the panoramic view of Paris. 'But the city isn't where I could spend my days forever. A vineyard would be a good start.' He winks.

'Yes, but if you drank all the wine, you wouldn't own it for very long, and you probably wouldn't live too long either.'

'You're too practical, Cath.' He shakes his head jokingly. 'Okay, somewhere by the sea. Some rugged beach on any part of the Brittany coastline would suit me. How about you?'

'As you know, I'm not very well travelled … but being here right now, I'm not just seeing the view, I'm feeling it.' I don't really have the words to explain what I mean, how it isn't just the stunning vista, the wonderful man by my side and the fizz of giddiness in my head. It's like I'm bathing in a cocktail of it all and I don't want it to end. I know he gets it because this is what he's wanted me to experience all along.

'Hopefully, this is just the beginning of your adventures.' He clinks his plastic flute against mine.

'Hopefully,' I echo.

When we've finished our drinks, we take the lift down to the second floor, where we visit the souvenir shop. There is just about anything you'd want an Eiffel Tower emblazoned on in here. I buy a novelty tin of biscuits for Kieran, reasoning that he loves biscuits and the tin will be useful for storing knickknacks in after. I lose sight of Olivier, but when I step outside, he comes up behind me and wraps me in a hug.

'I bought you a gift,' he says, holding up a small white paper bag.

I cast an intrigued glance his way and take it from him. Inside, there is a small, metal key ring with a miniature Eiffel Tower dangling from the ring.

'It's to remember this day.' He says it in such a way that I know that what he really means is that it's to remember *him* by. A huge lump forms in my throat and I have to swallow hard before I can thank him.

In the first-floor restaurant, we're led to a window seat. I don't know how we swung it, but we did. The couple who'd been queuing next to us scowl a little as they're seated towards the centre of the restaurant, and for the first time in my life I don't even care.

'This is amazing,' I say, running my hand over the thick, white tablecloth after we've taken our seats. We're handed the set menus and offered wine immediately. 'And the service is pretty good too.'

When I look to Olivier for agreement, I can tell he's not really listening because he's looking at me pensively with his chin resting on his fist.

'I'm not ready to say goodbye to you, Cath. Could we see each other again?' Despite the fact I sensed his brooding, the question takes me by surprise.

'I thought we'd been through this. How could we?' I speak gently and he shrugs, defeated.

'I don't know, but I'm only an hour from Calais; you're only an hour or so from Dover. It just seems that the distance shouldn't be an issue.'

'We live in different countries. There's the expense, for starters …' The waiter returns with our drinks and I take a much-needed sip.

'I can make it over a few times a year.'

'I can't commit to coming here a few times a year. Olivier, this trip has cost me everything I have.' I didn't mean to say that aloud but it's true. 'You'll meet someone else more local and forget about me.' I keep my tone light, but really, I know this will happen and the thought churns my insides. It's my attempt at self-preservation. I reach across and put my hand on his, glancing upwards to meet his eyes. 'Can we just enjoy the time we have left together?'

'Of course.' He smiles weakly. 'I have plenty more facts about the Eiffel Tower to entertain you with.'

I giggle. 'Perfect.'

The rest of the meal passes with pleasant conversation, but it's false and I can sense a deeper sadness. We've chucked a blanket over the elephant in the room but its big, fat presence is there weighing heavily upon us. I've zoned out. I don't want to listen to any more trivia, or talk about books and movies, because what's the point in getting to know someone only to lose them soon? It's like dieting before an all-inclusive holiday, or spending a whole day preparing beef Wellington for dinner just to wolf it down in two minutes.

I watch his strong jawline tense as he chews between snippets of conversation. His shirtsleeves have been rolled back, exposing his thick forearms and a smart, chunky watch, beneath which I can see the edge of a white mark that the sun didn't catch. His top button is open, exposing that fine sprinkling of chest hair that I still want to rub my hands over.

There's only one more thing Olivier can give me.

***

It's a short distance back to the hotel. We're walking hand in hand and swaying slightly with the merriment a few glasses of wine has brought.

'I've never been on a date before,' I confess, spinning on my heel to face him. His body crashes into mine just a split second later and our faces are just inches apart, sending sparks between us.

'What, never?' He sounds surprised.

'Nope. Not before you. The people who I knew all just fell into being couples after group nights out with work or mutual friends. Formal dates weren't really a thing when I was in my prime.'

'You're still in your prime.' His words send small eruptions through my chest.

'So have you been on many dates?' I ask, taking position back by his side so we can continue walking.

'A few. You have to remember, Elena is my sister and her main goal in life is to see her hero brother happy.'

I smile. 'But she hasn't found you *the one* yet?'

'No, her philosophy has been more along the lines of *someone* rather than *the one*, and I've never been on a second date. Other than with my old girlfriend, that is.'

'Ever?' I can't imagine why unless he's incredibly fussy.

He shakes his head. 'I think that's why she's been subtler with you. She knows with you something is different and is frightened I'll get hurt.'

There's not really anything I can say to that, but I can keep up the pretence that we both know what we're doing, and we won't get hurt.

'Someone must have been worthy of a second date.' I won't believe him if he says there wasn't anyone.

'I think I was the one not worthy of a second date,' he says bluntly.

'I find that hard to believe.' Unless it was during his struggling years, though I doubt even Elena would have been matchmaking back then.

'Nobody seemed interested in a second date. I suppose they thought I was boring as I've very little to talk about other than my work. I don't have great life experiences or anything.'

'Well, anyone who thinks that simply doesn't deserve you.' My words hang in the air until we stop outside the hotel.

Olivier turns to me and cups my face in his hands. 'I don't care about anyone else. Tonight has been the most perfect evening and I'll always have it to remember. I don't care if I never meet another woman again.'

Pressure builds inside of me. I know exactly what he means. I've been fine on my own for so many years that I know I'll be fine once I'm home, but something about this experience has changed me. It's like a button has been flipped in my head and while I know I'll be okay all alone, I don't want to be. His eyes bore into mine, hypnotic blue, powerful and encompassing. 'It's the perfect weekend and we'll always share our memories,' I say.

He places a gentle kiss on my lips, sending a surge through me. The familiar smell of his skin is magnetic, and I pull him closer. The lights from nearby buildings cast romantic background lighting and the moment is so perfect my chest heaves and moisture fills my eyes.

We walk back to the hotel in silence. Olivier has his arm around my shoulders and I'm tucked cosily into the nook of his arm. We bypass the bar and head straight up to the room and out onto the balcony. I lean on the rail, looking right, towards the tower, and Olivier snuggles up behind me, placing his arms either side of mine. I hadn't noticed before just how strong his upper arms are. *Such safe arms to be wrapped in. But they won't be there when I fall.*

The breeze sends a shiver through me, and goose bumps rise on my bare arms. Olivier presses his warm body against mine, shielding me from the cold. He runs his hand up my arm, but it has an adverse effect on my goose bumps and more seem to arise. He kisses my neck softly, working his way up from my collarbone, making them worse, and soon his hands are on my hips, pulling me closer. I throw my head back, enjoying every one of his delicious kisses until I can take no more and turn around to kiss him back. I manoeuvre him back towards the patio doors and into the room and start to unbutton his shirt, running my hands over the soft hair on his chest when it falls open. He places his hands on my outer thighs, beneath the hem of my sundress, and glides them up to my hips, kissing me as he does.

I push him down onto the bed and watch him as he looks at me in a way I've never seen before. His blue eyes are fixed on me but narrowed slightly, and his head is tilted to the side. It gives me a surge of confidence and, caught in the moment, I slip my dress off over my head, and stand there in just my underwear. His eyes drink me in, his lips falling apart slightly as he reaches for my hand and pulls me into his lap. His huge hands cup my bottom as he kisses me intensely, then he stands up and turns around, laying me down on my back. In that moment, I stare up at him, willing him to come to me.

'Are you sure you want to do this?'

I bite my lip and tug the waistband of his trousers, pulling him down to meet me. I've never wanted anything more in my life.

Chapter Thirty-One

We're standing on the platform and I can't believe it's time to say goodbye. After last night, it feels wrong, like it shouldn't have to happen. This thing between us has now been cemented and our bond feels too strong to break.

After we'd made love, I'd fallen asleep in the safety of his arms and that's where I'd woken up this morning, but the dream is now over and relishing the warmth and safety of being in his arms this morning was the last sweet drop of it.

Leaving him now we're at the train station feels akin to tearing off a limb and casting it aside for the sheer hell of it. The point of leaving feels lost, and while I know I'm going home *for* my son, I'm not going home *to* my son. Perhaps if I knew Olivier better, I could justify some toing and froing to France, but the fact of the matter is, it's been just four weeks. The rational-thinking side of my brain is vying for a promotion.

Olivier's blue eyes are rinsed with sadness and a deep V forms a crevice between his eyebrows, mirroring the pain inside me. He wraps me tightly in a hug and I crumble into him. His strong arms support me, keeping me upright. His head is resting on mine and as he pulls away to look at me, I feel dampness where his cheek had been. It's enough to send a torrent of emotion surging through me and tears sprout from my own eyes. Once they start flowing, I can't stop them.

'This is one of the hardest things I've ever had to do.' My words come out broken between sobs. My floodgates are open and Olivier is the dam. *Without him, I'll never be able to stem the flow of sadness.*

'I know,' he whispers. 'Me too.' He kisses me on the head and holds me silently for a little while longer as more and more people start to mill around the platform. My chest thunders as it gets closer to departure time and I search and scour my head for a better plan, but Mrs Rational-Thinking has left me in the lurch.

'Why does doing the right thing feel so wrong?' I say. He looks down directly into my eyes, and I can see his pain so vividly that I'm not sure if it's mine or his I feel puncturing my chest – or both.

His body sags. It's just an impossible situation. 'Your being here has brought a light into my life that hasn't been there in a long time.'

I have no words for that. My heart is tight and painful. It's been wrung out and the saggy, empty shell of it rests somewhere low in my stomach. There's no cure other than time. He steps forward and leans in, placing his soft lips on mine. They're salty and moist with the meld of our tears. He kisses me slowly and I respond, letting the pain dissolve for just one more moment. The crowds around us become a blur of noise and colour that begins to fade out the longer the kiss goes on. I allow myself to float in the moment one last time before the burdens of shopping and buses takes me back to reality. Warmth fills my veins and creeps across my skin and nothing can take away the memory of being in this right now.

Most of the people are on the train now and there is just one minute until departure. 'I have to go.' I'm not quite able to believe I've said the words. Concrete fills my cavities and the warmth lifts, leaving no imprint, just its numb residue. It feels too soon.

He nods in agreement, bowing his head to the floor. I stand on my tiptoes to kiss him on the cheek and he whispers his goodbye. It still doesn't feel real as I tear myself away and go to the train door.

'Cath, wait,' he says. I turn to look at him. 'Don't go. You don't have to. Stay, and let's work things out.'

With one foot on the step, I want to run back and throw my body onto his. I want to wrap my arms and legs around him and smother him in kisses and never leave him. Instead, I blow him a single kiss allowing my lips to linger on my fingers for a moment as though that would enable me to pack in everything I feel for him. My heart tears in two as I pull myself through the train doors and find my seat on autopilot. I'm on the platform side of the station and as I go through the motions of stowing my coat and case, I can feel him watching me. I can't look.

Once I'm in my seat, I throw my head in my hands. I must look a puffy mess but I'm finding it hard to care. *I'm going back to my life. The life I've always been content with*, I tell myself. The train rumbles to life and I steal a glance outside. He's standing there looking forlorn and my heart aches for him too. I know he'll meet someone – he just needs to let them in and now he's tried it with me, he'll have no trouble doing it again. That brings me some comfort – he deserves to be happy. I will be again too, once things are back to normal. I just need some time to transform myself into a shape that fits perfectly back into my old life.

Slowly, the train pulls away, tearing an invisible tether from my chest. He's gone in a flash. Just like that – ending a summer to remember and one I now need to forget.

Chapter Thirty-Two

When I turn the key and cross the threshold of my house, everything is normal. The smells of my life waft from the carpet fibres
and curtains. The faint smell of the lino flooring in the kitchen
and the slightly damp smell near the soggy plaster by the front
door are all equally familiar, but something is off. The house feels
smaller but that isn't it. It feels empty. I know if I speak my voice
will echo because with Kieran and Gary gone, there is little life
left in the place to absorb the vibrations. Quietly, I say 'hello',
knowing that nobody is there to answer and knowing that it will
sound hollow. It does.

After dumping my bags on my bed, I go to wash the travel
grime from my face and notice the mirror in the bathroom.
Gary has done a good job. I smile, hoping it's a sign he's turned
himself around. Back in the bedroom, I flick the TV on for
background noise, and David the weatherman is on so I ignore
my unpacking and sit down to see what he has in store for me.
'Rain,' he says. Something about a big band coming in from the
Atlantic. Typical. My mind is thrown back to my last run-in with
the Atlantic and a single tear rolls down my cheek as I remember
the day at Le Touquet. The tear is salty and it stings my sun-
weathered skin but I don't wipe it away. I want to feel something

because otherwise, I'll feel nothing. Like this house, I'll be a hollow shell.

As I watch David, I notice things about him I hadn't before. He doesn't look as much like Olivier as I'd thought – he's all polished and shiny. The thick TV make-up gives him a weird 'too perfect' look at first glance. But if you really look, his hair is thinning on top and his nose is a funny shape. He does a weird mouth-closed smile where one corner turns down instead of up. I used to think it was sexy, but now I wonder if it would be safe to be near him in a dark alley.

My phone pings and I jump. It's Kieran.

Are you home? Hope you had a good trip. Can't make it back this weekend because there's a fancy-dress ale trail thing. Sorry. xx

My upper body sags. I'll have to get used to this.

Once everything is neatly back in my wardrobe I go downstairs, expecting it to need a good clean, but the place is spotless. I know Gary won't apologise for the things he said. When I next see him, he'll be chipper and friendly like nothing ever happened. Cleaning the house is his way of saying sorry and thank you and everything else he should have said, and I accept that.

The next morning, I go through my routine. Shower, breakfast and coffee. Why? The word pops into my head. Why did I shower? Why put make-up on and style my hair? Why did I make sure my T-shirt hung right over my jeans? I probably won't see another person today unless I go to the shop. I'll see another person at work tomorrow, but I have a uniform for that. I let out a humourless laugh for nobody's benefit when I realise that I could probably give nearly all my clothes to charity now and be largely unaffected.

The trouble is, I've been spoilt. I was perfectly happy with my life until I had the taste of something different and now I want more. Like a child who plays at their friend's house and thinks their friend's toys are better and their own boring. Is it so wrong

271

to want more from life? Is it so wrong to realise I want more at this stage in my life? I don't know the answer, but I do know things won't ever feel the same again.

'Pull yourself together, woman; live for the now.' For some reason, Martha's voice fills my head and the words ring true. I can sit here and wallow in self-pity, or I can get out there and live; otherwise, what is this all for? My great-grandfather's words echo now. Without wasting a second unpacking, I grab my phone and start looking for local language classes. Bingo. There's a French class on a Wednesday evening that I can sign up to now. I take my bank card and enrol before I have the chance to talk myself out of it. I could even do a cookery class – the world is my oyster. I'll learn a skill, meet people … Why haven't I done this before?

Once I've finished, I pick up the keys and rub my new Eiffel Tower key ring gently with my thumb. Who knows – after opening myself up to a man, maybe in time, I could even learn to love again.

Chapter Thirty-Three

'It's great to be home,' I say at work. I'm unconvincing at best as I spout out the same line I've been using all week. I've come up with a bank of useful clichéd phrases to convince my colleagues that I'm fine. They range from: 'France was wonderful but you can't beat an English cuppa,' to: 'It's good to be back in my own bed.' People are buying them too because it's what they expect to hear. I just wish the words could suppress the empty, hollow black hole that's been upsetting my stomach since I got home.

Kaitlynn leans on my checkout during a lull. 'So, how does it feel to have had your Gary surgically extracted?' She's just back from a week off in Wales, and we haven't had a chance to catch up properly yet. She knows all about the Olivier situation because she rang me when I was on the train and practically incoherent. She knows better than to ask at work.

'A relief, to be honest. It's nice to have the TV all to myself again.' I also have a bank of clichés for Gary-based questions because I'm not as overjoyed by his absence as I'd thought I would be. It's as though I don't want to think about anything or talk to anyone anymore. I've been back from France a week now and I'm mopey to the point people are starting to ask me what's wrong. Or whether I have the holiday blues. For my own sanity,

273

I've banned myself from thinking about Olivier and if I'm not super strict with myself, I find myself doing it anyway so I've come up with a strategy that I've even given a catchy slogan to: 'A romcom a day keeps memories of Olivier at bay.'

So, when my mind has really started to wander on an evening when I'm at home alone, I've been sticking on a good old-fashioned romantic comedy because lusting after some unobtainable Hollywood hunk is much more palatable than dwelling on a Frenchman who was so close to obtainable, but so unobtainable it was cruel. He sent a text to see if I got home okay, but I didn't reply. It just seemed like I'd be opening up a can of worms. I'd agonised over sending a quick 'yes, thanks', which seemed cold or a more honest 'yes, and I miss you so much'.

In the end I just left it and I feel terrible but it's for the best. I'm going cold turkey. The romcoms are working for the most part and getting out of the house for my French class on Wednesday worked a treat. I have a great book to read when I'm alone in bed, when the house is quiet and still, because that's when I'm really at risk of slipping into a fantasy life with Olivier. I'm worried that if I do, I won't be able to pull myself back out and I'll be found decomposed in bed by Kieran on one of his rare visits home. My headstone will read: 'Died of a broken heart' when really it should say: 'Died of a full heart, of a love so powerful it took her.' Literally. What? *Shut up, Cath.*

That's if he finds me at all, of course. I guess I'm just boring old Mum to him now and probably won't ever be needed much by him again. It probably should feel liberating – I have my freedom back, after all – but really, I'm still on a leash. I can't go off to France and live happily ever after with Olivier because Kieran does still need me to be here. He needs his home here at least.

I haven't told Kaitlynn yet because she'll be devastated, but I've been thinking of a career change. Gary's words about me being stuck here resonated a little and after working with the children on the train ride in the Somme Valley, I've been thinking about becoming a teaching assistant. I've even made enquiries about qualifications and I'm quite excited about it.

A customer plonking her shopping on my conveyor belt disrupts my train of thought. Eggs, chicken, bread, milk, and I'm back in real life with a beep, beep, beep. 'Would you like any help with your packing, madam?' I say with a smile, thankful for the routine of it. She shakes her head, as ninety per cent of the customers do and I continue scanning her items, with the odd bit of small talk thrown in as per my training as she packs them up. 'Forty-three fifty-two,' I say, waiting for her to enter her card and PIN.

The next customer has already started loading the conveyor belt and I know it's the start of my favourite time of day: the mid-morning rush. I don't even look up because this is where I excel – speedy scanning. I love seeing the conveyor belt clear at the end, ready for the next customer – it's like my own personal challenge, clearing the belt before it's filled up again. Cured meats, Camembert, a freshly baked loaf, cured ham, and a bottle of wine that looks familiar – *Louis Jadot, Macon Village Chapelle aux Loups*. The sight of it paralyses me for a second before my till beeps and the 'check twenty-five' message pops up. I look up to assess the customer's age and the sight of him sends me into shock. My mouth is too dry to speak.

'*Bonjour*, Cath.' There's no smile on his face and his blue eyes are wide and sad.

'Olivier?' My whole body is shaking. 'What are you doing here?'

'Would you believe me if I said I was in the neighbourhood?' He shrugs.

'Not really.' I stand up so I can look him in the eye, unable to absorb the fact he's really here.

'Cath, I—'

A middle-aged man plonks a joint of beef of the conveyor belt and, simultaneously, both Olivier and I bark: 'This checkout is closed.' The man opens his mouth to speak but, instead, huffs and walks off.

'Why are you here, Olivier?' My voice trembles with nerves, excitement and shock all balled up into one.

He looks down to his shopping. 'Two reasons,' he says simply. 'The first is that I needed some groceries.' I cock my head to the side. 'Okay, that's not a reason. The first is that I missed you, Cath. I know we haven't known one another very long and my being here probably seems ridiculous to you.'

I shake my head. 'Not ridiculous, exactly,' I say, but he doesn't seem to hear me. It's like he has to get something off his chest.

'But I can't seem to concentrate on anything or think about anything other than you.' For the first time, his eyes meet mine straight on. Those familiar electric-blue bolts.

'You've become my *raison d'être.*'

My eyes widen and my chest swells. His reason for being. He's looking at me with hopeful, expectant eyes but I don't know what he wants me to say. His feelings echo my own but what does it change? Him being here, wanting us to be together, is no different to me being there and wanting to be together. The location and timing are different but our circumstances are the same.

'Olivier, I …' I'm stuck. There's so much I want to say, yet I have nothing. I want so much to agree, and tell him I've been lost without him and I've missed him so much that I've had to employ distraction strategies. But what good is it when all it will do is prolong the recovery period we both need? 'Olivier, we still live in different countries. Your business is in France and my son is here. I miss you too but you must understand that there isn't a version of "us" that could ever work. Nothing has changed.' My brow crumples, a bit like my soul.

He takes a deep breath and holds my gaze for a moment before nodding slowly. 'You're right.' He smiles tightly. 'Too many movies perhaps.' He hands me thirty pounds to cover his shopping and

I take it silently as he bags it up. When I hand him his change, he holds onto my hand for a moment.

'I'm sorry, Cath. It was wrong of me to come.' He turns to walk away.

'Wait,' I blurt, causing him and a few shoppers to look round in surprise. 'What was the second reason?' He looks at me, puzzled. 'You said you came here for two reasons, but you only gave me one.'

'Oh.' He looks sheepishly at his bag. 'I was going to see if you wanted to join me for a picnic.'

'Yes.' It pops out of my mouth before I have time to think about it properly. 'Since you're here anyway, I mean, and we're friends. I don't see why not. How long are you here for?'

'I leave tomorrow morning. What time do you finish work?'

'Five.'

'I'll meet you outside at five.'

And then I'll have to say goodbye all over again.

Chapter Thirty-Four

It's five on the dot and I'm standing outside work in my familiar polyester uniform and pleather shoes. My hair is flat and desperately in need of a wash and my half-hearted make-up feels like it's done a slalom down my face. To top that off, it's piddling down with rain as expected. David might not be as attractive since the removal of my rose-tinted glasses, but his weather reports are still the best. I've no idea where we could go for a picnic because the sights of Berrybridge don't really compare much to the beautiful rustic towns of France.

My heart flips. He's walking towards me, so I have a frantic, last-ditch attempt at smoothing down my flat-yet-defiantly-frizzy hair and I run my finger underneath my lash lines in the hope I don't have panda eyes.

He's close now and there's a small, uneasy smile on his face. He's so close, in fact, I need to make a snap decision on how to greet him. Kiss on the cheek? Hug? I feel panicky. He's too close now and if I don't decide, there will be an awkward scenario where we both go in for something different and I end up kissing his ear. I hold my hands behind my back and kink my knee a little, and now I feel like an idiot for curtseying to him.

He doesn't seem to notice and instead pulls me into an all-embracing hug and I melt into him, allowing every muscle in my body to relax as our pieces fit together and the panic dissolves. My knees almost buckle beneath me, but even if they did, I wouldn't notice because he's got a firm grip on me. His warmth and fresh, familiar scent soothes away all my doubts to the point where I can't remember them anymore. A warm tear rolls down my cheek and I'm thankful to the rain for masking it.

'I have no idea where we're going to go for a picnic,' I say, patting my face dry with the sleeve of my denim jacket.

He holds me with outstretched arms and tips his head to the side. 'I have somewhere already in mind.'

'Where?' How can he possibly know where is good to have a picnic on a wet day in Berrybridge?

He taps the side of his nose. 'Follow me.'

We walk in the rain umbrella-less, because despite David the weatherman's warnings, I'd forgotten mine as usual. For once, I don't care. It feels cool and refreshing after a day at work, and it completely negates the bad hair issue. Five minutes have passed and we're still nowhere particularly picnic-worthy. In fact, we're approaching the car park by the park. I say nothing and instead just wonder if perhaps it's a French thing to dine al fresco even in the rain. It's unlikely.

Then I see where this is going. The red coach sits proudly in the far corner of the car park, shining like it's been polished for an occasion. 'It's not the Seventies and that's not a VW Campervan,' I joke, but he frowns in confusion as a weak laugh escapes him.

'Welcome aboard,' he says, opening the doors. As I step inside, I gasp. Rose petals are scattered down the aisle. The overhead lighting is warm and yellow, and the seats at the back have been covered with the red and white gingham tablecloth from our picnic at the vineyard. A bunch of hand-tied tulips is set neatly on one of the seats next to a tray holding two wine glasses.

'Olivier!' I'm gobsmacked. 'Nobody has ever done anything

like this for me before. It's lovely.' I add the last bit on, but it's by no means an afterthought.

'Cath, I …' It's unusual for Olivier to be lost for words but he is, until he changes tack. 'It's not quite the champagne region of France, but it's very close to the champagne aisle of your super-market.' I smile, appreciative of the mood-lightening comment.

'Shall we?' I say, gesturing to the back seat.

Soon we're sitting down and Olivier is pouring the wine. 'I almost put pictures up of the vineyard but thought that might have been a step too far.'

'Definitely. You're in England now and it's the law to enjoy, embrace and endlessly complain about the bad weather,' I joke. 'You can't just mask it, you know.'

'Ahh yes. The Great British weather.'

He shrugs off his coat, revealing a casual blue polo shirt under-neath, then starts slicing bread and opening the cheese and other things. I watch his upper arms tense and the muscles move under the skin as he hacks at the crusty bread while I sip my wine, enjoying the feeling of being spoilt one last time.

'So how's life back in Blighty?' He hands me a paper plate of cheese and bread.

'It's good to be back.' The lie trips off my tongue as easily as it has done all week.

'That's good,' he says quietly. 'Life in France has been quiet.'

'Is the business okay?' I ask. Surely quiet isn't good when you're in tourism – the season isn't yet over.

'The business is thriving. We're turning down requests. Next year we want to expand the business and take on more guides. Maybe even another coach.'

'That's fantastic, Olivier.'

'I meant things are quiet without you.' I knew what he meant; I just didn't want him to say it. The words are too hard to hear.

'I know. Things are quiet without you too. I'm sorry I didn't text you back – I thought it would complicate things.'

'I understand.' We fall silent and I pick at a thread on the hem of my tunic. The air becomes thick between us and the atmosphere heavy. Olivier takes my plate from my hand and places it down on the empty seat beside me.

'The truth is, Cath, everything I have seems pointless if you're not there to share it with. I know I did it before, but now I've seen what it's like to have you there, I can't go back to just … existing.' He lets his arms flop down beside him.

'Saying goodbye to you was the hardest thing I've ever had to do.' My voice quivers.

He pulls me into a hug and I sob quietly into his shoulder, hoping he can't hear. When I've composed myself, I pull away and look at him. '*Je manquer tu.*'

He lets out a soft laugh.

'What?' Heat rises up the back of my neck. '*Je te manque?*'

He shakes his head.

'What? How is that still wrong?' I make a 'hmph' sound. 'I had a really rubbish French tutor, you know.'

'*Tu me manques.* You are missing to me,' he says. 'Not I miss you.'

The words warm my chest. 'Ah, that makes more sense. The person missing should be the subject, because they are the focus.' I meet his eyes and whisper, 'They're what matters.'

'Exactly.' His eyes are intense. 'Because the person missing from your life is the most important.'

My eyes fall to my lap and the muscles in my forehead tense as the sadness inside me manifests on my face.

'So why are we torturing ourselves?' he says, placing his hands on my shoulders. 'What if there is a way to make this work?'

'How?' My chest lifts even though I can't think of a way.

'Well, as I've said, the business is growing all the time. We need more staff and although the Somme region is our bread and butter, we're expanding further afield and we're bringing people across to the UK all the time.'

I'm about to protest and say how we can hardly base a relationship on a few trips to the UK each year but I'm intrigued to see how he thinks it will work. 'Go on.'

'Julien and Elena want to try for a family soon and so being in the Somme Valley will really work for them whereas taking over the UK operations might just work for me …'

'How often are we talking?'

'Well, in summer, I could run at least one trip here a week. The London tours are so popular as are the Scottish and Welsh trips. In the winter, we could run a busy Christmas shopping schedule. And then you'll have holidays too; you could come and stay with me. I don't know the ins and outs or if it will work but it seems foolish not to at least try, don't you think?'

'I thought I'd settle back into my life and be happy with the memories we shared but truth be told, it's been so hard. I've never felt pain quite like it,' I say honestly.

'Me too,' he replies. 'And how do you feel now I'm here?'

'Better.' I entwine my fingers in his. 'Happy. Cured.'

'Me too,' he says softly.

'Being together is like pain relief, so, I suppose we need to see one another for medicinal purposes. Something of an addiction.' It comes out as a joke, but I regret it instantly. I bite my lip. 'Sorry. I didn't mean—'

'Don't worry,' he says. 'I know what you meant.'

I have to ask him – it's been playing on my mind. 'Did you, you know, need the tablets?'

He looks puzzled for a second and I'm tense with anticipation, primed and ready to pounce on any denial that comes my way. It doesn't matter either way to me because I can help him through it, but I know it matters to him. He pulls the bottle out from his coat pocket and shakes it. 'You're talking about these?'

'Yes! I know things have been hard and if you needed to take one I understand, and I can help you.'

'Cath, these tablets are eighteen years old. Even if I wanted to

282

take one, I don't think they'd have the desired effect. What made you think I'd start taking these again?'

I chew my bottom lip. 'I saw them by your bed. I wasn't snooping, I promise, I just wanted to see the view from upstairs and—'

He clasps my hands in his. 'I'm flattered that you're worried, and that you wanted to see my bedroom—' he winks '—but I keep these with me as a reminder to show me how far I've come. The day I decided to stop taking them, I had eleven pills left and I've always carried them with me because I know if I can resist them, I can do anything.'

I breathe a huge sigh of relief. 'That's fantastic, Olivier. You're stronger than you know.'

'I can't say I didn't want to take something similar when you left,' he says, shoving them back in his coat. 'When I was tempted, I came clean to Elena instead, and she's been a big help.'

'That's great. I knew she'd understand.'

'I know, she did. To be honest, she saw it as no worse than the marijuana that she smoked in college, which, by the way, I did not know about.'

I laugh. 'And I'm guessing she still thinks you're an amazing brother?'

'It's like there's no stopping her.' He shakes his head. 'She said that if I didn't need them when you left, I wouldn't need them again so asked why I kept them. I didn't really have an answer.'

'You kept them to prove you didn't need them,' I say.

'I know, but I don't need them, and I don't need proof. They're also probably a customs risk so I'd like to throw them away.'

'If you're sure, there's a bin by the entrance to the car park.'

We brave the rain and scurry across the tarmac to the bin where he throws the bottle.

'Are you okay?' I ask as we climb back aboard.

'More than okay. Besides, they were so old, they'd have probably killed me.'

We spend the next few hours chatting and eating, and once the wine is gone, we clear everything away.

'What time do you need to pick up your guests tomorrow?'

'Ten o'clock.'

'Then I guess you've got plenty of time to come back to my house?' I say, with mischief in my tone.

'Well, madame, if you insist.'

Chapter Thirty-Five

The front door slams shut and I sit bolt upright. The house is usually so still, and not even Gary has a key anymore. I glance to my right and Olivier is there, sleeping. I don't want to wake him, but someone has either just come in or gone out of my house. I slip my dressing gown on and tie the belt tightly around my waist before tiptoeing down the stairs as quietly as I can to investigate. There's rustling in the kitchen. I look around the hallway for something I can use as a weapon, but there's nothing apart from the umbrella I'd not taken to work yesterday. I clutch it and peer around the door to see the back of a man who is rooting through the cupboards.

'Hi-yah!' I shout as I whack the umbrella around the back of his head as hard as I can.

'Ouch!' The man turns around and I gasp.

'Kieran. Oh my God. I'm so sorry, love.' I pull my lummox of a son into a hug. 'What are you doing here?'

He pulls away. His brow is crumpled as he rubs the back of his head. 'I thought I'd come home and see you. Didn't think you'd batter me with a brolly, though.'

'Sorry, I thought you were a burglar.' Other than Olivier, the house hasn't had a visitor since I've been back.

'There's nothing here to burgle. You haven't even got any biscuits.' My mind is cast back to yesterday; I didn't exactly have much time for shopping after work.

'Sit down and let me make you some tea.' I feel terrible.

'Is everything okay?' Olivier is hovering in the doorway, thankfully fully dressed. The weirdness of Kieran and Olivier standing in my kitchen together renders me speechless.

'I heard shouting,' he continues.

'Olivier. This is my son, Kieran,' I say. 'Kieran, this is Olivier.' I hope that Kieran listened when I mentioned Olivier on the phone call in France and that he needs no more introduction.

'It's so good to meet you. I've heard a lot about you.' Olivier's typical friendly demeanour is particularly welcome.

Kieran raises an eyebrow and hesitates. I hold my breath. Other than Gary, this is the first man I've ever brought into my home.

When he leans over and shakes Olivier's hand, I exhale with relief. 'It's good to meet you.'

I want to ask Kieran when he had become so polite, but I bite my tongue, not wanting to break this fragile moment of bonding.

'Well, I'm glad it was just you anyway. I could have sworn I'd heard the Karate Kid down here.' Olivier shoots me a playful glance.

'Excuse me! I thought there was a burglar in the house. Notice how I didn't wake you up? I just came down to deal with the task of burglar-bashing myself – I'm an independent woman remember, so don't mock me!' I prod him playfully.

''Er ... I'm going to put my bag in my room.' Kieran excuses himself and heads upstairs, leaving me feeling guilty for ignoring him and talking to Olivier just now.

'I'm going to see if he needs a hand,' I say and Olivier nods sympathetically.

When I reach Kieran's room, I have to stop myself from just

286

barging in. He's an adult now, with manners apparently, so I should knock. I tap three times on the door.

'Come in,' he shouts.

When I enter, he's unpacking his bag and putting clothes into his drawers. *Is this even the same person?*

'Kieran? I think I've got some explaining to do.'

'I wasn't expecting to find some bloke here, if that's what you mean.' He carries on unpacking and I can't tell if he's cross.

'Kieran, I—'

'Relax, Mum. It was bound to happen at some point. I'm just glad it's now, y'know, that I'm an adult. I get it, but I couldn't have handled it when I was a kid.'

My chest cracks. 'Oh, Kieran. It's something of nothing really. Olivier lives in France and I live here so it's nothing serious. He's more of a friend, really.'

'Well, my girlfriend is from Edinburgh.'

Girlfriend? What – Kieran has a girlfriend? This is a first. This is brilliant! I'm sure she'll be lovely and want to do all the things Kieran never did, like go shopping and get pedicures.

'Mum?' Kieran breaks into my thoughts.

'Sorry, what?'

'Nothing, you went all weird. I'm eighteen now, I'm allowed a girlfriend, you know.'

I smile. 'Of course you are. I'm over the moon. Come here.' I give him a squeeze and he lets me for a few moments before pulling away and holding me at arm's length.

'I was trying to say that the distance doesn't have to be a big deal. Not if you don't want it to be. Chloe and I see one another when we're at uni, and when we go home, we FaceTime and stuff. If you like this guy, give it a go.'

My insides come over all peculiar. It's a mixture of embarrassment and warmth, because taking relationship advice from my son is uncharted territory, but, particularly, his perception and thought is something new too. This girlfriend business has changed him. I don't reply – if all that comes out he'll get all embarrassed, and besides, as much as I appreciate his words, I'm not comfortable discussing Olivier with Kieran. It's all just a little too odd.

'I'm going to get dressed,' I say once Kieran's bag is unpacked. I assume Olivier will have made himself some tea or rustled up a Danish pastry or something.

I come downstairs as soon as I'm ready because I don't want to miss Olivier, and there isn't much time left. As I approach the doorway to the kitchen, I hear him and Kieran laughing so I hang back, not particularly wanting to eavesdrop, but not wanting to ruin their moment either.

'It's good you got her to try,' I hear Kieran say.

'She wanted to. She's a determined woman really,' Olivier replies. My whole body tenses. I know they're talking about me.

'I know. She's the best,' Kieran says, and my chest swells. I can't listen any longer because it doesn't feel right.

'Who's the best?' I say as casually as I can when I walk in.

'You are,' Kieran says. *Awww.* 'Olivier was just telling me you'd been learning a bit of French.' Hence the laughter.

'That's right. I suppose he told you all about my faux pas too, did he?' I shoot Olivier a look of mock-scolding and he stifles a laugh.

Kieran looks quite amused and rubs his chin as if to conceal it. 'He might have mentioned one or two actually.'

I fold my arms. 'Oh, did he now?'

Olivier walks over to me and wraps me in his arms. 'I'm sorry to throw you under the bus, I was just trying to bond with your son.' There's mirth in his tone and while I maintain a look of mock-grinchiness, I'm thrilled to see them getting along.

While I scramble for a witty retort, I notice the time and gasp. 'Olivier, you need to get going, it's twenty past nine.'

'Oh dear.' He sighs. 'I don't want to leave just yet.' He squeezes me tighter.

'And I'm not ready to let you go, but you must.' He kisses my neck as I speak.

'Er, and on that note, I'm popping to Dan's. We're going for a catch-up and a full English,' Kieran says. 'It was great to meet you, Olivier – and, Mum, he's a nice guy.' He nods pointedly towards Olivier and though his words and gestures were minimal, I know it's Kieran's way of giving me his blessing; but before I can say anything he's out the door.

'Nice kid you've got there,' Olivier says. 'You've raised him well.' I daren't tell him that this new improved version of my son is a product of half a term at uni and not eighteen years' worth of die-hard single parenting.

Once Olivier is ready, we amble back to the coach in our signature, companionable silence. There's no awkwardness, just a sense of company that brings me comfort. I suspect it's the same for Olivier. Seeing him this weekend has been like the bonus feature on the DVD of our time together. It's drawn out our movie, extended the warmth and joy but it still has to end.

'I can't believe we have to say goodbye all over again,' I say as those familiar spears start jabbing at my chest once more.

'What if I told you I'd be doing this exact same trip next month and I'd like to see you again?'

I pause for a moment, biting my lip.

'I suppose it wouldn't make this goodbye so bad.'

'So are you saying you'd be happy to see me next month?' He entwines his fingers with mine.

'I don't suppose it would be *so* bad.' I match his grin.

'Okay then. I will see you next month.' He pulls me in for a full-on kiss and I melt into the familiar velvety embrace. My heart grows, filling my chest and belting away the spears.

'This is the kind of goodbye I can do.' I speak aloud the thought as it hits me. Seeing Olivier sporadically is definitely better than not seeing him at all. We're both used to being alone, happy even.

So living that way shouldn't be any different, and there's this as a cherry on top.

He holds me tight, the familiar connection of all our lumps and bumps slotting together perfectly once again as he inhales the scent of my hair. I don't know what the future holds, but I know it's one with Olivier in it.

Chapter Thirty-Six

I ring the buzzer apprehensively. Gary hadn't wanted me to visit until he had the flat perfect and that time has now come. 'You need to expect Elena-style cooking, minus the good sense to purchase backup baguettes,' I say to Olivier as we enter the lift to head up to Gary's flat. I'd tried to suggest to Gary that inviting Olivier round too might be a bit much for his first attempt at hosting a dinner party (of sorts), but he insisted on him coming as a thanks to me for helping him out of his fug and he even went on to invite Kieran and Chloe (his girlfriend, who is lovely by the way and actually does like shopping and pedicures. She even washes the dishes after dinner).

It's a month after Olivier and I agreed to keep things going and he's back in the UK for a few days. I thought it might be too soon for a family gathering but he seemed ridiculously excited when I'd mentioned it.

'Good evening,' Gary says, swinging the door open on our arrival. He's ironed his T-shirt, I note.

We exchange greetings and he shepherds us into the lounge. 'Well, well, well. This is very nice,' I say truthfully. 'Nice mirror.' I gesture to the large silver-framed piece above the electric fire that forms the focal point of the room.

'Hi, Mum.' Kieran and Chloe come out, each carrying a bottle of beer, from what I assume is the kitchen.

As I head over to greet them, I hear Olivier ask Gary if he's done the place up himself, and as I hug Kieran and Chloe I hear Gary say: 'Oh you know, a lick of paint here, a few pictures there.' As though it was the easiest thing in the world. I smile as Olivier gives him the credit that he's due, and for all Gary's faults and niggles, he has come a long way in a short time and Olivier knows that. The fact he offered him praise and no words of negativity is why I love him.

Yes, I love him.

And he loves me.

Suddenly, I look around and everyone is sitting down staring at me. 'What?' I ask uncomfortably.

'Sit down, Cath,' Gary says.

'Mum, this is an intervention.' Kieran looks very serious all of a sudden.

'What on earth is an intervention?'

Kieran draws a breath. 'We've been chatting to Olivier, on WhatsApp and stuff.'

'Oh,' I say, unsure where this is going.

'He's told us he's asked you to move to France to join the business but you won't. Because of me.' Kieran's face is full of emotion and it sets my bottom lip off.

'Cath. Before this goes any further, I just want to say that this was all Kieran's idea and I respect your decision.' I glance at Olivier as he speaks, then back to Kieran.

'I want you to live a better life, Mum. I know the sacrifices you've made for me and it's time to do something for you. Go to France.'

I look at him and then Chloe, who smiles encouragingly.

'Mum, you can sell the house and go. I've never seen you so happy as when you're talking about France – you love it there.'

'I'm not selling that house,' I say.

Olivier takes my hand. 'You won't have to.'

'I see you less than once a month as it is, Mum, and if you worked with Olivier, you'd be back once a month anyway and me and Chloe would come to France to visit,' Kieran adds.

'And me,' Gary pipes up.

'I can't just up and leave. I start my course in a few weeks. I'm changing career.'

'That's entirely your decision,' Olivier says, kissing my hand. 'We do have schools in France too though, and our coach company is partnering up with more and more UK schools. If that was something you'd be interested in I would love you to head up that department.'

I think about what Kieran is saying. I consider what living and working in France might be like. I think about Olivier's house and cooking and visits to the vineyard, the beach and Paris. People do it, don't they? Jenny in Thiepval did it and she's very happy with her life. Is it so wrong to want more? To dare to be selfish for once and follow my heart?

I take a deep breath and look to Kieran and then Olivier.

'If you're sure that this is what you want. That it will work out and I don't need to sell my house then ... *oui*.' A smile cracks on my face. 'Yes. Yes.' Olivier wraps his arms around me and thrusts me into the air and I glance down at him.

'Okay.' I squeal. 'But I'm going to need a better French teacher.'

One Year Later …

'*Bonjour*,' Elena coos as she lets herself in. 'Where do you want this?' She's got an oven glove on and is carrying a crockpot with gravy juices oozing from the lid. It smells good but I know better and raise an eyebrow.

'Oh no, no, no, I don't want to upset a pregnant lady but what is that?' Olivier pops his head out of the kitchen.

'Relax brother, I have a new recipe. That American lady, Martha, who friended me on Facebook sent it to me. This is the one that will leave you begging for more.' She grins, walking to the kitchen.

Olivier and I exchange wary glances. 'Did you at least bring sandwiches?' he asks her as she places it on the counter. The question earns him a lashing with the oven glove.

'I'm being serious. Cath made the *tarte aux pommes* for dessert. This whole evening could be a disaster,' he teases.

'Hey,' I say. 'You taught me.'

Elena places her hands on her hips and glares at him. 'Try it.'

'Do I have to?' She whips him again. 'Okay, pass me a spoon.'

I look on, intrigued, as he spoons a lump of beef into his mouth. The air is thick with tension.

'Well?' Elena asks.

'It's good.' He nods. 'Really good.'

'Thank goodness for that – I've peaked! I can give up now.' She giggles as there's a knock at the door.

My heart races. 'Oh my God, oh my God. I'll get it,' I say, dashing to the door. Elena and Olivier are behind me as I swing it open.

'Hello,' I cry, clutching my hands to my face before launching myself at Kieran and Chloe, pulling them into a hug. I move on to Gary next. 'You found us okay then?'

'Easy,' Gary says.

'I can't believe how quick the journey was, a few hours to the tunnel and then an hour from Calais. It would have been worse if you moved up north,' Kieran jokes. 'Seriously, Mum, this is fine and look at you – you look so healthy, and happy.'

My eyes fill up. 'Oh, come here, you.' I grab him again and kiss his cheek. 'It's great to see you all.'

Olivier welcomes everyone in and we make our introductions before spending the afternoon catching up by the pool. Chloe and Kieran seem sweet together and they're pretty solid now after being together over a year. My heart swells with happiness. Gary has got himself a girlfriend and has even been promoted at work. As I watch him pronounce the *t*'s at the ends of his words and the aitches after all his *w*'s I can't help but wonder whether Olivier has been the positive influence he needed in his life to gee him on a bit.

Julien joins us for dinner and we spend the evening enjoying (yes you heard it right) Elena's food and my dessert. It's hard to imagine life back in the UK now. I've been working with children just as I'd wanted but I decided the coach company suited me better than the classroom because now I get to see that beautiful scenery my great-grandfather wrote about, every single day. I get to share his story and it helps to know he didn't die in vain. I still chat to Martha and Cynthia in our Chitchat group and I even met up with Jackie on her annual trip to Arras a few weeks

295

ago. Kaitlynn is never off Instagram and I feel like I know more about her life now that I ever did before.

As everyone is sat by the pool chatting, I take some clean towels up to the spare bedrooms and go to change my shoes in our room when I stop by the bedroom window. Olivier has gathered everyone close and he's talking. His expression is serious.

When I head back downstairs I hover at the patio doors. Julien sees me and clears his throat, causing everyone to turn around.

'What?' I say, feeling incredibly self-conscious.

Olivier rises to his feet and takes me by the hand. 'Cath my love, come and sit down.'

'If this is another intervention or whatever, I'll not be impressed.' I sit on a lounger and fold my arms.

'It isn't, I promise.' Olivier kneels down and wraps his hands around mine.'

'If you've come to beg for the last piece of apple tart you can think again. It's mine.'

'I haven't.'

'What is it then?' I'm starting to feel a little worried and the beady eyes of our nearest and dearest upon us aren't helping.

'Cath, I love you so much. Having you in my life has been more than I could have ever wished for and, I think, I hope you feel the same way. I see a light in you that gets brighter each day and you light me up too. Your confidence and initiatives are great for the business and your apple tart is second to none. But most of all, I just love to be around you. I love your presence, your company and your funny little phrases.'

'Of course, I feel the same way, you fool.' I laugh nervously.

'Then I hope you'll answer my question with a yes.' He takes a deep breath and squeezes my hands. 'Cath, *veux-tu m'épouser?*'

Will … you … I'm trying to process the words. *Will you marry me?* I gasp, clutching my hands to my face as I well up. Then I spot the black fuzzy box he's taken out and is holding in front of me.

'Oh my goodness, yes. A thousand yeses.' Tears stream down my face as Olivier pulls me into his arms and there are whoops and cheers from our audience.

When Olivier eventually pulls away he looks visibly relieved.

'I'm so sorry for springing this upon you in front of everyone. I uhmed and ahhed about taking you to Paris or the countryside to do this in private but when I thought about what matters to you the most, it's family. I hope you don't mind the audience.'

'Olivier, it was perfect. Having everyone I love here in one place is amazing. Now let me see that ring.' I wipe my eyes and take the box. 'Ahh, it's beautiful.' I take out the sapphire, set in diamonds on a platinum or white gold band, and place it on my finger.

'It's a French cluster ring from the Edwardian era, made in around 1910. I couldn't get one guaranteed to be from 1917 but figured this was something special that was around when your great-grandfather was.'

I'm now sobbing. 'It's perfect – it means the world to me that you'd do this. Thank you, thank you so much, for everything.' I wipe my face again. 'You're perfect. I love you.' I pull his collar in and kiss him, spurring on more ahhs from the crowd. 'And I love you lot too,' I add when I pull away.

We spend the next few days showing Kieran, Chloe and Gary around our haunts including the vineyard, where we've decided to have the wedding and Le Touquet where we may go for a few days after. We have plenty of fun things planned before our guests go home but tomorrow, we're all visiting the Menin Gate.

Acknowledgements

This book wouldn't have been possible without the help and support of several awesome people. Hannah Smith, thank you so much for taking on this book and for your early advice on the plot. Cara Chimirri, for your honest, constructive feedback, knowledge and fantastic editorial notes. Katherine Trail, once again thank you for your invaluable advice and notes. Also, thank you to HQ Digital for publishing this book and designing the wonderful cover and Helena Newton for your wonderful copy edit notes.

I'd also like to thank my friend, Linda Benalia for her kind help and advice with the French translations that made this book possible. I can wholeheartedly say, I was a bit of a pest but you were always happy to correct my many mistakes. Thank you to Elizabeth Marsland for sharing your passion for WWI history with me and to you, Dad, for your input.

Finally, I'd like to give a special mention of thanks to The Edward Thomas Fellowship for their assistance and good wishes.

Dear Reader,

I just wanted to say a huge thank you for taking the time to read *It Started with a Note*. This book is quite personal to me as I took a similar trip to Cath in 2017 to visit the Thiepval Memorial to the Missing, where my great-grandfather is commemorated. It was a humbling trip whereby I learnt a lot and returned with so much respect for those who lived through the World War I era, both at home and on foreign soil. The Calais region of France is a fascinating place and offers access to some of the most insightful WWI sites in northern France and Belgium.

In my own special way, I wanted to write something that would serve as a reminder of the war and a tribute to those who gave their lives or suffered loss, injury, trauma and displacement, particularly as the year of release ties in with the centenary year; hence *It Started with a Note* was born. I hope you enjoyed the love story, but I hope you found the historical elements both interesting and touching too. If you've ever visited any of the sites mentioned in the book I'd love you to get in touch and share your story – you can find me on Facebook, Twitter and Instagram.

Reviews long and short, good and bad are incredibly valuable to authors. They let us know how we're doing, how we can improve and give us warm fuzzy feelings when people like our work. If you can spare a few minutes to leave one on your chosen retailer's website, I'd love to hear your feedback.

Finally, thank you again for your support in purchasing this book and, if you liked it, please check out my others.

Best wishes,

Victoria Cooke